CASE CLOSED
DANGER ON THE DIG

THE CASE CLOSED SERIES

Case Closed: Mystery in the Mansion

Case Closed: Stolen from the Studio

Case Closed: Haunting at the Hotel

Case Closed: Danger on the Dig

LAUREN MAGAZINER

CASE CLOSED

DANGER ON THE DIG

PICK YOUR PATH,

CRACK THE CASE!

KATHERINE TEGEN BOOKS
An Imprint of HarperCollins Publishers

Katherine Tegen Books is an imprint of HarperCollins Publishers.

Case Closed #4: Danger on the Dig
information address HarperCollins Children's Books, a division of
HarperCollins Publishers, 195 Broadway, New York, NY 10007.
www.harpercollinschildrens.com

ISBN 978-0-06-320736-3 (trade bdg.)
ISBN 978-0-06-320735-6 (pbk.)

Typography by by Andrea Vandergrift and Torborg Davern
22 23 24 25 26 PC/BRR 10 9 8 7 6 5 4 3 2 1
❖
First Edition

To Hali Baumstein and Jessica Sears,

Long live the Clue Crew. . . .
There's no one else in the world
I'd rather crack a case with.
Thanks for always being
my two favorite co-detectives!

(Of course, it is—
what else did you expect? ☺)

WE WAIT FOR our luggage to arrive from the plane, and there's a one thousand percent certainty that Frank is going to ride the baggage carousel.

"He's going to do it," I say to my best friend, Eliza.

"No way!" she says. "He's almost seven. He's older now! More mature."

Eliza is very smart—the smartest, most logical person I know—but she's totally overestimating her younger brother. Frank is absolutely going to do it.

"Bet you anything," I say. "Bet you a euro."

Eliza's eyes flash. "No. Winner gets to pick which suspect to talk to first."

Of course she would bet that. She's been trying to steal my role as team leader for over a month now. And things have been unbearably uncomfortable between us. It's like . . . we're in a fight, but we're not actually fighting about anything? We're just awkward, maybe drifting apart.

It all started when Mom and her partner, Cole, agreed to let our pictures go on their website as official junior detectives. Our last three cases were high-profile and brought Las Pistas Detective Agency a lot of good press. We saved a millionaire from death threats, found a kidnapped actress, and uncovered the secrets behind a haunted hotel.

We were so excited when our detective profiles went live . . . but Mom said that our status as junior detectives was dependent on us having regular training sessions—to keep our detective skills sharp in between cases.

At our first (and only) mock case, Eliza started grabbing clues out of my hands, making decisions, and bossing me around. She was even asking our fake suspect questions—which is usually *my* job. Our team-work totally fell apart, and it wasn't because we were rusty.

It was because Eliza turned into a one-woman show. She totally forgot that we are on a team, and we all have specific roles to play. When we started fighting about who's the decision maker and who's the puzzle solver, Eliza stormed out of our house.

We never finished our training, and it's been tense between us ever since. Mom tried to make me feel better by telling me that change is a part of growing up. But that made me feel even worse. I don't want things to change with my best friend. Even if they already have.

"Well?" Eliza says as Frank wiggles to the front row. "Are you betting me or not?"

"You're on."

At first Frank sits down on the edge of the carousel, like he's tired and needs a bench. But slowly he rolls onto the spinning conveyor belt. Then he starts surfing on top of a bag.

"WE HAVE BEGUN OUR DESCENT!" he shouts, and Eliza groans.

"Frank!" Mom yells, spotting him from where she's trying to collect our luggage. "Get down from there! It's dangerous!"

"Danger? I eat danger for breakfast! And lunch! And dinner! And maybe as a snack too! And definitely for dessert!"

Frank is way too hyper for his own good.

I laugh and turn to Eliza. "I win!"

She folds her arms. "You don't have to gloat about it."

"I'm not gloating," I say. "I'm stating a fact."

She grabs her backpack and runs toward Mom. I had hoped that with our first international case in Greece, we'd snap like rubber bands back to our old dynamic, but I guess not. This is also the first case where the client asked for *us*, not Mom or Cole, but Eliza barely seems excited about that.

I sigh and walk over to Mom. An airport worker,

who keeps gesturing wildly toward the luggage carousel, is scolding her and Frank in Greek. Mom looks apologetic. Frank does not.

When the airport worker walks away, Mom lets out a sigh.

"Frank," Mom says. "What did we say about misbehaving?"

"Always miss behaving!" Frank says.

He's hopeless.

With our bags in tow, we head to the exit. Next stop? An archaeological dig!

I've read the case file a million times, and I know every weird detail of this case. I run through the facts again in my mind.

During an excavation outside Delphi, Greece, archaeologists stumbled upon a mysterious entranceway to underground catacombs.

The catacombs are made up of a series of tunnels. And the writing on the wall (literally) in the entranceway seems to suggest that there's a mythical treasure hidden somewhere inside.

But in the archaeologists' attempt to retrieve the treasure, the leader of the dig (named Keira Skelberry) accidentally fell into a booby trap and got gravely injured.

Since then, a special treasure-hunting task force had

been assembled to go retrieve the treasure.

But as soon as the special task force arrived, valuable artifacts began disappearing from the drying racks.

The head of the special task force, Orlando Bones, isn't sure which of his team members he can trust.

And Orlando Bones is afraid that the treasure in the catacombs is about to be stolen, just like these priceless artifacts.

So he hired us to find the artifact thief.

I can't wait to meet all the suspects. And as we walk toward the airport exit, I realize that's about to happen sooner rather than later. A young white woman is holding a sign for Las Pistas Detective Agency.

"That's us!" Mom says, walking up to the woman.

She is young. She looks like she might be in college, but she dresses like she could be in her fifties. She's wearing a pencil skirt, a blazer with a lapel, and high-heeled shoes. Her brown hair is slick straight and shoulder-length. She wears glasses with thick frames. She's got rabbity features: a small nose, prominent front teeth, glossy eyes, and an alert energy that makes me feel like she's ready to scamper at any moment.

"I'm Marta Higgins, but soon you'll see that everyone on the dig calls me Smarty Marty," she says. "I'm the lead archaeological consultant on the special task force. I will be your liaison today."

My mom checks the case file. "Ah, yes, Marta Higgins, also known as Smarty Marty. Lead archaeological consultant, you say? Huh. My records say you're the intern."

Smarty Marty flushes an angry, splotchy red. "I—okay, fine. I'm an intern. But not for long!" She grabs one of our suitcases and stomps toward the parking garage. When Smarty Marty's back is turned, Mom winks at me.

Man, she knew *just* what to say to get Smarty steaming mad. Mom is the master at work.

We pile into Smarty's car. Adults in the front, kids in the back.

"Are we there yet?" Frank asks.

"Smarty Marty hasn't even turned on the ignition!" I say.

Smarty starts the car, and soon we're on open stretches of road. The farther from the airport we get, the more the landscape transforms into stark mossy mountains and grassy valleys. The sky is so bright and clear.

Occasionally we drive by pillars and ruins. They're like nothing I've ever seen before. It's kind of funny how something so new to me could be so old in general. Because these ruins are *thousands* of years old.

"We're not too far away now," Smarty Marty says. "To be honest, I'm not sure why Mr. Bones even hired you. It's not like we need a whole team of detectives."

Huh? "You don't?"

"But haven't artifacts been going missing?" Eliza asks.

"They have," she says carefully. "But I told Mr. Bones I was *more* than capable of handling the case myself. I've read every detective novel I could get my hands on. I know all about investigative work. I know everything about many things—and if I don't know it, I *will* with an hour of research," she boasts. "I'm a quick reader and a fast learner. I graduated summa cum laude, you know."

That means nothing to me, but Smarty definitely thinks it's worth bragging about.

Suddenly Frank starts gagging. I look over at him, and he has both of his hands inside his mouth.

"Frank, what on *earth* are you doing?" I ask.

"I haf a loof toof!" he says, still about to swallow his own fists.

A loof toof?

"Oh!" It hits me what he's trying to say. "You have a loose tooth!"

"Frankie, that's great!" Eliza says. "I'm so proud of you!"

"Proud?" Smarty whispers incredulously. "Of *that*? Everyone loses their baby teeth! That's nothing special!"

"I don't like you," Frank says. "GUILTY."

Smarty clenches her jaw, and the veins in her neck bulge.

I slink down into the car seat. Oh, Frank!

Frank grins at me, but his tongue is still working that tooth. "Think the tooth fairy will find me in Turkey?"

"Frank, we're in Greece."

"We are?"

"Some detective," Smarty mutters as she shows her badge to a security guard. He waves her through.

Smarty parks in the lot with a dozen other cars. Then we get out of the vehicle and stretch our limbs. It's been a *long* day of travel, and the time difference is exhausting. I try not to think about how it's two in the morning at home. The not-thought makes me yawn.

We cross a roped off walkway to get to the actual excavation area. It's more crowded than I was expecting. Lots of people in hats and cargo shorts, holding tiny spades and brushes. Everyone seems to be carefully wiping dirt away. The site itself seems large, with sandbags and trenches everywhere. One area of the excavation is covered by a tarp roof. But the other area is in direct sunlight, with no overhead covering.

"Welcome to the excavation site," Smarty says. "The entrance to the tunnels is beneath the covered portion."

"Did you go into the tunnels?" I ask.

"Briefly," Smarty says. "They're dark. And filled with snares."

Frank perks ups. "Hares?"

"Snares."

"Pears?"

"*Snares.*"

"Bears?"

"Ignore him," I say. "We all do."

Frank sticks his tongue out at me, and Mom sighs.

"This way," Smarty says, leading us to the outskirts of the site. Here, there are dozens of tents set up, some big, some small.

"What are the tents for?" Eliza asks.

"Artifact storage, lab techs, sleeping, eating, medical. There's a tent for everything. But our tents are back here. The green ones are for anyone on the special task force." There are seven green tents that Smarty points out to us. "Those three"—she points at the three tents closest to the edge of a rocky hill—"are where we sleep. Completely off-limits."

Off-limits doesn't really mean anything to us when we're on a case. I try to catch Eliza's glance to see if she agrees, but she's scribbling in her notebook. I look to Frank, but he's just walking back and forth while wiggling his tooth.

"These four tents are the only ones you'll need. This

one on the far right is where you're going to sleep. Let me drop your suitcases off." She rolls our suitcases into the tent, which is empty except for four cots.

"The bathroom?" Mom asks.

"You don't want to know," Smarty Marty says darkly, with a head jerk toward a row of porta potties a long walk away. Eliza grimaces.

"This next tent," Smarty says, pointing to the biggest one, "is the bosses' tent—where Mr. Bones and Ms. Nadeem work. Do *not* disturb them. Second from the left is the work tent for the rest of us. Basically, it's where we store any artifact we find—and yes," she says to Mom with an annoyed huff, "before you ask, it *is* the location of the thefts. You'll find me in there often, along with Zip, who creates maps of the tunnels, using laser scanning."

"Lasers! Fun!" Frank says. I turn and look at him just as he trips, falls to the ground, and accidentally punches himself in the face with the hand he's been using to wiggle his tooth. "Ow!"

"Well, I suppose our last tent is fortuitous," Smarty says snidely. "This is the tent for medical. We on the task force have our own special physician, Dr. Mandible."

"Is the doctor in? I'll get Frank an ice pack," Mom says. Without waiting for a response, she charges in. A Black woman with braided hair looks up from her phone. She smiles widely, and she has shiny teeth. Forget doctor—she could be in a dentist commercial. She's got a kind, round baby face and a bigger body. I *think* she's about Mom's age, but I'm bad at guessing adult ages.

"Welcome, welcome! Are these the detectives?" the doctor asks Smarty, who rolls her eyes. "Aww, they're so cute! And little!"

"I know you are, but what am I?" Frank hollers.

"Uhhh . . . cute and little?"

"I know you are, but what am I?" Frank repeats.

This could go on *forever.* I have to step in. "We are Las Pistas Detective Agency. That's Detective Serrano. I'm Carlos. This is Eliza. And that's Frank."

"MR. FRANK TO YOU!" Frank says.

I sigh.

The doctor hands him a lollipop, and just like *that,* Frank brightens up. "Just what the doctor ordered!"

"I'm Dr. Amanda Mandible, the physician for the special task force. I have a decade of experience in medicine, so if you ever find yourself in a medical emergency, please come find me."

"What about a lollipop emergency?" Frank asks hopefully.

"Those too." She hands him another lollipop.

"I like her!" Frank says. "NOT GUILTY!"

"We don't know that yet, Frank," I mumble.

We leave the medical tent. Smarty pulls us into the tent next door—the work tent—to meet a person hunched over a computer. There's a name tag on the desk: ZIP TAYLOR. MY PRONOUNS ARE THEY/THEM.

"This is Zip," Smarty says. "Zip? The detectives."

Zip turns around, and their dark eyes have an I've-been-staring-at-a-computer-screen-too-long zombie sort of glow. The computer is the only light in the tent, and it shines on Zip's dark skin.

Zip has a stubbly face and is also wearing bright blue eyeshadow and pink lipstick. They're wearing a plain white muscle shirt and a very flowy, vibrant skirt. Their hair is buzzed short, and they're wearing a flower headband.

"April showers bring May flowers!" Frank says, pointing to the flower.

"Yes, but Frank, it's March," I whisper.

Frank shrugs. "I like flowers. I like you. NOT GUILTY."

"You have to stop doing that!" I grumble.

Zip nods. "It's true—I am not guilty. Nice to meet you."

"Is Zip a nickname?" Mom asks.

"Not anymore," Zip says.

"Zip," I say. It sounds almost like a superhero name.

"Is that because you're really fast on the computer?"

"Or because you work with zip files?" Eliza asks.

"Or because you like zippers?" Frank suggests.

Zip laughs. "All of the above."

"What do you do here?" Mom asks.

"Right now I'm making maps. Basically, we set up a terrestrial laser at the mouth of the entrance into the tunnels. I scan with the laser, then come back here to make 3D imaging models using the measurements. It's a mathematical process of determining where we're going, so we're not wandering recklessly. Every time we reach a new spot in the tunnels, I come back and make maps."

"That's so *cool*," Eliza says in awe. She's practically drooling over that laser.

"Okay, that's enough chatter!" Smarty Marty says. "We can't be late for Mr. Bones!"

She ushers us outside. Immediately, we run into two older white men of wildly different sizes arguing in front of the work tent.

"You *can't* be serious!" says one man in a deep voice. He is short and stocky, with arched eyebrows and a prominent goatee. "Artifacts belong to the public—they're meant to be enjoyed by all!"

"The average philistine cannot enjoy that which he does not understand," the other man replies in a thick

English accent. He is tall and gangly, with thinning gray hair, wire glasses, and a downturned mouth. "In the hands of academia, these artifacts can be properly examined—and thus give us a superior knowledge of history. A gallery is a waste."

"A waste?" the first man splutters. "A *waste*? With the time, money, and resources of a museum, we can do so much more than your precious university!"

"I would beg to—"

"Ahem!" Smarty says loudly. "We have guests."

Their argument melts away, and their fake smiles don't quite reach their eyes, which are still hot with anger.

"Oh, don't let *us* interrupt," Mom says. "Sounds like you were having a heated argument."

"What about?" I add.

They look at each other. The glance is half embarrassed and half indignant.

"Sounds like you were arguing about where artifacts should go after they're found," Eliza says. "Whether they should be placed in the hands of academics for experts to study, or in a museum for all to enjoy." She thinks for a moment, and I can see her working up the courage to say something. "But you're *both* wrong to think of taking these artifacts out of their country of origin. They should go back to the government of the country they're found in. In this case, Greece."

14

At that, both men burst into laughter.

"How absolutely absurd!" says the lanky British man.

"You are naive," the squat man says. "But what can one expect from someone so juvenile?"

Eliza flushes angrily.

And so do I. We might be on awkward terms, but Eliza is still my best friend, and I can't let them insult her. "Hey! Eliza is the smartest person in the world! What do you know, anyway?"

Frank blows a raspberry. "I don't like you, and I don't like you either. GUILTY!"

"My sincerest apologies, young academic," the British man says to Eliza. "I did not mean to slight you. I am Phineas Alistair Worthington, professor of classical studies at Bonington University."

"I am the lead curator for several museums in North America. My name is Richard Leech."

"And you're sorry," I insist.

"Sure," he mumbles, looking down at his feet.

"How did you two come to be working on this special task force?" Mom asks.

Richard Leech rubs his goatee. "Orlando Bones and I became acquainted on a dig in North America. Many of the artifacts he found ended up in my possession."

"You mean your *museum*'s possession," Eliza says, correcting him.

"Potato, potahto," he mumbles.

Professor Phineas Alistair Worthington snorts. "Well, I am here not through tenuous connections to Mr. Bones, but rather because I am the upmost authority on the Necklace of Harmonia."

"The what?" I ask.

"Oh, we don't have time for this!" Smarty says, tapping her foot impatiently. "Mr. Bones is expecting you now. He's a very busy man, and I'm a perfect intern." Smarty doesn't notice, but I do: Richard Leech and Professor Worthington *both* make mocking faces behind her back. "You can always come back for a history lesson!"

"I look forward to it," the professor says with a tip of his head.

Finally Smarty pulls us into the bosses' tent. This one is big and well lit, which is surprising, coming from Zip's dark work environment.

"Oho! You're here!" bellows a boisterous white man. He's wearing a fedora, and his face underneath is a little sweaty and dirty. He looks like he's in his forties, or maybe fifties. His forehead has a few deep grooves, and he's got lines like parentheses that connect his mouth to his nose. His warm brown eyes look tired, but his smile is bright. "Thank you so much for rolling the dice on this case."

"Thank you for flying us," I say. "And for hiring Las Pistas Detective Agency."

"Well, when the chips are down, I've got to get professional help in here. I'm sure you're exhausted, but we have much to discuss, if you don't mind. That'll be all, Smarty."

"Can I stay?"

"Can a two and a seven win a hand of poker?" Bones replies. Smarty looks confused. "No," he clarifies.

Smarty opens her mouth, and she seems like she's halfway between yelling at her boss and asking for a promotion. But instead she says, "Yes, sir, Mr. Bones." Then she turns on her heel and marches out.

"Got rid of Smarty much easier than usual!" Orlando Bones says. "Don't know if you noticed, but she's kind of a know-it-all. Nadira's hire. She introduced herself as Smarty on the first day. Says it's her nickname from grade school, but I'd bet my bottom dollar it wasn't supposed to be a compliment. Anyway, enough about Smarty. Let's chat."

"Okay," I say. "Can you describe—"

"Not here!" Bones says with a wave of his hand. "Somewhere private."

"This isn't private?" Eliza asks.

Orlando Bones shakes his head. "Nadira's back here. *Nadira!*"

The curtain divider rustles, and a woman pops her head out. "Did you need me, Mr. Bones? I have an appointment in ten minutes," she says. She has an accent that I think is French. She's wearing a pale pink hijab that is shockingly clean, considering all the dirt on the dig site. She's got light brown skin, thick eyebrows, and prominent cheekbones.

"This is Nadira, my number two."

Frank snickers. Of course.

"No, not *that* number two," Orlando says, horrified. "Let me start over. This is my right-hand woman, Nadira Nadeem. Second-in-command. Expert archaeologist. We're the ultimate treasure-recovering team. We're two of a kind!"

"In that case," Mom says, "would you want to have this initial conversation together?"

"No, no, Nadira's busy."

"Perhaps I *should* stay," Nadira says. "I have strong suspicions about who might be taking our artifacts."

Orlando Bones blanches. "Oh, well, uh . . . I'm sure you can talk to Nadira later."

"Unfortunately not. Busy, busy day—Zip and I are doing some imaging scans for our next voyage into the tunnels later. Professor Worthington and I are scouring an ancient Greek text for mentions of Harmonia. After that, our team is supposed to go into the tunnels, no? Oh, and I almost forgot—I'm supposed to contact Keira's relatives and update them on her emergency surgery." She checks her watch and whimpers. "Oh, dear! I'm already behind in my work. Now's the only time I can squeeze you in today!"

Nadira seems organized and frantic, both at the same time. Kind of how Eliza gets right before a big test. I wish I could give Nadira an A+. I know that always helps Eliza breathe easier.

Bones stares at us, basically begging with his eyes. He clearly doesn't want Nadira around for this conversation. Does that mean he suspects her? After all that two-of-a-kind talk? Did we call his bluff?

If we include Nadira in this chat, then Bones might withhold information. On the other hand, it sounds like Nadira has some suspicions we need to hear.

I don't want to miss out on what either of them has to say, but this conversation can only go one way.

TO TALK TO ORLANDO BONES ALONE,
TURN TO 359.

←——→

TO INVITE NADIRA NADEEM TO PARTICIPATE
IN THIS CONVERSATION, TURN TO 384.

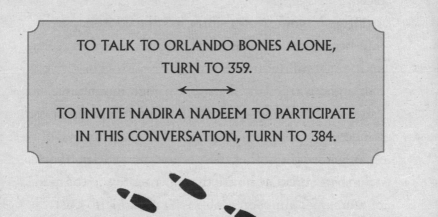

I DECIDE TO give in to what my best friend wants. "Let's go to the ruins. You win, Eliza."

The smile on her face is so bright that it's almost worth putting my plans on pause. "Oh, thank you, Carlos! You won't regret it! Let me get the address from Professor Worthington."

"I'll see if I can borrow Smarty Marty's car," Mom offers.

"And I'll . . . DO IMPORTANT STUFF TOO," Frank says as he plops onto the dirt and starts wiggling his tooth.

I sit down next to Frank. Even though this choice means putting the catacombs on hold, and even though it wasn't my idea, I'm actually excited to see these ruins and possibly learn the dark, cursed history of the necklace.

Fifteen minutes later, Eliza has the address plugged into her phone, and Mom has the keys to Smarty's car, and Frank still hasn't removed his tooth. The drive is half an hour from the dig site, through mountains and valleys, with the wind blowing through our open car windows.

When we get to the ruins, at the top of a hill, there's no one around. The house that burned down was made of tan stone, but there's almost nothing left—just the bones. Frank climbs into the center, and Eliza follows him. Not to be outdone by the Thompsons, Mom and

I hop in too. I'm standing in what must have been the living room. The paint on the walls is fading, the rock is crumbling, and there's an old, rusty clockface on the wall that I'm surprised has lasted this long.

I walk through the ruins, but this house is just a skeleton of its former self now, with a few vertical columns and a few horizontal ones. Moss blankets everything. We can't see any of the char marks from the fire. Time must have worn those away.

"Well, it was a good try, Eliza. Should we go back to the catacombs now?" I say eagerly.

"Wait." She is staring intensely at the clock with no hands. I wonder if they burned away.

"I saw that too . . . it's really sturdy. Can't believe that's the only thing that survived the fire!"

"It shouldn't be here." Eliza pulls on the clock, but it's totally stuck to the wall. "Clockfaces weren't invented until the eleventh century—hundreds of years after the fire supposedly happened."

"So?"

"So . . . someone came along later and attached this to the ruins. It's a clue—I know it." She searches the sides and cries out. "Look! A sequence of numbers! Carved into the metal here. It has to do with the clockface, I'm sure of it."

"Sequence of numbers for what?" I ask, just as Frank hollers, "LAND HO!"

I look up. Frank has climbed near the top of a column in record time. I roll my eyes. Typical Frank.

"Frankie!" Eliza shouts. "Get down from there! It's dangerous!"

"Danger is fun!" Frank says.

"You have until the count of three," Mom yells.

"NO!"

With Mom and Eliza distracted, I can solve the clock puzzle and prove my worth. I just have to figure out what the numbers are for. Do I add them up? Do I have to trace the numbers in order? Is there a pattern I need to understand? I'm determined to get this.

~~10~~ ~~12~~ ~~2~~ ~~8~~ ~~4~~

~~8~~ ~~6~~ ~~4~~ ~~10~~ ~~12~~ ~~2~~ ~~8~~

~~1~~ ~~11~~ ~~9~~ ~~3~~ ~~5~~ ~~8~~

THE SOLUTION TO THE PUZZLE WILL LEAD YOU
TO YOUR NEXT PAGE.

←——→

TO ASK ELIZA FOR HELP, TURN TO PAGE 388.

I CAN'T BELIEVE I'm doing this.

"Okay, Frank. You can feed your garlic bread to the snakes." It sounds far-fetched, but maybe they'll like Italian food? I know I do!

"Here, Buster. Come here!"

"Buster?"

"I named them. That's Buster. That's Buster Two. That's Buster Three."

"I get the picture."

"That's Penelope. That's Alexandra. That's Benjamin. That's Mike, Michael, Mikey, and Michelangelo."

"Frankie? Focus!" Eliza says.

"Here you go, Rumplesnakeskin," Frank says, tossing the bread at a particularly thick snake. It quickly glides away. "Nooooo, stop running away when I'm trying to share! Sharing is caring! Now take my garlic bread!"

It's the oddest thing—any time Frank approaches a snake with garlic bread, it slithers away from him. It's like he's wearing snake repellent or something.

"Serpents must hate the smell of garlic!" Eliza says excitedly. "This is amazing! Science at work!"

We each take two pieces of garlic bread and hold them in front of us. The snakes hiss angrily, but they back away. Each step we take clears a path.

At the end of the room is an archway, and we find ourselves at the top of a staircase, looking down at a huge maze.

24

"A labyrinth," Eliza says breathlessly. "They're so pivotal in Greek mythology."

"What's a lab or rinse?" Frank asks.

"A *labyrinth* is a giant, elaborate, unsolvable maze meant to hold the Minotaur."

"Oh. And what's a minosaur?"

"The *Minotaur* is a monster with the head and tail of a bull and the body of a man."

I frown. "So basically we're facing an unsolvable maze and there might be a monster inside?"

"Precisely." Eliza kneels, reaches into her backpack, and retrieves a book. "See those symbols? In ancient Greece, letters stood in for numbers, and I think that's what's happening here. Oooh, look at this chart in my book!"

"So . . . why are these numbers in the maze?"

"They must be markers that guide your way. We should pay attention to which ones we pass, so we don't get lost."

Ancient Greek Number Chart								
Alpha	Beta	Gamma	Delta	Epsilon	Digamma	Zeta	Eta	Theta
A	B	Γ	Δ	E	Ϛ	Z	H	Θ
1	2	3	4	5	6	7	8	9
Iota	Kappa	Lambda	Mu	Nu	Xi	Omicron	Pi	Koppa
I	K	Λ	M	N	Ξ	O	Π	Ϙ
10	20	30	40	50	60	70	80	90
Rho	Sigma	Tau	Upsilon	Phi	Chi	Psi	Omega	Sampi
P	Σ	T	Y	Φ	X	Ψ	Ω	Ϡ
100	200	300	400	500	600	700	800	900

ADD UP THE NUMBERS YOU PASS THROUGH IN THE MAZE, AND TURN TO THAT PAGE.

←——→

TO ASK ELIZA FOR A HINT, TURN TO PAGE 184.

"SO . . . WHAT EXACTLY is this treasure in the catacombs?" I ask Bones, and Eliza leans forward eagerly in her seat.

"Something more valuable than all the gold in the world," Orlando Bones whispers, swiveling his desk chair as he slowly and dramatically looks at each of us.

"Bubble gum?" Frank says. "Bubble wrap? Bubble baths!"

"It doesn't just have to be bubbles," I say.

"Oh," Frank says. He thinks for a moment. "Cats!"

I look over to Orlando Bones to see if he regrets hiring us yet, but he seems amused.

"More valuable than riches," Eliza says thoughtfully. "Knowledge. Is it a library?" Only Eliza would think that a library is more valuable than all the gold in the world!

Mom consults her notebook. "Earlier, two different people—Nadira Nadeem *and* Professor Phineas Alistair Worthington—mentioned something about Harmonia. Perhaps that's a clue for us. Mr. Bones, can you elaborate on what that is?"

He grins. "Bingo! At the end of the tunnels . . . we think . . . lies the Necklace of Harmonia." He pauses like he's waiting for oohs and ahhs, but the shock and awe never comes.

"What's the Necklace of Harmonia?" I ask.

27

"It's an ancient necklace, said to bestow eternal youth and beauty."

Eliza snorts. When we all turn to look at her, she flushes. "Well, that's impossible, isn't it?"

"Why do you say that?" Bones says. He's disagreeing with her, but he's not argumentative or angry about it—it's like he's excited by the possibility of a good debate. "Open your mind! *Impossible* is a word for the terribly unimaginative."

Eliza looks wounded. I dislike *how* Bones said that . . . but I can't disagree with the content of what he said.

This isn't the first time Eliza and I have disagreed about the supernatural. Eliza's a big believer in logic. To her, everything can be explained with sound reasoning and thorough analysis. But me? I know there are things in this world that defy explanation—things that are magical or mystical.

Maybe this Necklace of Harmonia is one of those things.

"What makes you so certain that the Necklace of Harmonia is down there?" Mom asks.

"Because of this," Orlando Bones says, gesturing behind him. He turns around, opens a locked cabinet, and fetches a disk out of it. He puts it on the table, where we all can see.

28

It's old. *Very* old. It's circular, made of stone, and has painted golden snakes curling their way across the face. There are letters all around the edge . . . Greek letters.

"We found this artifact sitting on a plinth right inside the mouth of the catacombs. It tells us everything we need to know."

Frank leans forward. "It does? It's all Greek to me!"

"Me too," Bones admits. "But Nadira has studied Greek, and she translated. The inscription around the side tells of an ancient and powerful necklace that lies deep within a tomb, for anyone brave enough to seek it out."

"I'm brave!" Frank shouts.

Bones bounces excitedly in his chair. "That's just what I wanted to hear."

TO ASK FOR MORE INFORMATION ABOUT THE HISTORY OF THE NECKLACE, TURN TO PAGE 328.

←——→

TO ASK TO EXAMINE THE DISK, TURN TO PAGE 402.

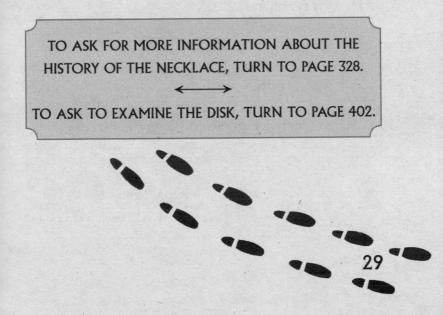

"WHICH ARTIFACTS HAVE gone missing?" I ask Nadira.

"Too many," she says. She consults her clipboard. "From the archaic period, three vases. From the classical period, a bust and a hair ornament. From the Hellenistic period, coins. And a golden armband that we found near the catacombs, which was stolen before we could catalog it. Altogether, these artifacts are worth hundreds of thousands of euros."

"So when did the thefts start?" Eliza asks.

"One day after the special task force arrived. The same day Keira Skelberry was put in the hospital. Before then, no issues. That's why Mr. Bones and I are convinced the thief is part of our team, and not Keira's. Right, Mr. Bones?"

He grunts noncommittally.

Is it just me, or is Orlando Bones being sulky about letting Nadira stay in the room? He reminds me of Frank when someone tells him no.

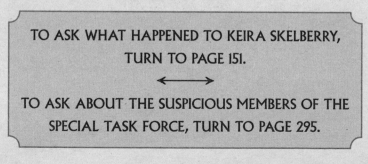

TO ASK WHAT HAPPENED TO KEIRA SKELBERRY, TURN TO PAGE 151.

←——————→

TO ASK ABOUT THE SUSPICIOUS MEMBERS OF THE SPECIAL TASK FORCE, TURN TO PAGE 295.

WE DRIVE FOR a long time. It must be at least an hour or two before we stop at a town and purchase supplies for hiking and water so we don't get dehydrated. We also grab sandwiches, which we eat back in the car. After lunch on the go, Frank wiggles his tooth aggressively until he falls asleep in the back seat. Eliza is reading, of course. Mom and I are quietly talking about the case, about school, about nothing at all.

I start to notice it about halfway through our journey: a silver car behind us. Its front windows are tinted dark, so I can't see who's driving it. It's staying far enough away that it's not immediately on our tail. But after it keeps pace with us for fifteen minutes, my alarm bells are ringing.

"Mom, Eliza . . . maybe I'm just paranoid, but I think that silver car is following us."

Mom looks in her rearview mirror, and Eliza stops reading to turn around.

"What should we do?" Eliza asks.

There's not much we can do. Especially when we need to reach Mount Olympus as soon as possible—we just can't afford any detours. As far as I see, we have two options. Ask Mom to floor it and go so fast that we lose our pursuer. Or ask Mom to slow down, so we can catch a glimpse of our pursuer's face.

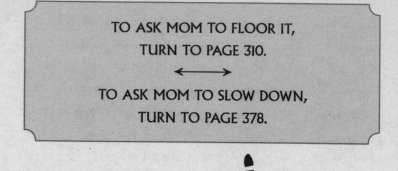

TO ASK MOM TO FLOOR IT,
TURN TO PAGE 310.

←→

TO ASK MOM TO SLOW DOWN,
TURN TO PAGE 378.

32

"HAVE YOU SEEN my mom?" I ask Dr. Amanda Mandible.

She shakes her head and looks confused—the first genuine expression I've ever seen her make. Either that, or she's a good actress. "What do you mean?"

"She disappeared at some point yesterday," Eliza admits. "And we don't know where she is."

"What are your symptoms?"

"Huh?"

"Depression? Anxiety? Do you find it hard to get out of bed? Are you worried constantly?"

"Right now, I'm annoyed and angry," I offer. "So, you haven't seen her?"

"Not since yesterday morning. When I met all of you."

"And you haven't seen her in the tunnels?" I ask.

She gulps. Then that smile comes back—that eerily fake grin. "I have never been in the tunnels," she says. "I don't go into the tunnels."

"But what about when—"

"Oh, you know what? I forgot about a . . . erm. A very important doctor's appointment I have to get to."

"But *you're* a doctor," Frank says. "Can't you just . . . doctor yourself?"

She giggles. "Doctors have doctors, who have doctors. But you know what they say—an apple a day keeps the doctor away!" She scurries out of the tent with a huge stack of papers and folders.

I sigh. Back to the drawing board.

But when I turn around, Eliza is grinning. She's holding a piece of paper.

"Thanks for being the bait, Carlos," she says. "I knew if I had a spare second, I could nick something useful from her pile of papers. Something that would tell us more about the ingredient list."

"But . . . you don't nick things," I say, confused. This is just like our mock case last month when she wanted to play every role on the team. "That's Frank's job."

"YEAH! Stop stealing my job!"

Her good mood curdles. "I'm not at all sorry for getting the job done."

LOOK AT ELIZA'S CLUE ON PAGE 361.

WE DID IT! Thirty-five is the number that's going to open Dr. Amanda Mandible's drawer. Now I can get into her files.

Inside is a series of charts and scribbled notes. It's hard to read because Dr. Mandible's handwriting is *terrible*.

> Magnesium rich, especially.
> High levels of iron, sodium, potassium, and calcium.
> Combine with honey, charcoal, milk, aloe vera, avocado, green tea.

"What's all this?" I ask.

I can feel Eliza looking over her book. She's interested in what I've found. I've got her hook, line, and sinker.

As a truce, I hold the papers out to her, and she comes over to look.

"Hmm . . . it's like an ingredient list, almost," Eliza says. "But I'm not sure what for."

The tent flap moves, and I *slam* the drawer shut.

Just in time! Dr. Amanda Mandible walks in. Her white lab coat has dirt stains at the bottom, and a few beads of sweat drip down from the braids at her scalp.

She seems surprised to see us inside her tent. But she recovers almost instantly with a wide, toothy smile.

"Oh, hello, adorable young detectives! How can I help you? Have a boo-boo? Need a lolly?"

"Always!" Frank says, grabbing three from her jar and sticking them into his mouth until his cheeks bulge.

"How have you been today? Are you acclimating to Greece?"

Is she just going to *ignore* the fact that we saw each other in the tunnels earlier? Perhaps I should ask her about that—or maybe I should cut right to the chase and ask her about the ingredient list we found.

TO ASK HER WHAT SHE WAS DOING IN
THE TUNNELS, TURN TO PAGE 410.

←——→

TO ASK HER ABOUT THE INGREDIENT LIST,
TURN TO PAGE 163.

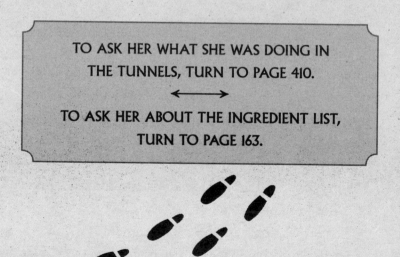

"ELIZA, YOU'RE SO amazing at puzzles. You're the smartest person I know!" I say, buttering her up. "Can you help me?"

She flips the page in her book. "Nope."

"What do you mean, *nope*?"

"I told you. I did my part already."

"Okay, but we're part of a team, and your job's not done if we haven't cracked this password."

"You have everything you need to solve this."

"But you always help when I get stuck with puzzles!"

Eliza puts her book down. Her gray eyes are blazing, and she looks *livid*. "You want to be the leader? Then lead."

"I *am* leading! But it's impossible to lead when you won't follow."

"What's your problem?" Eliza says, standing up and slamming her book on the ground.

"What's *your* problem?" I shout.

"Maybe you should use some of your detective skills and figure it out!" she says.

"Yeah? Well . . . same to you!"

Frank puts his hands over his ears. "STOP FIGHT-ING!"

"No!" we both shout.

Before I know it, all three of us are throwing things in frustration—Dr. Mandible's tongue depressors, gauze, the stethoscope, the blood pressure squeezey thing. It feels so good to let out some of my anger on the stupid fluffy cotton balls.

"What's going on in here?" Dr. Mandible bellows from the entrance to the tent. She sees the mess we've made—her medical supplies all over the ground.

"This was all sanitized, and you've sullied it!" she gasps. "You're going to make me break my Hippocratic oath! If I can't treat the wounded, then people might *die*."

"What can we do to fix this?" Eliza says.

Dr. Mandible pulls a container of sanitizing wipes out of a drawer. "Thank you for making amends. I need you to wipe everything down. Then do it again. This place needs to *glisten*."

Every time we think we're done, Dr. Mandible comes in with a magnifying glass to inspect our work and finds more areas of dirt that we missed. We are cleaning, scrubbing, wiping every tongue depressor, every cotton ball, every surface, every tool. Our hands burn from the cleaning solution on the sanitizing wipes.

Will this torture ever end? Because we are wiped out.

CASE CLOSED.

I LOOK AT the wall, and I realize with a jolt: the image shows a hammer. The symbol and tool of the god Hephaestus. My eyes dart between the necklace in the center and the hammer in the stockpile of items. I think it's pretty clear what we have to do.

Eliza realizes it too. "No, Carlos—there has to be another way!"

"There is no other way. There's a spot on the rock that perfectly fits the necklace. The wall has a hidden hammer. I point to all the objects meticulously lined up against the back wall. There's even a hammer in the cave, Eliza. This can't be a coincidence. It's clearly telling us to break the curse of the love triangle by destroying the necklace."

"But," Eliza squeaks. "But we *can't* obliterate an artifact."

"Eliza, we have to. The directions say—"

"Oh, and if the directions told you to jump off Mount Olympus?"

"Wheeeeeeeee!" Frank says. "Splat."

"This is different, Eliza. The necklace is cursed. It literally kills people who wear it. It destroyed Harmonia and countless others after her. It's an object of evil."

"But . . . it's also an ancient and beautiful relic. It has so much history. It's lived more lives than we ever will, and there is not another one like it in the world. Carlos, it is unethical to destroy it."

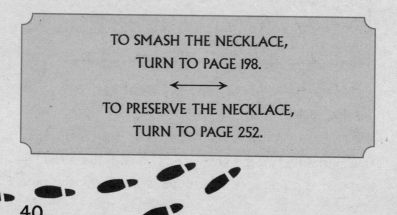

TO SMASH THE NECKLACE,
TURN TO PAGE 198.

←——→

TO PRESERVE THE NECKLACE,
TURN TO PAGE 252.

IT'S CLEAR THAT the Necklace of Harmonia is more important than the other missing artifacts. It seems like Bones's whole career depends on it, and he is our client! We have to switch focus.

"Sure, Mr. Bones," I say. "We can shift our focus."

I feel like I'm doing a great job, pleasing the client, but then I glance at Eliza, who looks back at me with confusion. I shrug, which only makes her brow furrow deeper. What is she thinking?

I look to Mom for validation instead, but . . . her eyes are set on Orlando Bones, not a hint of emotion on her perfect poker face. When this case is over, I have to get Mom to teach me how to do that! "Isn't finding the necklace the job of the task force? That's *not* what we do."

"I'm not asking you to treasure hunt. I'm asking you to investigate—"

"—in the catacombs, underground, alone, in darkness," Mom says, snappier than an alligator. "Mr. Bones, I'll be candid with you."

"Candy?" Frank says, perking up.

"Candid," Eliza whispers. "It means frank."

"Frank? It means *me*?"

Eliza groans softly. "It means honest!"

"A nest?"

"He's hopeless," I mumble to Eliza as Frank grins at me.

"Mr. Bones," Mom repeats, "we're not going back there. We've seen the catacombs briefly, and they are claustrophobically tight. Possibly unstable—and in danger of collapsing. And there are booby traps." I notice she doesn't mention that *we* got caught in one. "It's too hazardous to explore. I don't want my kids in those tunnels."

"I thought I was hiring professional junior detectives, not kids."

"They're both," Mom says. "And I have to put my foot down. I'm responsible for them, and I'm not risking their lives for a necklace, even a valuable one."

Disappointment registers on Orlando's grimy face, and annoyance jolts through me—I thought *we* were the lead detectives on the case, not Mom. I thought she was here to support us, not babysit us.

Mom stands up and holds out a hand for Mr. Bones to shake. "We will, of course, continue to investigate the missing artifacts for as long as it takes to find the thief. And if we hurry, we can catch the thief before they get anywhere near the necklace. Your undivided attention can be spent finding it now."

Mr. Bones stands up and shakes Mom's hand. "I respect that. You know when to hold 'em and know when to fold 'em."

We all get up, and as we cross through the flap into

the morning air, Frank says, "What's holding and fold-ing mean?"

"It's poker speak," Eliza explains, "for knowing when to keep placing your bets . . . and when your cards just aren't good enough to keep playing."

"So we're dropping out," I say glumly.

"Not out of the case, Carlos," Mom says. "Just out of the catacombs."

"That's the best part!" Frank whines.

"No, it's the most dangerous part."

"Danger *is* the best!" Frank says. "Danger and death and . . . doughnuts!"

There are archaeologists bustling about, grabbing trowels and heading into the pit. We see the special treasure-hunting task force in a huddle, listening to instructions from Nadira Nadeem. They're all about to head into the catacombs with Zip's map.

At least *someone* gets to investigate down there.

Still, seeing everybody reminds me that we still have things to look into: Nadira's flashlight and the way Mr. Bones didn't want to discuss the case in front of her; Richard Leech's squirrelly behavior and the way he freaked out on us and bolted yesterday; Zip and the way they were in the catacombs alone before we got there; Smarty and her attitude. And Professor Phineas Alistair Worthington, who Bones wants us to talk to.

And Dr. Amanda Mandible, who we haven't seen yet.

"Okay, team, let's head out!" Nadira Nadeem says.

With everyone (except Orlando Bones, apparently) gone in the catacombs, this is the perfect opportunity to snoop through people's belongings. And I won't lie—Richard Leech and Nadira Nadeem are at the top of my suspect list.

"So, what do you want to do?" Mom asks me, Eliza, and Frank. "Short of going into the catacombs!" she quickly adds, for Frank's benefit. He harrumphs.

TO SEARCH NADIRA NADEEM'S DESK,
TURN TO PAGE 422.

←→

TO SEARCH RICHARD LEECH'S TENT,
TURN TO PAGE 312.

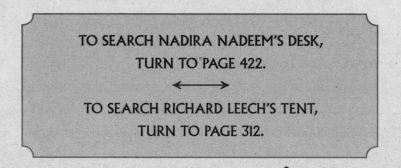

44

WE HAVE TO mess up Smarty's work—I know that's the only way to get rid of her. I run to her desk and push the papers off. They fall to the ground and scatter everywhere. Smarty looks at me, and for once, she is speechless. Her jaw drops.

After watching me, Frank suddenly has a mischievous gleam in his eye. "MUST. DESTROY. ALL." He grabs papers off the floor and starts ripping them straight down the middle.

"*No!*" Smarty shouts. "That's all my work over the past year!" And then she starts crying. More like blubbering.

Guilt twists inside me . . . but not inside Frank, apparently, who is dancing amid the wreckage.

"How could you be such a bad example for him?" Eliza says, horrified.

"But it worked—Smarty's distracted!" I say as Smarty lets out a racking sob. "Let's go, Zip!"

Zip shakes their head. "No, I'll be staying here to help my coworker fix her research. I won't talk to you anymore. And I'll make sure no one else on the team does either. Ripping up her work like that? This was unforgivable."

I don't even blame them; I don't really want to talk to me anymore either. Speaking of rips . . . RIP, case.

CASE CLOSED.

I THINK IT'S time we got out and did some of our own investigating. "Thank you so much, Mr. Bones," I say. "I think we have everything we need for now. Except . . ." I eye the disk sitting on the desk. "Can we take it with us? I think I know what to do with it."

"Smash it with a hammer?" Frank says, and I elbow him. Hard.

"He's just kidding. He has a *hilarious* sense of humor. Can we please take it with us?"

Bones has a look of horror on his face. "Absolutely not—you cannot! This is mine!" His hands curl around the artifact, his nostrils flare, and his eyes dart between us. He looks like a dragon guarding his hoard. "I need to keep this safe! With all the artifacts going missing—I'm sure you understand. This can't go missing too. It's too valuable."

"But—"

"No dice!" he says, putting the artifact back into his drawer and locking it. "I've had enough things go missing on me! I'm on a losing streak. So go save the treasure in the catacombs for me, eh? Go now!"

Outside, we huddle. "We have to talk to the professor," Eliza says. "Professor Phineas Alistair Worthington knows all there is to know about this Necklace of Harmonia. We need more information. What Bones told us was basically worthless."

"What do you mean?" I say. "He gave us a ton of information!"

Eliza ignores me. "Come on, even Bones suggested we talk to the professor. I'm dying to hear what he has to say!"

"Okay," Mom says. "Let's go!"

No fair! Since when don't I have a choice in the matter?

TO TALK TO PROFESSOR PHINEAS ALISTAIR
WORTHINGTON, TURN TO PAGE 386.

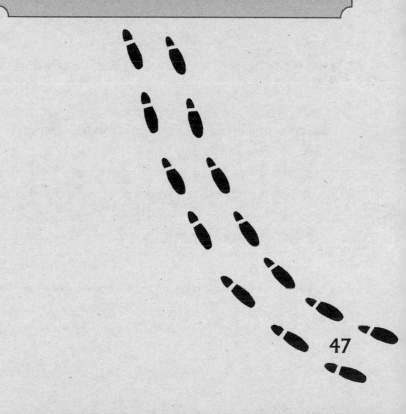

TRYING TO FIND Nadira's password with this calendar puzzle is making my head spin.

"Here, let me!" Eliza says, yanking the calendar out of my hands before I can even ask her for puzzle help. Rude. "We should work backward with this one. Since we know that today is Thursday, we know that yesterday is Wednesday, and the day before yesterday is Tuesday, right?"

"Wrong," Frank says.

"So when the riddle says 'Four days before the day after the day before yesterday,' you can substitute it out by saying 'Four days before the day after Tuesday.'"

DAILY PASSWORD: Four days before the day after the day before yesterday						
Sunday	Monday	Tuesday	Wednesday	Thursday	Friday	Saturday
126	142	178	236	259	284	321

That does make it easier, and I know I should heap praise upon her like I normally do. But I'm not in the mood. I can't take how hot and cold she is!

Eliza doesn't even acknowledge me. She continues, "Then if the day after Tuesday is Wednesday, we can replace even more of the riddle. So now it reads 'Four days before Wednesday.' And then it's entirely solvable."

THE SOLUTION TO THE PUZZLE WILL LEAD YOU TO YOUR NEXT PAGE.

THE MORE I think about it, the more I realize Eliza's theory makes sense. It just doesn't work logically. We saw my mom this morning. And for this letter to be true, someone would have had to kidnap her in daylight, in plain view of dozens of witnesses.

Ignoring the letter may seem like I'm doing nothing . . . but it's actually the hardest action I've ever had to take.

But I know it's the right one. If Mom isn't in the catacombs, then she might be in danger somewhere else. And we have to find her.

"So how do we trick a trickster?" I ask Eliza.

Eliza thinks for a long time. She twists her hair around, which is her nervous habit, and then finally an idea jolts through her like a bolt of lightning. She stands up suddenly. "Have you ever heard of a forgery?"

"Like a fake piece of art?"

"Yes. Let's make one."

"But isn't that a—"

"Crime?" Eliza says. "Yes."

Frank rolls over in bed and says loudly, "And we're partners in crime!"

"We're not selling it. So . . . *technically*, it's an arts and crafts project."

Frank perks up. "I love arts and crafts! But not as much as I love *farts* and crafts!" He toots.

"Very mature," I say.

He grins.

I turn back to Eliza, and she's looking down at her notebook—at a sketch she made of Harmonia and the necklace, painted on the entrance to the catacombs. She looks up at me again with a mischievous twinkle in her eye. For a moment, she almost looks like Frank. "Do you trust me?"

"You know I do."

"Good. Now, follow me."

An hour later, we're crouched in the parking lot. There are a ton of cars here, but nearly no foot traffic.

"This is never going to work," I say. I open my backpack. There are about twenty trowels inside. It's honestly a *miracle* we didn't get caught stealing them. Once the archaeologists discover that their tools are missing, they'll need to go into town—a hardware store—to get more. And that's where we'll hitch a ride.

Of course . . . the plan seemed a lot smoother than the execution. The late afternoon sun is beating down on us, and even though the parking lot is dirt, not asphalt, I still feel like a bagel in a toaster.

"Look!" Eliza whispers as we crouch behind a blue car.

Smarty Marty is grumbling as she walks to her

car—and we know which one it is, since she's the one who picked us up at the airport. With a good distraction, we can get to her car without her seeing us.

I rummage through my backpack. I obviously have twenty trowels. And I have snacks.

There's not much I can do with either of these except toss one across the parking lot—and hope Smarty looks in that direction.

TO TOSS A TROWEL, TURN TO PAGE 401.

←——→

TO TOSS A BANANA PEEL, TURN TO PAGE 176.

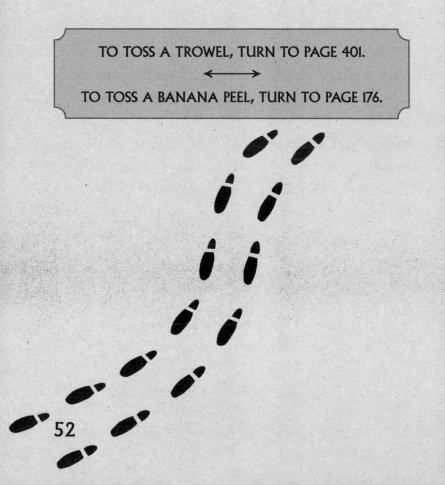

52

"DID YOU STEAL the missing artifacts?" I ask Smarty.

"Why would I do that?"

"To make Nadira look bad," Eliza suggests. "If the artifacts disappeared on her watch, she'd look incompetent."

"Or to make yourself look like a hero," I say. "If you stole the artifacts, you could stage a whole scenario where you magically find them again, and maybe Bones would be so happy with you that he'd promote you."

Smarty snorts. "Okay, but on the flip side, if I were caught, I would literally *ruin* my career prospects. Forever. Theft is a blemish that does not wash off an archaeologist's permanent record. Do I seem like the type of person who would be willing to risk my career?"

"No," Eliza agrees. "But you're a pretty arrogant person."

I choke on a cough—I can't believe she said that. Then I look at Mom, whose jaw has also dropped in disbelief.

"Arrogant?" Smarty says angrily. She stands up from her desk and smooths her skirt. "What on do you mean, *arrogant*?"

Eliza gulps. "I just mean . . . theft is only a risk if you get caught. And I'm sure you'd believe that you're too smart to get caught."

"BUT WE'LL CATCH YOU!" Frank says.

Like a rubber band snapping back into place, Smarty regains her composure. She sits down on her office chair. Then she picks up her fake glasses and puts them back on her face. "I take it back," she says. "I was wrong about being wrong about you."

That was a bust. All because Eliza had to go and insult the suspect.

We exit the tent, and it's already early evening outside. Eliza frowns. "I'm sorry. I don't know what came over me. It just sort of burst out."

Mom rubs Eliza's back. "It's okay, Eliza. I was shocked at first . . . but I actually think that was an interesting tactical move. You were able to break through Smarty's very smug veneer; for just a second, Smarty was stumped. I think that's a good way to handle her."

Eliza nods eagerly. In just one minute, she's really perked up. "I'm glad you think so too, Ms. S! I mean . . . it was an accident, but kind of a happy one, right?"

"You did incredible work today, Eliza. In the biz, this is what we call a hot streak! I'm very proud of you."

Mom has been paying my best friend so many compliments today, acknowledging Eliza as a detective in ways that *I* want to be seen. I guess it makes sense, since all of Eliza's leads panned out, and every idea she had was genius. Whereas . . . what did *I* do? Practically nothing.

The irresistible smell of supper wafts toward us: some kind of baked pasta dish called pastitsio, according to the dinner-preview menu I saw hanging up at lunch. I perk up a little bit, because I'm extremely hungry.

But after dinner, I feel just as glum again. Eliza's always been smarter than me. It's just a fact. But I finally found my calling with detective work, especially in making decisions and talking to suspects. But now it's like . . . Eliza's in my space. Even getting praise from my mom.

We worked so well together on three cases before this. We always got along. We never bickered about our choices . . . like we've been doing ever since that mock case last month. Why does Eliza want to change the way we are together?

As we get ready for bed, my mind drifts to the Necklace of Harmonia, which is supposed to grant the wearer eternal youth. If I had the necklace . . . I wonder if it would pause time. I wonder if it could keep things from changing between Eliza and me.

It's the first time I've ever seen the appeal.

I crawl into my cot and pull up the blanket. As my

eyes adjust to the dark, I realize I'm facing Eliza's cot, and she's facing me back.

"You've been awfully quiet tonight," Eliza whispers to me. "Are you okay?"

"Yeah. Fine."

"You know you can talk to me, Carlos."

"I know. Good night."

I turn my back to her and fall asleep.

"WAKE UP!" MOM whispers in my ear, and I groan. "Shhhhh!"

"What time is it?" I grumble, looking at my phone. "Four thirty! Mom, have you lost your mind?"

"Shhhhh!" she says again as she gently wakes up Frank, who pops out of bed like a jack-in-the-box. Then Eliza, who acts like an opossum playing dead for a few minutes.

Mom has already laid out our clothes and shoes, which makes me wonder how long she's been up.

"What are you doing?" I whisper, as Eliza finally sits up in bed.

But Mom just zips her lips and hands us mints to freshen our breaths. When we're all dressed, she leads us outside. No one is awake, and it's still dark.

We walk single file to the excavation pit and climb down the ladder in silence. Even Frank, which is— frankly—impressive.

The pit is empty. Spooky too. We have the moon and our flashlights, but every time a breeze blows through the pit, I jump. When we reach the archway, it feels like a cold breath is blowing on us. Like the entrance-way is the mouth of a monster, and we shouldn't go in.

But we have to go in.

"Now that we're far enough away from everybody else," Mom says, "I can tell you why we did this."

"It's to avoid attention, isn't it?" Eliza says. "If we go in the dead of night, before everyone wakes up, we can be in and out of the tunnels before anyone even realizes we've been down here. And whoever is trying to steal the necklace won't be able to follow us, which means we are less vulnerable."

"Excellent deduction skills!" Mom says. "You're an essential part of the team, Eliza. Right, Carlos?"

I nod, but a twinge of jealousy flushes through me. It's a hot, ugly feeling.

"Please don't do anything rash," Mom says. "I'm talking to you in particular, Frank."

"Rashes make me itchy." He scratches himself all over to prove the point.

"Good." Mom steps past the threshold, into the cat-acombs. One by one, we follow.

Inside, the dark feels like it's crawling. Spiderwebs cling to every corner, and the stone walls are cracked. I huddle close to the rest of the team. Eliza is breathing hard, and Frank is humming to himself.

Mom swings her flashlight from left to right and back again.

58

Eliza stops walking, and I run into her.

"This isn't going to work," she says. "We need to split up. Two of us on the left side of the catacomb. Two of us on the right side."

Splitting up? In these conditions? Sounds like a recipe for disaster. "I don't know. . . ."

"We're never going to find the keyhole like this," Eliza says. "We have to cover more ground, and we have to get closer to the wall. Walking in the middle like this is just not thorough enough."

"I CALL CARLOS!" Frank shouts.

"Why?" I say incredulously.

"BECAUSE I LOVE YOU!"

"Why, *really*?"

"Because you let me get away with the most stuff."

I roll my eyes.

"Actually," Eliza says in a small voice, "I was hoping to talk to you, Carlos. Would you come with me?"

My stomach drops. I feel like some sort of ominous conversation is about to happen. I really don't want to hash things out with Eliza. But I know I should.

"PLEASE!" Frank shouts.

"Please?" Eliza whispers.

TO EXPLORE WITH FRANK, TURN TO PAGE 182.

←——→

TO EXPLORE WITH ELIZA, TURN TO PAGE 265.

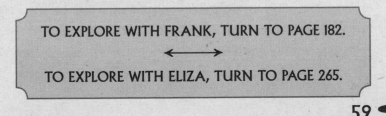

ELIZA'S THE FINGERPRINT expert, not me! I nudge her and whisper, "I'm having trouble telling them apart."

"It's really hard work," she agrees. "Especially since the one on the artifact was a little smudged and faded. But I still think we'll be able to tell. First let's figure out the shape of it. There are loops, whorls, and arches." She draws out the different fingerprint patterns for me in her detective's notebook.

loop   whorl   arch

"What do you think?" she asks.
"Definitely a loop."

"I think so too. So next we eliminate all our suspects that have whorls or arches."

"Now what?" I ask.
"Now we determine which one is the closest match."

1. Richard Leech.
2. Nadira Nadeem.
3. Smarty Marty.
4. Orlando Bones.
5. Zip.
6. Amanda Mandible.
7. Phineas Alistair Worthington.

TAKE THE NUMBER OF YOUR SUSPECT AND ADD THREE HUNDRED. THEN TURN TO THAT PAGE.

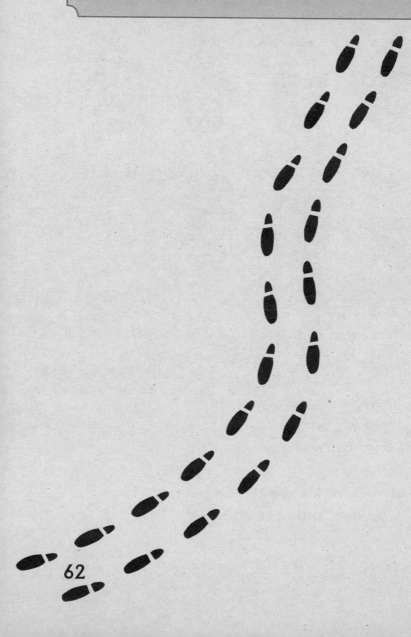

62

AFTER THINKING ABOUT it, I decide to support Eliza's idea. After all, we could always visit the catacombs next, but I don't tell her that part.

"Oh, Carlos!" she says, throwing her arms around me in a big hug. "Thank you so much for backing me up!"

With Eliza in the lead, we head to the work tent, where the artifacts are being stored. It feels weird to be following Eliza. I think I got kind of used to calling the shots, of knowing more about detective work, just because of all my years of living with Mom and watching her work. But now that Eliza and I have solved cases together, we're no longer the amateur detectives who don't know what we're doing.

It's like . . . we both have strong opinions, and we both have gut instincts. Ever since our mock case went terribly wrong, it's like our hunches are in two different places, and we don't agree on anything anymore. Everything just feels different.

"Hello?" Eliza says, peeling back the entrance of the work tent. "Anyone here?"

"Will you be quiet?!" Smarty Marty snaps at us. "I'm trying to work here! How on earth am I going to show Mr. Bones that I deserve a promotion with *all this racket?*"

"Sorry!" Eliza drops her voice to a whisper. "We just wanted to check out the—"

"Shhhhhhh! Don't care! Working here!"

"Have you ever played the quiet game?" Frank says. "My parents like to play the quiet game ALL the time. It's when you have to be quiet, and whoever's quietest the longest wins! Wanna play?"

"Will it get you to be quiet?" Smarty Marty says rudely.

"Sure! One, two, three, GO!" He's quiet for all of three seconds. "Oooooh, look—a penny! Wait, that's not a penny! It's just a button! WHOOPS, I LOSE! I forgot to tell you, I *always* lose at the quiet game!"

"I wonder why," Smarty Marty grumbles.

We shuffle to the artifact shelves for a closer peek. Every artifact is inside a clear plastic baggie and cataloged. I do notice a few empty spaces, where it seems like artifacts have been taken. But there's no pattern to the shelf, no rhyme or reason. And I don't see any clues left behind. Without a literal trail to the missing objects, I don't know how we're going to find them.

Eliza seems to find the half-empty artifact shelf more interesting than I do. She scribbles in her notebook and thoughtfully paces in front of the shelf. Personally, I can't think of a more boring direction we could have taken this case. This is like the exact opposite of a secret, mysterious, treasure-filled catacomb.

"Can I go talk to Smarty?" I ask Eliza as she crouches

over a bin. I figure I might as well start questioning more suspects. Sure beats whatever Eliza's up to.

"What? Oh, yeah. Sure."

Mom stays with Eliza, but I take Frank with me. "Hey, Smarty, can I talk to you for a second?"

"SMARTY MARTY, SHE'S A FARTY!" Frank sings.

She looks up from her computer, and her eyes narrow. "No."

"No?"

"Go away."

I know she doesn't want to talk, but I have to press on. She has information we need!

TO ASK ABOUT RICHARD LEECH,
TURN TO PAGE 258.

←——→

TO ASK ABOUT ZIP, TURN TO PAGE 423.

"WHO DO YOU suspect, Zip?"

Zip thinks for a moment. "I'm sure you heard about Richard Leech being kicked out of the work tent. He was getting awfully cozy with those artifacts. I heard he was promising them to donors. Ones that weren't his to promise."

"Where did you hear that?"

"From Smarty Marty, but I wouldn't trust her either. She'd do anything to get ahead."

"Okay. Is there anyone else you suspect?"

"Nadira," they say.

"PLOT TWIST!" Frank gasps.

"Why Nadira?" Eliza asks.

"Because she suspects me, right?"

"Yeah, but that's it?" I say. In the detective business, that's not really enough to go on.

"Sure. I know I'm innocent, so it's highly suspect that she's pointing the finger at me. Anyway . . . was that honest enough for you? I'm sorry, but if you have any more questions for me, you'll have to follow me back to the work tent. Orlando Bones expects me to have a new map in an hour. I've already told him it's just not possible, but . . ." Zip sighs.

"Is he a good boss?" Eliza asks.

Zip sighs again. "He's demanding. He's very excited about getting to the necklace. A little nervous too."

"Nervous?"

"Yeah. Always blathering on about how someone's going to steal it before he gets there. Constantly complaining that the deck is stacked against him. That puts a lot of pressure on me, and these things take time—maps and 3D imaging."

Eliza swoops down and begins picking up some of Zip's files that have scattered on the tunnel's floor. "Here, let us help you. We don't want you to be late for your deadline." She picks up a piece of paper and frowns. "Why does it say Map Version Four?"

Zip quickly snatches the paper out of Eliza's hands. "Because I messed up on the first three maps."

"But aren't you a professional?" I ask.

"I'm human too!" Zip says quickly. "And humans make mistakes all the time."

"It's true! Pobody's nerfect!" Frank says.

Zip grabs the lantern with one hand and the tripod in the other, and then—true to their name—they zip toward the tunnel's exit.

"Well, that was weird," I say.

"Now that Zip took our light source," Mom says, "do you think we should go back too?"

"We still have our phone flashlights, Mom. What if we went just a little farther? What do you think, Eliza?"

Very faintly, almost soft enough to miss it, she whispers, "I still think we should have looked at the crime scene first."

"Is anyone going to ask *Frank* for his opinion?" Frank says. "I think . . ." And then he farts so loudly that the tunnel nearly collapses. Nice. Classy.

TO GO FARTHER, TURN TO PAGE 392.

TO GO FARTHER, TURN TO PAGE 392.

←——→

TO TURN BACK, TURN TO PAGE 152.

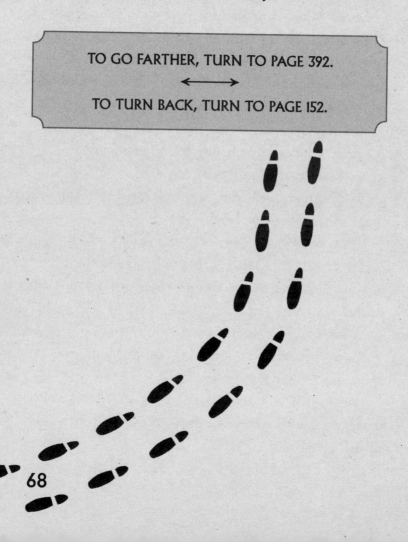

I FILL THE boxes of the nonogram into a diamond shape. Not bad!

Suddenly the bottom of the cabinet drops out, and the artifact crashes to the ground. It breaks into a hundred pieces. It's just crumbled rock now—completely unsavable. Unusable. Nothing more than a relic of a relic.

CASE CLOSED.

STOMPING ON THE stone feels like the right thing to do. It *is* loose.

"One, two, three, JUMP!" I shout. Frank and I use the full force of our body weight to stamp on the stone. The room rattles.

Uh-oh. Maybe we jumped *too* hard.

Suddenly glowworms rain down from the ceiling. They cover us head to toe.

"Get them off me!" Eliza shrieks. She does *not* like bugs.

"Cool!" Frank says. "I'm neon!"

I start to feel tingly.

"Um . . . Eliza?" I say, my voice thick and my tongue lazy.

"Glowworms are poisonous," she says. "They can secrete toxins that immobilize their pray."

That explains why I suddenly can't move my arms. Or my legs. Or my face. Uh-oh.

CASE CLOSED.

LEECH STORMS OVER to us, and we have to confront him. I'm not scared of him—he should be scared of *us*. After all, we know the truth, and we're the ones holding the evidence.

"Give me back my phone," he growls when he reaches us.

"What are you talking about? Your phone is in your hand," I say, which gets Leech even *more* fuming mad.

"The other one! You can't just go through people's stuff!"

"You're about thirty minutes too late for that," I say.

Eliza clears her throat. "Does the name Chad DuPont ring a bell?"

Richard Leech's face goes ashen. He rubs his goatee nervously. "Not. Here."

"Follow us," I say, and we lead him past the dig and halfway up the hill Frank and Mom must have hiked this morning. We need to be close enough to the dig that we could call for help, but far enough away that no one will overhear us. The view of the valley below is breathtaking, but I can't enjoy it. Richard Leech's face is contorted in fury. His overarched eyebrows look like they might pop off his face.

"Congratulations on the private collection," I say sarcastically. "I hear you have some real *steals*."

"You listened to a new voicemail," he says, halfway

between enraged and nervous. "It's the only explanation, because I wipe that phone clean every time I hide it back in that bust."

"So you're the artifact thief."

"I don't know what you're talking about."

"LIAR LIAR PANTS ON FIRE!" Frank bellows.

I waggle the phone in front of Leech, taunting him. "We have documented proof that you've stolen the artifacts."

"You don't know what you're talking about," Leech says. "Just like kids to come in and fling accusations around without any regard to the consequences!"

"So . . . you've never stolen a single artifact in your life?"

He squints. "I didn't say that."

"So you've stolen artifacts before," I say.

"I didn't say that either. I never claimed that!" He looks around to make sure no one is near us. When he's satisfied that we're the only ones on this hill above the excavation site, he leans in and whispers, "I'll deny we ever had this conversation. All I can say is that the archaeologists here run a tight ship. Everything is cataloged instantly. Smarty Marty caught me checking the catalogs and artifacts multiple times, hoping for something that wasn't documented—or at least was documented improperly. Don't look at me with such disgust, children. I'm doing the world a favor."

"How do you figure?"

"Art is meant to be shared, enjoyed, viewed widely. Oftentimes artifacts that end up in the possession of the government get shoved in a back room somewhere, never to see the light of day."

"So that's how you justify your thievery?" Eliza says with disdain.

"Imagine what a tragedy it would be if the world never saw . . . the *Mona Lisa*. Or the Nefertiti bust. Or the mask of Agamemnon. In my possession, every artifact—every magnum opus—finds an adoring audience."

Eliza snorts skeptically. "Don't pretend like you're doing this for the masses. In your private collection, you stand to make twice as much money as in the public museum you curate. You're enriching yourself."

Leech's nostrils flare. "I think you'll find that this is a mutually beneficial relationship. I benefit, the public benefits, everyone wins."

"What does Mr. Bones think about that?" I ask. "He's the reason you're here—he brought you onto his task force. You'd really betray his trust like that? I thought you two were friends."

Richard Leech smiles, and it's a very smarmy sort of grin. His teeth are unnaturally big and white. "This is all hypothetical," he says. "Because I *didn't* steal the artifacts."

"But you just said—"

"I would."

"Right."

"But I didn't."

Frank shouts, "Woulda, shoulda, coulda!"

Richard Leech clucks his tongue. "*Somebody* beat me to it. And now that the bust, the armband, the coins, and the vases have gone missing, the security on the other artifacts is even more tight."

I feel like my thoughts are all jumbling around. It's the first time I've ever heard someone admit to *wanting* to do a crime, if only they'd gotten there first.

TO ASK LEECH WHO BEAT HIM TO THE PUNCH, TURN TO PAGE 186.

⟵——⟶

TO ASK LEECH ABOUT HIS PLANS TO STEAL THE NECKLACE, TURN TO PAGE 406.

I CAN'T LIE to Eliza. Even when I'm upset with her, she's still my best friend.

"The truth is, Eliza, I'm frustrated."

"Oh, Carlos!" she cries, throwing her arms around me. "I didn't mean to forget about your mom! That was so thoughtless of me! I was just in the moment."

"Well, about that," I say. "I don't know how to say this. . . ."

"Just tell me."

I look into her familiar gray eyes. She looks a little worried. "Eliza, I feel like you've been stealing my thunder all case."

"Stealing . . . your thunder," she repeats in a flat tone.

"It just feels like we're out of sync, you know? Always disagreeing. And we used to get along so well during cases."

"Yes," Eliza says, "because I always went along with what you wanted."

"I guess I thought we had a dynamic that worked . . . and now we don't. You were the brain, I was the lie detector, Frank was the finder."

She crosses her arms. "Well, was it a dynamic that worked for *all* of us? Or just you?"

I *thought* all of us—we were solving cases. And everyone seemed happy with their job. Or so I thought. But the way Eliza has phrased the question, and the way her body language is all closed off, makes me think that she feels differently.

"Carlos, I'm a multidimensional human being! You realize that I'm more than a brain, right?"

"Of course!"

"Because I don't want to apologize for having investigative convictions of my own, even if they conflict with yours."

"I—I didn't mean . . ." I'm feeling flustered. And guilty. Because I really *did* want each of us to fit into our neat little boxes, our perfect assigned roles.

"I'm happy being a puzzle help line, but that isn't *all* I want to be. I'm not a one-trick pony."

"What do you mean?"

She flushes. "I . . . you're not the only one who wants to be a professional detective when you grow up. I want that too. Which means I have to hone all my skills, even the positions that used to go to you and Frank."

"Did someone say Frank?!" Frank says, skipping over to us. He tugs on my sleeve until I lean over. Then he whispers in my ear, "Two words: lolly. Pop."

I swat him away. Then I turn back to Eliza. "Where do we go from here?"

"I don't know," she admits. "I can't go back to the way things were. I like using my voice."

"I like that too," I say.

"Do you? Because you've been pretty miserable about it."

Okay . . . I have to correct myself. "I *will* like it. From here on out. I just need to learn to compromise more."

"I don't think it's about that," Eliza says. "I think it's about trusting each other, believing in each other's hunches, and talking it out. We haven't really been talking, you know. You've dug your heels in about your hunches, and I've dug my heels in about mine, which is why it feels like a huge tug-of-war between us."

"How about a hug-of-war?"

She squeezes me tight. "Best friends again?"

"We always were!"

"Ahem!" Someone near us clears their throat. Eliza and I separate. Smarty Marty stands before us, barely concealing an eye roll. "It looks like you're having a *moment* and all," Smarty says derisively, "but Mr. Bones is looking for you."

"Mr. Bones?" I say, perking up.

Smarty points us to the picnic tables. Orlando Bones greets us with a solemn nod, which is a *huge* departure from his lively, energetic attitude yesterday.

"Please sit," he says.

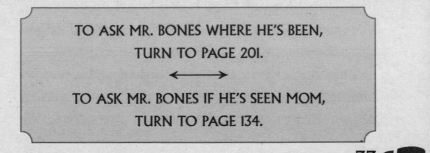

TO ASK MR. BONES WHERE HE'S BEEN,
TURN TO PAGE 201.

←——→

TO ASK MR. BONES IF HE'S SEEN MOM,
TURN TO PAGE 134.

I PULL THE necklace over Frank's head.

"HEY!" he cries.

"If you want it," I shout at Orlando Bones, shining my flashlight in his eyes, "go and *get it*!" I pitch the necklace so fast and so far that my Little League coach would be proud. The necklace plops into the river and quickly disappears in the dark water.

"Noooooooooooooooo!" Bones wails. He runs past us and dives into the river. "Where is it? Where is my jackpot? WHY WOULD YOU THROW THE GAME?"

But we are already running away, scurrying through the crawl door, dashing toward the exit. And at last we race through the archway—and find ourselves in the excavation pit again. Dawn is just starting to break over the horizon as we climb up the ladder. And once out of the pit, we run through the dig, screaming until we have no more breath in our lungs.

Two hours later.

It took fifteen Greek police officers to drag Orlando Bones out of the water, where he was diving over and over again (in vain) for the necklace. Rumors spread like wildfire around the dig that he nearly drowned two officers with all his flailing.

They hauled him above the surface and after two minutes of pressure, Orlando Bones cracked like an egg and told the authorities everything, including the location of Mom: on his boat docked in a nearby bay. As a few officers went to retrieve Mom, Nadira Nadeem brought the three of us some hot chocolate.

"Thank you," Eliza says.

"Where's the whipped cream?" Frank asks, and I elbow him.

"He means *thank you*!"

Nadira sits down with us. "All these rumors flying around about Mr. Bones and you three and the Necklace of Harmonia, and I just have to ask . . . did you really find it?"

I nod.

"Only to immediately lose it?" she says sternly.

"We didn't *lose* it, we *trashed* it," Frank says. Clearly he somehow thinks that's better, but it is definitely worse. Nadira lets out a wail and walks away.

"I think we've broken everyone's heart today," Eliza says, the corners of her mouth turning up into a smile.

"Well, we did chuck a priceless treasure."

"Don't worry. We still have a priceless treasure," Frank says. And he reaches into his pocket, grabs his front tooth, and holds it up to the sky. "TA-DA!"

Eliza and I snicker.

"This tooth will be worth something one day," Frank says.

"Yes, twenty-five cents tonight," I reply.

He grins at me.

"Perhaps the real treasure," Eliza says, "was the friends we made along the way."

We look sideways at Nadira, Smarty, Leech, Zip, Professor Worthington, and Dr. Mandible, who are all glaring at us.

"Or . . . perhaps not."

We continue sipping our hot cocoas, and I can't keep my eyes off the parking lot. Even with assurances from Orlando Bones (as he was escorted to a police car) that Mom was okay, I know I won't feel relief until I see her for myself.

But at last I see flashing lights in the distance, and I know it's Mom. She gets out of the car and runs across the dig to me—and I run to her. We meet in the middle of all the columns and I hold her tight.

"Mijo," she says, kissing my forehead.

And in that moment—with Bones apprehended, and Mom safe, and Eliza grinning, and Frank showing off his new gap to a bunch of archaeologists—everything is perfectly as it should be. Not bad for our first case as the lead detectives.

As for whether we'll take another case? I know in my heart that Eliza, Frank, and I will do this again, come hellhound or high water.

CASE CLOSED.

80

"OKAY, ELIZA," I say. "I guess we can talk to Richard Leech."

She squeals in delight. And she can't stop grinning, even as we climb out of the excavation pit and wander around the dig.

Finding Richard Leech turns out to be easy—he's sitting in a chair in front of his tent, smoking a cigar.

It smells *awful*. Sickly sweet and musky at the same time. Eliza and I both grimace . . . then we make sure to stand upwind.

"Pee-yew!" Frank says. Then he clenches his face. He looks like he's squeezing real hard.

"What are you doing?" I ask warily.

"Trying to fart," Frank says. "To improve the smell."

Richard Leech scowls. "You're ruining my smoke break."

"We just have a few questions. Then we'll be out of your hair."

"I don't want to answer any questions."

Too bad! We have a job to do. "Mr. Leech, do you have any reason to be suspicious of your fellow task force members?"

"I *said* I didn't want to talk to you," he says.

I soldier on. "You stole the artifacts, didn't you?"

Leech chokes on a huge puff of smoke. Then he starts wheezing and coughing. He blinks at us with watery, bloodshot eyes. "What? What are you talking about?"

"We know you were cozy with the artifacts," I say. "And that you had to be escorted from the tent."

"I . . . what a ludicrous—I don't want to answer any questions!" He dabs his face with a bandanna. His goatee twitches slightly, and his eyes dart. Definitely the body language of the guilty.

"We heard you promised your donors you'd have these artifacts in your museum—"

"I—I've gotta go!" he growls. He tries to extinguish his cigar in the dirt, but he leaves it still smoldering on the ground as he dashes into the bosses' tent.

Well, that backfired. I never took him for the squirrelly type.

"Amateurs," says a woman's smug voice in the tent's doorway (or technically, flapway). It's Smarty Marty. "I could do a better job."

"We know what we're doing, thank you," I say coldly.

"If you say so," Smarty says. "But I'm the one who actually has a clue right now. Not you."

Eliza perks up. "Would you share it?"

"Perhaps," she says cryptically.

I really have to restrain myself from rolling my eyes.

Frank lets out a huge yawn. "I'm sleepy," he says. "Time for bed. We'll talk to you tomorrow."

I must admit—I'm *exhausted*. To be honest, I'm not sure how sharp of a thinker I am when I'm this bone-tired. But the thought of walking away from a potential lead is almost unthinkable. Of course, Smarty could be bluffing.

"Smarty Marty, why didn't you give this clue to us earlier? We spent so much time with you today!"

"I didn't feel like it. And I didn't know if I could trust you."

Frank yawns, which makes Mom yawn, which makes Eliza yawn, which makes me yawn. Jet lag is pulling us under. My head feels suddenly heavy.

"Of course," Smarty Marty says snidely, "you can always choose beddy-bye."

TO ASK SMARTY MARTY ABOUT HER LEAD,
TURN TO PAGE 145.

←——→

TO GO TO BED, TURN TO PAGE 260.

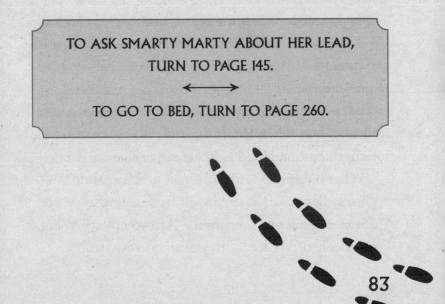

83

I HAVE TO throw this necklace off the mountain. There's only one thing he wants, and it isn't us.

"Hey, Mr. Bones!" I shout. I wind up. I pitch the pieces of the necklace straight over Orlando Bones's shoulder.

The remains of the Necklace of Harmonia arc through the air. The necklace pieces fly fast—and soar over the edge of the cliff.

"NOOOOOOOOOOOO!" Bones cries, and he turns on his heels and dives after it. Right off the side of the mountain. Eliza, Frank, and I run outside to see if we can see him—but we can't. Not from this angle.

"Is he . . . ," Eliza asks tentatively.

Right now I only care about one person. I get up and follow the shelf around the corner. "Mom? *Mom!*"

She is facedown on the ledge. I nudge her, and she begins to stir. After a few moments, she sits up against the mountain. "Ouch, that hurts," she mumbles, holding her head.

But she's okay. I laugh in relief and sweep her up into a big hug. Then I start digging into my first-aid kit for anything that could help her inevitable headache.

"What did me in? A head clonk or a rockslide?"

"Bones got you!"

"Bones?" she says, surprised. "Are you okay? Where is he now?"

I point to the edge of the cliff. "He jumped after the necklace."

"El tonto," she mutters, rolling her eyes.

After a few minutes, I help Mom to her feet, and we head toward the cave. There's one last thing we have to do. . . .

When we smashed the necklace, I heard a click. Now I have to find the source. I search the back of the cave and find a tiny door, slightly ajar. Before I can even look inside, Frank elbows me and Eliza out of the way. He crawls in.

"What do you see, Frank?"

His voice comes back, a little muffled. "Aw, this is worthless."

Bummer. I try not to be disappointed. Someone set up this wild-goose chase over a thousand years ago, so *of course* it didn't pan out. I don't know what I was expecting. "You can come out now, Frank."

"There's *no pizza* in here!" Frank says, clearly miffed. "Only gold, and you can't eat gold."

"Gold?" Eliza says. We each grab one of Frank's ankles and yank him out of the doorway. We shine our lights inside. There's a single object. Eliza reaches forward and pulls it out. It is some sort of belt made with gold so fine and delicate that it looks like lace.

"Is this . . . ? It can't be . . . Aphrodite's Girdle,"

Eliza whispers. "Forged by Hephaestus. It's said that if you wear it, everyone around you will fall in love with you."

"Romance. YUCK," Frank says.

"Okay, but if you wear Aphrodite's Girdle, do you die a horrible death?" I ask Eliza. "Was it forged in anger and revenge? Will you be cursed forever?"

"Nope!"

"Great! Then we traded up!"

One month later.

I'm doing homework at the table when Eliza bursts in through the front door. "Did you see this? Did you see?" Eliza shouts, holding her dad's laptop. She sets it on the table and looks around. "Where's your mom?"

I sigh. "Off on another case. She's been really popular these days. We were the lead detectives, and she reaped the benefits," I joke. "Why, do you need her?"

Eliza opens her dad's computer, and there's an article about Aphrodite's Girdle, which has spent a few weeks being studied by Professor Phineas Alistair Worthington and other leading minds in classical studies. He was gleeful about getting to examine it, even for a short time. Now that his university's lease is over, the belt is about to be moved to a museum in Greece, where anyone can come see it.

I smile, thinking about a month ago. When we returned from Mount Olympus with the girdle, Nadira Nadeem was shocked. We sat down with her first and told her everything—about the necklace, about the catacombs, about Mount Olympus, and about Orlando Bones.

When we finished our story, Nadira let us know that—like Eliza had said—intentionally destroying a relic is a crime, even if the artifact is cursed. So, in order to protect us, Nadira told everyone that the necklace slipped out of our hands and broke on the fall down the mountain. Luckily, after one look at Frank's adorable, newly toothless face (he wiggled out his loose front tooth on the way back from Mount Olympus), everyone instantly forgave our accident.

The authorities were sent after Bones. They scoured Mount Olympus for days, but they didn't find Bones *or* the Necklace of Harmonia pieces. They found only one thing: a fedora resting gently on a rock. It was placed in such a precise way that the special investigators in Greece don't think it fell that way naturally. So Bones survived the fall and is on the run.

Two weeks after we left Greece, Nadira emailed us from a different dig, where she is going to be the lead archaeologist. Apparently Nadira did not take Smarty with her, but I think Smarty's going to be okay. From some light online stalking, we discovered that Smarty is self-publishing a memoir about her experience as such an *important* archaeologist on a critical treasure-hunting mission.

"Carlos, are you reading the article?" Eliza says.

"What? Oh, yeah."

But my eyes glaze over as I start to read. No offense to whoever wrote the article, but I can't believe they could take the most exciting few days of my life—mythology and history that is so totally interesting—and turn it into such a snooze.

Eliza grows impatient with me. "Just look there!" she says, pointing to the bottom of the article.

> This artifact was uncovered, all thanks to three young children detectives from the United States of America: Carlo, Aliza, and Fred.

"Who?" I choke. "They didn't even get our names right!"

"They got close, though!" Eliza says, her eyes twinkling. "Isn't this exciting?"

I can't help but feel like our close proximity to the Necklace of Harmonia made the curse wear off on us . . . just a little bit.

"Maybe this publicity will get us more cases!" Eliza says.

"Yes, I'm sure Carlo, Aliza, and Fred have great adventures in front of them."

She grins and shoves my arm playfully. Even if we are slightly cursed now, we're in this together, and I have to admit . . . I dig it.

CASE CLOSED.

"WHO IS HARMONIA?" I ask.

Professor Worthington peers over his glasses at me. "Do you know the Greek gods?"

"Like Zeus and Hera and Athena and Poseidon?" Eliza asks.

"Indeed," the professor says. "Only this story starts with Aphrodite, goddess of beauty and love, and her husband, Hephaestus, god of fire and metalworking. You see, Aphrodite was having an affair with Ares, the god of war. When Hephaestus found out, he was furious. He told Aphrodite that he would curse any child that resulted from that union. But of course there was a child."

"Harmonia," Eliza and I say together.

"Precisely," Professor Worthington says. "Hephaestus bided his time while the child grew up. But seized his opportunity for revenge when Harmonia was of marrying age. Mad with jealousy and rage, Hephaestus forged the fateful necklace. Legend says it is adorned with gemstones and jewels—shaped like two snakes twisting around each other, their mouths meeting at the clasp. Hephaestus gave the necklace to Cadmus, the first king of Thebes and Harmonia's betrothed, who then presented it to Harmonia on their wedding day. Along with a robe, but very little is discussed about the robe."

90

"Did Hephaestus make the robe?" Eliza says.

"Is the robe cursed too?" I ask.

"Is it terry cloth?" Frank adds.

"I don't know any of that," the professor says. "The important thing is the necklace! You see, little did Harmonia know . . . pain and misfortune are bestowed to all who wear it."

"All?" Mom says. "Who else wore the necklace?"

"Oh, there are stories of it being passed down from owner to owner. And yes, calamity befell all of them. At last the necklace was passed down to two brothers; they soon wanted to rid themselves of the object. They asked an oracle for advice, and the oracle said to offer the necklace as a sacrifice at the temple of Athena in Delphi—and leave the necklace there. They did so, and that should have been the end of it. But a tyrant stole the necklace from its resting place and brought it to his mistress, the last known wearer of the necklace. While wearing the necklace, she perished in a house fire, intentionally set by her son."

"Wow, that's dark," Mom says.

"The history of the necklace is dark. What were you expecting? This is Greek mythology, not Mother Goose."

"So where is the house that burned down?" Eliza asks.

"What happened to the necklace after the fire?" I say.

"And speaking of gooses, what came first—the chicken or the egg?" Frank says.

"The ruins of the house are reasonably close by. I can provide an address, if you like. After the fire, the necklace seemed to vanish from existence. Of course, now that we've found these catacombs—and now that I have seen the entranceway for myself—I have two hypotheses: either someone returned the necklace to a resting place that already existed here, or someone created a resting place specifically for this necklace. All I know is that this entranceway and the Necklace of Harmonia are most certainly entwined."

"And the chicken versus the egg?" Frank says.

"Oh, I nearly forgot." He adjusts his glasses and looks seriously at Frank. "The egg."

"Crack goes the egg and down it goes," Frank whispers as he tickles his sister's head. "And now you've got the *chills*!"

I do have the chills, but not from Frank. This story gives me the shivers.

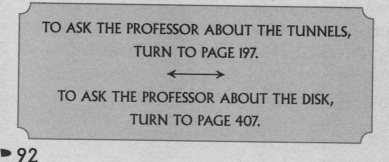

TO ASK THE PROFESSOR ABOUT THE TUNNELS, TURN TO PAGE 197.

←——→

TO ASK THE PROFESSOR ABOUT THE DISK, TURN TO PAGE 407.

I HAVE TO start with a green gem.

I thread the whole thing. Then when Frank is done with his clay part, we press the ends of the beaded chain into the clay . . . and voilà! I step back to admire our handiwork.

Only my side of the necklace looks a little off. Especially next to Eliza's.

She hums. "Are you sure you threaded it right?"

I was pretty sure, but I'm not anymore.

"It's okay," she says. "We can just try again."

We go to pull the gems off, but they're kind of stuck.

"Pull harder!" Frank says. "Heave ho!"

Eliza and I yank up on the twine. Half the beads break off and go rolling into the cracks of the wooden platform floor beneath our tent. The other beads are stuck to the clay but are bent or crooked now.

There's no way *anyone* is falling for this forgery anymore. This break destroyed our fake.

CASE CLOSED.

"I'M CONFUSED," I say to Nadira. "Where did these items come from? And if these aren't artifacts, then why were you so nervous about us finding your account?"

"Because I shouldn't be selling these things! Even if they're not stolen."

"You own all this . . . fancy stuff?" I ask, looking her up and down. It's not that I can't imagine her with fancy things. But . . . it is a little jarring. She's pretty casual, here on the dig.

"Some of these items were gifts. One is an heirloom."

"Wait, Ms. Nadeem. I don't understand. If these pieces of jewelry are just your personal items, why were you so secretive about selling them? And why were you so nervous that we found out?"

She grimaces. "Because one of the pieces is not mine. But it's the one that's worth the most. The emerald and diamond necklace belonged to my soon-to-be ex-husband's late grandmother."

I grimace. "You shouldn't sell something that doesn't belong to you."

"Why not?" Frank says. "Finders keepers losers weepers! That's the rule!"

Nadira sighs so heavily that she crumples onto her desk. It takes her a few moments before she lifts her head again and says in the smallest voice, "I've been

94

backed into a corner." She straightens up and smooths her hijab. Her tone is stronger now. "But I take my work very seriously—not a single item for sale is an artifact. You can look through my account."

"We will," I say.

"I can't believe you thought that I would be stealing artifacts and selling them in a public space online. That would make me a *very* unwise criminal!"

TO ASK NADIRA WHY SHE'S SELLING THE ITEMS, TURN TO PAGE 127.

←——→

TO ASK IF SHE HAS ANY SUSPICIONS ABOUT WHERE THE ARTIFACTS ARE, TURN TO PAGE 367.

WE CAN'T OUTRUN the spiders . . . we have to climb the pedestal and hold on.

"HURRY! CLIMB!"

We move like lightning. Frank goes first and gets to the top in no time. I follow. Then Eliza is beneath me. Mom is on the other side of the trunk from her.

Just in time, Mom pulls her feet up, and the spiders come racing through the room. They're making clicking noises. And I even think I hear a weird hissing—can spiders hiss?

"Carlos?" Eliza says. "Um."

"What's wrong?"

"My hands are so sweaty. . . . I can't hold on!"

"You have to!"

She shrieks.

"What happened?"

"One of my hands slipped!"

"Nooooooooo!" Frank cries. "MUST SAVE SISTER!" He crawls across me, stomping on my fingers, and nimbly inches down to her. "Got you, Eliza! Ooooops."

"Ooops, Frank? What oops?"

"I dropped the necklace. It fell out of my pocket."

No! I let go with one hand and pull the flashlight out of my pocket. I search for a moment—then spot a glint of gold!

There it goes! Riding away on the backs of a spider stampede.

Tears sting my eyes. Our one shot at cracking this mystery is gone forever.

My mood?

Cloudy with a chance of tarantula downpour.

CASE CLOSED.

I CLICK ON the spreadsheet that Orlando Bones has open. And I am overwhelmed with numbers.

DATE	EVENT / GAME	BET AMOUNT	RESULT	WIN / LOSS / EVEN
March 1	Sports Betting Football	$9,500	-9,500	LOSS
March 3	Track Horse Race	$8,300	$18,050	WIN
March 4	Online Betting Blackjack	$3,100	-$3,100	LOSS
March 5	Poker Game	$7,500	-$7,500	LOSS
March 7	Track Horse Race	$11,300	-$11,300	LOSS
March 8	Sports Betting Football	$7,800	9,600	WIN
March 8	Sports Betting Wrestling	$15,400	-$15,400	LOSS
March 11	Online Betting Blackjack	$3,900	$3,900	EVEN
March 12	Poker Game	$7,500	-$7,500	LOSS
March 13	Track Horse Race	$11,800	-$11,800	LOSS
March 16	Online Betting Blackjack	$200	-$200	LOSS
			-34,750	

"Wow," Eliza says. "He loses a lot."

I laugh. "Yeah, he's not very good at this."

"If he's losing this much money every week, he must be hundreds of thousands of dollars in debt."

"What kind of salary does an archaeologist make?"

"His whole yearly salary is probably about twice what he lost in just the past two weeks."

I whistle. "So he's got a gambling problem."

TO READ ORLANDO BONES'S EMAIL,
TURN TO PAGE 430.

"BUYING TIME?" I ask Zip.

"I'm waiting for the Anti-Grave-Digging Society to drum up support. There's going to be a massive protest outside the perimeter. With enough public outcry, we can stop progress on the dig."

"But *why* would you want to do that?" Eliza asks.

"Because these objects do not belong to us, and we should respect the burial rights of the dead. How would you like it if someone robbed *your* grave one day?"

"I'd be dead," Eliza says logically. "So I would neither like it nor dislike it."

"So you're just a fake engineer? The maps don't exist?" I ask.

"I'm not a fake. And sure they do. I just won't reveal them to anyone."

"Including us?" Frank says, throwing his bottom lip out in his most adorable pout.

"Including you."

"But we're CUTE."

Zip smiles. "Yes, but your mission is antithetical to mine. Nothing is more important to me than halting all progress on the dig and keeping this site intact. There's just nothing you can say that would change my—"

A piercing screech emanates from outside, and we all put our hands over our ears. A garbled voice echoes from the loudspeaker across the dig.

100

"Attention! Attention! Las Pistas Detective Agency, please report to Orlando Bones in his tent immediately. This is urgent."

I sigh. "What now?"

REPORT TO BONES ON PAGE 229.

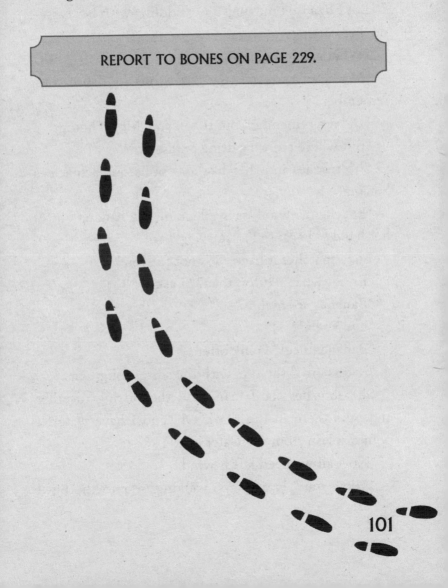

101

WELL, THIS IS the end of our adventure. We've reached a dead end, because there's no way we'll get our hands on gold or potassium or whatever.

"It was a good try," I say, turning around.

But Eliza isn't moving. She's fiddling with her ears—no, her earrings.

"What are you doing?"

"My mom gave me tiny gold studs for Christmas, remember?"

I did not remember, but thank you, Mrs. Thompson.

"But where are we getting potassium?"

She reaches into her bag and pulls out a snack: a banana.

"Excellent," Frank says, plucking the banana out of her hands, "because I'm *starving*!"

Eliza snatches it back. "It's not for you."

"Er . . . what is it for, then?" I ask.

"Bananas are high in . . ."

"Uh. Peels?"

"Banana juice!" Frank offers.

"Potassium!" she says with the softest of groans.

She smushes the banana and the earring together and puts them in the bowl. Oh, and I have water! I pour a splash from my water bottle.

"Now all we need left is wind."

"Allow me!" Frank says, walking over to the bowl

and farting. I guess that's one way to do it.

Suddenly we hear a soft *click*. The bottom left square on the wall swings outward, like it's on a hinge, and we can crawl through it.

Frank goes first, mostly because he slips through before we can stop him. Eliza goes next, and I hear her inhale sharply, and when I'm through, it's my turn to let out a surprised noise. Because on this other side of the wall, I see something I never ever *ever* in a million years would have expected down here.

There is a full river. Not a puddle. Not a pond. An actual *river*. The water looks inky black, and for some reason, I know we shouldn't touch it.

Creepiest of all—there's a boat waiting for us on the shore. I don't know what's across the river. Even with the flashlight, I can't see that far. All I know is . . . I know we have to see this through.

"The River Styx," Eliza whispers.

"The what?"

"In Greek mythology, the River Styx serves as a bridge from the human world to the underworld. This is an incredible imitation."

I'm glad she's so certain it's just an imitation. Because it looks real to me.

I walk over and climb into the boat. Eliza hops in after me.

And immediately the boat starts sinking.

"Eliza! GET OUT!" I shout.

She jumps out of the boat.

"MY TURN!" shouts Frank as he hops into the boat.

Immediately, again, the boat starts sinking.

This time I scramble out of it.

"Did people weigh less back in ancient Greece," I gripe, "or were they trying to make sure that the only one who could reach the treasure was a house cat?"

Eliza tentatively takes a step into the boat with Frank. Together, the Thompsons float . . . just barely, but passable.

"Great, so it's just me. Should I swim across?" I say sarcastically.

"We'll take turns crossing," Eliza says. "If Frank and I can travel together, and Carlos, you have to travel alone, we just need to figure out the minimum number of times we have to cross the river to get us all on the other side."

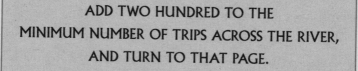

ADD TWO HUNDRED TO THE
MINIMUM NUMBER OF TRIPS ACROSS THE RIVER,
AND TURN TO THAT PAGE.

←——→

TO ASK ELIZA FOR A HINT, TURN TO PAGE 143.

WE FINALLY FIND the pathway of the electricity, and we're able to flip those circuits closed. The barrier immediately stops buzzing. But the fact that there's a trap with electricity in here in the first place . . .

"Do you think the culprit set up these traps to keep people out of the catacombs?" I ask as we kick down the fence and start walking, more carefully, to the exit.

"It's not enough that there are ancient traps—there are modern ones too!" Mom says. "This is too dangerous for us."

When we reach daylight, it takes my eyes a moment to adjust. It's like I've looked directly into a camera flash—and I'm seeing dots. I blink a few times, and then everything comes into focus.

"And the person behind us escaped while we were trapped," I say, disappointed.

"Well, if they set it up, they knew to avoid it," Eliza says.

I sigh. It feels like we're stumbling along. What we need is a tangible clue.

"Flashlight tag, you're it!" Frank says, whacking me on the leg with a flashlight.

"Ow, Frank—that really hurts!"

"Apologize," Mom says, "and turn that over."

"I apologize," Frank says. He blinks at me innocently. "NOT."

"Where'd you get that thing anyway?" I grumble,

yanking it out of his hands. "And why didn't you use it when we were in the tunnels?"

"I just found it! Thirty seconds ago. No, thirty-one seconds ago. No, thirty-two seconds ago."

"I get it."

"Thirty-three seconds ago."

I let Frank count on. I turn the flashlight over in my hands. NN is written in marker on the bottom. "It's Nadira's flashlight," I say, showing everyone the initials. "NN. Nadira Nadeem."

"Okay?" Eliza says. There's a long pause. I can tell Eliza's not really into my theory by the way she avoids my glance. My own excitement deflates like a punctured balloon.

"What's wrong, Eliza?"

She shakes her head. "Nothing. Never mind."

"Nothing, never mind! NN!" Frank says brightly.

I can usually read Eliza like a book, but not today. She looks just as frustrated as I feel. Why does every clue, every choice in this case, have to be a fight?

"Just tell me what you're thinking," I say to Eliza.

She tucks a few wispy loose strands of her pigtail braid behind her ear and finally meets my eyes. "It's just," she says hesitantly, "anyone could buy a flashlight and write NN on the bottom. And even if it is Nadira's, anyone could steal her flashlight from her workspace. It doesn't mean she was here. I think we should forget about the flashlight and go talk to Richard Leech."

Mom steps between us. "It's tough to work with a partner. Sometimes Detective Cole and I have different hunches when we work cases together. But being part of a team means listening to each other."

Eliza and I are both silent.

"Or taking turns?"

Eliza folds her arms. So do I.

Mom sighs. I can tell she's deeply concerned. "How about we flip a coin until you two can talk it out?" She pulls out a single euro coin and flicks it into the air.

"Tails!" Eliza calls.

It's heads. That means it's my choice.

I know what Eliza wants, and I know what I want. I wish I could please both of us—but I can't. The thing is . . . Eliza looks so hurt right now. She's wearing that face she gets sometimes at school, where she presses her lips together and doesn't blink for a scary amount of time. It's her I'm-not-going-to-cry-in-public face.

But why would she cry right now? I'm not sure I understand what's going on between me and my best friend—another mystery that needs untangling.

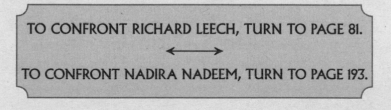

TO CONFRONT RICHARD LEECH, TURN TO PAGE 81.

←——→

TO CONFRONT NADIRA NADEEM, TURN TO PAGE 193.

WE HAVE TO keep going with the original plan. What's the point of even having a plan if we're going to change it?

I point to one of the column ruins near the edge of the dig. "We'll be putting the necklace at the base of that column in ten minutes. Only the culprit is allowed to come within thirty feet of the column. In exchange for the necklace, you will leave—on a notecard—the *real* location of my mom. And yes, we know she's not in the catacombs."

"DISMISSED!" Frank shouts.

Everyone disperses, and I put my backpack at the base of the column. I guard it until time is up, then I walk away.

Not more than a minute later someone runs by wearing—*no joke*—a blow-up T. rex costume. I guess that was their way of avoiding being identified as the artifact thief. The T. rex grabs the backpack, leaves an index card, and runs away faster than I knew it was possible to run in a blow-up T. rex costume.

We rush toward the index card. Where is my mom? We flip the card over to find out. It says, *Wouldn't you like to know?*

CASE CLOSED.

OUR BEST CHANCE at escape is to throw the robe on Bones's head. As cool as it would be to have two mythical relics, I can't risk Eliza's and Frank's safety.

Bones reaches for the necklace.

"RUN!" I shout, throwing the robe over him.

We dash past Bones as he struggles under the robe. We run down and up the stairs. Which brings us to the labyrinth.

"This way!" Eliza says, and *bless* her photographic memory.

We round the corner, and Frank lets out a yelp. "My tooth!" Frank says. "I lost it!"

"Congrats!" Eliza says.

"No, I mean I *lost it* lost it. It popped out of my mouth!"

We don't have time for this. "Pick it up, Frank! And let's go!"

Frank scours the ground with his flashlight. "I can't find it!"

"Frank, it's just a tooth—"

"I'M NOT LEAVING WITHOUT MY TOOTH!" he bellows.

Eliza and I turn our flashlights to the ground, looking all around the dirt for a baby tooth. Coming up with nothing.

Big, thundering footsteps are coming from the

bottom of the stairwell—Orlando Bones isn't far behind. We have to go!

"No use trying to escape, kids! I'm always playing with loaded dice!"

Just like in Greek mythology, we're in a labyrinth with a monster. Only instead of a minotaur, we've got a *mean*otaur.

I've got to do something. The labyrinth is impossibly large and winding. We could hide in a nook off the main path until he runs by us. He can't hurt us if he can't find us.

Or we could dash to the exit: through the labyrinth, past the snakes, and up toward the surface. I'm sure Bones wouldn't have dropped into the snake pit without some sort of exit strategy, like a rope or a ladder. And we're faster than Bones.

"I'M COMING FOR YOU!" His voice is dangerously close.

"Frank! I found your tooth!" I lie. "We have to go!"

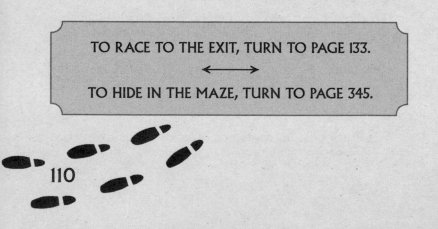

TO RACE TO THE EXIT, TURN TO PAGE 133.

←⟶

TO HIDE IN THE MAZE, TURN TO PAGE 345.

"TELL US MORE about the cursed necklace!" I insist. "How is it cursed? Why?"

Mom consults her notes. "Orlando Bones told us the necklace bestows beauty and youth upon the wearer."

"Oh, it does," the professor says. "But at the cost of pain and misfortune. Everyone who has ever owned the necklace has died a horrible and premature death."

"So . . . it keeps you young by killing you? *That* sounds worth it," I say sarcastically.

"Harmonia was the first, but she was hardly the last to wear this doomed necklace." He frowns, which makes his already downturned mouth look even more severe. "I fear what might happen if we *do* reach the end of the tunnels. Perhaps the necklace shouldn't be found."

TO ASK ABOUT HARMONIA,
TURN TO PAGE 90.

←——→

TO ASK WHY HE'S AFRAID TO FIND THE NECKLACE,
TURN TO PAGE 303.

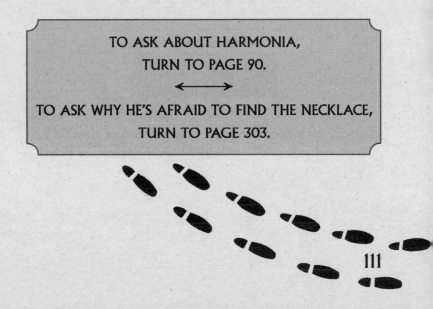

WE SHOULDN'T GET too close to the person in the tunnel. They could be dangerous. I have to call out to them.

"Hey!" I shout. "HEY YOU! WE CAUGHT YOU!"

The person stands up quickly. I can't see their face. They pick up their lantern and *run* deeper into the catacombs.

"Hey—stop!"

But they don't stop. They disappear into darkness. We dart after them, but . . .

Turn after turn, path after path—we get lost inside the catacombs, and we didn't leave bread-crumb trails to find our way back. We wander until our cell phones die, and then we wander in the dark, forever looking for our mystery suspect or a way out . . .

Welcome to our Greek tragedy.

CASE CLOSED.

"LET'S LOOK AT Orlando Bones's workspace," I say. "I'd like to know more about who's employing us."

We shuffle over to his desk. It's kind of a mess. There are playing cards and poker chips everywhere. All the pictures are of him, laughing, at casinos.

"It doesn't take a detective to deduce how much he likes gambling," Eliza jokes.

I'm honestly surprised he doesn't work at a casino—what on earth drew him to archaeology? I am so curious now.

TO SEARCH NADIRA NADEEM'S WORKSPACE, TURN TO PAGE 368.

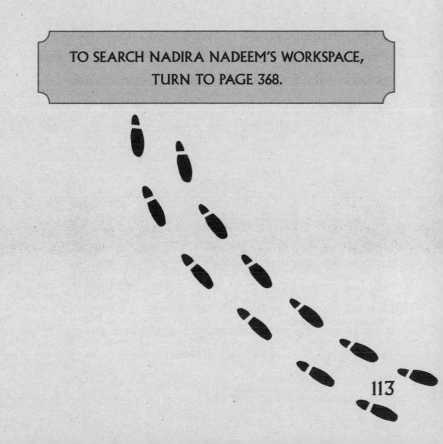

I READ THE last letter of each line aloud.

"Someone has taken your mother into the cata-combs. Be there in for teen minutes."

I collapse onto the bed—stunned, wounded.

Eliza pores over the letter again.

"We already deciphered the ransom note," I say irritably. "What else is there to figure out?"

Eliza doesn't answer me. The paper is so close to her nose, she could practically use it as a tissue.

Frank hops onto the bed next to me. "So Detecto-Mom is in the kitty combs, huh?"

"Yes, Frank."

"Are we going into the kitty combs?"

That's right—we could go after her. We *have* to go after her. She's in danger, and she needs us. I gather items—a flashlight, extra batteries, a trowel, a water bottle. Just as I'm zipping up my backpack, Eliza puts the letter down.

"Stop!" she cries. "We can't go down there."

"What? Eliza—we can't *not*! My mom is in danger!"

"Listen to me—"

"No, listen to *me*!" I say. "I don't know what's going on with you, but ever since the detective training we had last month, you've been different! Every time I want to go left, you want to go right. Every time I zig, you want to zag. I don't understand why we can't agree

114

on anything anymore. Are you disagreeing with me just to disagree? Or are you trying to make me feel stupid?"

She gets really quiet for a second, and for a moment, when she looks down, I think she's on the verge of tears. "I didn't know you felt that way," she whispers.

"How could you not? We've been clashing for a month!"

A long silence passes between us, with Frank darting his head back and forth like he's watching a tennis match or something. After a moment, Eliza looks up at me. There are tears in her eyes, but I can instantly tell—from the furious flush on her face—that they're tears of anger.

"Carlos, you're not stupid. And I would *never* try to hurt you on purpose!"

"Then why are you always fighting me on every choice?"

"Maybe it's not about you!"

"What does that even mean?"

She throws her hands up. "Detective work is in your blood—and you get to be around it all the time. Your gut instincts are always so good. And I . . . I've been studying so hard, playing catch-up to what comes so naturally to you. I got so many books from the library, learned all sorts of techniques, and I just—I wanted to step out of your shadow. I want to be your equal!"

"Eliza . . . what? You *are* my equal!"

She shakes her head, and her pigtail braids whip wildly. "No, no—I don't want to be *just* the puzzle girl. I want to make decisions too. I want you to take my opinions seriously, and I want to use my own voice." Tears roll down her face, and suddenly my hard shell cracks too.

"I didn't know you felt that way," I say.

She laughs and hiccups at the same time.

"Eliza, I hope you know that I never think of you as just a puzzle girl. And I value your instincts."

"Do you?" she says. "Because we do what you want to do most of the time."

I walk over to the tissue box beside Mom's cot and hand her one. "I'm sorry. I guess we both have a lot of opinions."

"ME TOO!" Frank says, wiggling his tooth.

"I suppose," Eliza says thoughtfully, "that we have to be okay with disagreeing with each other."

"And being flexible . . . which I haven't been," I admit. "I'm sorry."

Eliza smiles, then throws her arms around me in a big hug.

"HOORAY!" Frank says.

"So, to prove to you that I'm slowing down and willing to analyze the situation logically . . ." I put my backpack of tools on the ground and sit on the bed.

"Tell me why you don't think we should go after my mom."

Eliza sits on the bed across from me and Frank. "I want to go after your mom—*of course* I do, Carlos! She's like my second mom. I just don't think she's in the tunnels."

"Huh. Why?"

She smooths out the letter. "Something about this isn't adding up for me. For starters, *why* would anyone kidnap your mom?"

"Because she was on to them."

"But why would they take her down into the catacombs? That's kind of a funny place to keep her. We've also seen the catacombs, at least partly. They were extremely tiny."

"Frank sized!"

"True," I agree. "And Richard Leech told us none of the adults would fit down there. Mom isn't that much taller than us, and she barely fit."

Eliza passes me the letter. "This seems odd to me too. Why write us an anonymous letter with a secret message? If someone saw your mom being kidnapped, why wouldn't they just *tell* us about it? Or immediately tell Bones they know who the artifact thief is?"

Through my cloud of fear, something about my best friend's levelheaded logic reaches me.

"So you think whoever wrote this letter could be

luring us to the tunnels on purpose?"

"Making us think your mom is in the tunnels is the perfect way to get us down there."

This all makes sense. A *lot* of sense. "So if this letter is calling us down to the catacombs, you think we should just . . . ignore the call?"

"We could," she says with a nod. "But I understand if you want to go into the catacombs, Carlos. I really do. I'm trying to determine whether this letter is genuine or a trap. And if it *is* a trap, do we care? If going into the catacombs gets us closer to the culprit, should we take the bait? Or do we proceed with our *own* plan—and outsmart this kidnapper thief at their own game?"

"You choose," I tell her.

"No. Carlos, this one is yours. It's your mom. And I'll do whatever it takes to rescue her. I'm just glad you slowed down and listened to my logic, all the way through. I never wanted to take away your choices . . . I just wanted to be valued."

TO GO INTO THE CATACOMBS, TURN TO PAGE 237.

⟵——⟶

TO IGNORE THE LETTER, TURN TO PAGE 50.

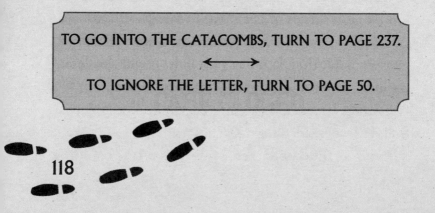

WE DON'T NEED to resort to stealing to get those maps. We can convince Zip—I know we can.

Back in the work tent, Zip is typing away on the computer. Luckily, Smarty is nowhere to be found. She *must* have caught on that Nadira's interview was a trick, right? So where is she?

Zip doesn't stop typing, even as we're standing right next to them. We tap them on the shoulder, and they jump.

"Sorry, we didn't mean to scare you," Eliza apologizes.

"No worries." Then Zip looks at me. "Heard about your mom. I'm sorry. That must be so stressful. Smarty told me," they add before I have a chance to ask. "If there's anything I can do to help . . ."

I take a step closer. "Actually, there is. You could lend us a map. The *real* one."

Zip winces. They look really pained. "You know I can't do that."

"If we don't have those maps—" I start to yell, but Eliza quiets me with a stern look. She pulls me behind her and steps closer to Zip.

"How did you become a part of the Anti-Grave-Digging Society? We've been meaning to ask you."

We *have*? That's news to me. But Zip lights up at the opportunity to answer her question. "In college, I joined a lot of activist clubs, but AGDS was very special to me. It was a passion that turned into a life mission. It's taken me all over the world. I met my partner protesting an excavation in Egypt."

"What about the society spoke to you?" Eliza asks. And even though I'm feeling so impatient that I'm practically itchy, I know she's going somewhere with this. I have to trust her.

Zip rubs their stubbly chin and considers Eliza's question. "I feel like I'm doing something important. I'm protecting something valuable."

"The artifacts," Eliza says.

"Yes! The history of people's lives."

"Human life is valuable," Eliza agrees.

"Exactly."

"So if you have the chance to save a life—Carlos's mom—wouldn't you agree that that's important too?"

"Of course, but—"

"The catacombs are going to become a tomb for someone very much alive. I know you know that an actual human life is way more important than even the most valuable artifact."

Zip frowns. "I empathize with what you're saying, but conservation is about more than just one person."

I huff angrily—we are getting nowhere, and Zip clearly doesn't care one bit about my mom. I want to throw something. Or maybe cry.

Eliza remains calm. She puts a hand on Zip's arm. "Zip, we understand you want to protect the integrity of the catacombs. It's a noble goal, really. But wouldn't it be harder to preserve if it became an active crime scene? Imagine all the detectives and police officers trampling through those catacombs. They'd have to demolish parts of it. A homicide is way more of a threat to the tunnels than we are."

Eliza gives her best puppy-dog face. Frank smiles widely, then breathes hard so his front tooth wiggles. I'm too mad to fake a smile . . . so I scowl.

"And," Eliza adds to seal the deal, "once we find Ms. Serrano, we'll destroy the map. No one ever has to go in there again, after us."

Zip considers for a moment. "You're right," they finally say. "I trust you kids to keep the catacombs pristine, more than I trust the police. Is it silly to put so much trust in you?"

"Not at all," I say.

They swivel the chair around, pull a key out of their skirt pocket, and dig through a drawer. Finally they find what they're looking for—a blueprint map. "This is the real map—as far as I could go, anyway. You're going to have to figure out the rest. I hope you find her."

"Thank you, Zip," I say sincerely. "Really. You saved the day."

"And remember—touch as little as you can! Wear gloves! And walk in each other's footprints, so you don't disturb the ground. And hold your breath, so you don't let too much carbon dioxide in there."

"Yup! Got it!"

We move to the exit.

"Oh, and don't bring food or water down there. Maybe you should consider wearing clothes that don't leave any particle residue behind—perhaps a poncho."

"Yup! Rain poncho—cool, cool!"

We escape the tent.

With Zip's map in hand, we dash to the entrance to the catacombs.

"Here goes nothing," I say, and we walk in. A chill goes through me. It's still so dark in here, not a peek of sunlight. It's suffocating, even with our flashlights.

I'm walking so fast that I'm nearly running. Every once in a while, we consult Zip's map, which helps us avoid two booby traps. Then the path slopes downward, like we're headed even deeper underground. I don't love the idea of that, but it's not like I have a choice.

"Mom?" I shout, crouching as the tunnel gets shorter and tighter. "Are you here? Can you hear me?"

"Ms. S?" Eliza calls.

"Detecto-Mom?" Frank yells.

But the only sound that echoes back at us is our voices.

At last, we reach a steep drop-off, and the catacombs open, just enough to let the three of us stand before a wall with very strange symbols on it.

"Ahhh, alchemy," Eliza says. "We got this."

"We do? Because last time I checked, you're not an alchemist."

"Yes, but . . ." She reaches into her backpack and pulls out a book.

Frank groans. "I thought we were crawling and sneaking, not studying!"

"We are—"

"I'VE BEEN TRICKED."

"Shhhhh," I say, just in case someone had any interest in following us.

Eliza flips through the book. "I knew we'd need a little extra alchemy knowledge as soon as we saw the archway outside. Remember how we saw that painted ouroboros snake—the symbol of infinity in alchemy? Of course, I didn't have an alchemy book with me. But Mr. Bones did."

I gasp.

"Wait, you *stole* a book?" Frank says with awe. "You

are the COOLEST SISTER."

"We needed to know about alchemy. He had the answers. I'm only borrowing it. I'll reshelve it before he even realizes it's gone."

She holds her flashlight over the book, then moves her light to the wall. She goes back and forth quite a few times before I realize I should be helping her out—and I focus my light on the wall.

$$\odot \quad \triangle \quad \triangledown \quad \female$$

"Interesting . . . it's a recipe."

"Like for a cake?"

"It's asking us for certain ingredients. And we're supposed to put them . . ." She moves her flashlight across the wall, and so do I, and so does Frank.

Something catches my eye at the bottom left edge: a small square outline in the wall. I wonder . . . Is it a door?

But I don't have much time to dwell on it before Frank cries out.

"There!" Frank says, shaking his light over a small divot in the floor. It looks almost like an offering bowl.

"Great job, Frankie," Eliza says. "Now if we can just figure out which ingredients to put in the bowl, I bet something will happen."

air   earth   fire   water

gold   iron   potassium   salt

silver   sulfur

IF THE RECIPE CALLS FOR GOLD, AIR, WATER,
AND POTASSIUM, TURN TO PAGE 102.

$\longleftrightarrow$

IF THE RECIPE CALLS FOR GOLD, EARTH, FIRE, AND
SALT, TURN TO PAGE 220.

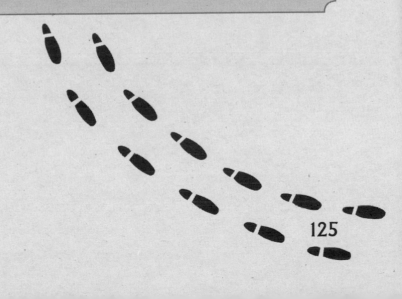

"YOU'RE STEALING THE artifacts, aren't you?" I say.

Dr. Amanda Mandible's stretched smile falters for just a second. Then she recovers. "You certainly have a lot of baseless accusations to make," she says. "I think maybe you should fix that mouth."

She leaps forward and puts sticky doctor tape across my lips. Then next thing I know, she's running around and around me with a bandage. She moves on to Eliza . . . then Frank! And when we're all mummified—covered completely everywhere except our eyes—she says, "Now that pesky accusation is under wraps!"

CASE CLOSED.

"WHY ARE YOU selling these items, Ms. Nadeem?"

She sighs heavily. "I never thought I'd be discussing my personal life with *you*, but . . . my husband and I are going through a very messy divorce. I'm about to be the sole caretaker of our three children. We're supposed to get equitable division of the assets."

"Huh?" Frank says.

"It means they're supposed to split all their money fifty-fifty," Eliza explains.

"But I know that my husband has a secret bank account, where he has hidden money away. The division won't be equitable. That's why I'm selling my engagement ring and all the jewelry and heirlooms. I'm just trying to make everything more fair, so that we *actually* get an equal split. And, well, I am already starting to worry about money. Childcare is expensive, especially when I'm on these digs. I'm overworked and underpaid . . . speaking of which—my meeting!" She picks up the phone. It rings and rings and rings. "Ugh, his voicemail is full. I can never reach Bones when I want to." She hangs up and tries again, talking to us over the ringing. "Things have been awkward between us ever since I asked him to take a break from archaeology."

"Your husband?"

"No, Bones."

Oh. That makes more sense. "You wanted him to quit?"

"He's been off lately. Distracted by the lure of treasure. I think he thinks it'll bring him fame and glory—" We hear Bones's voicemail again. Nadira growls and slams the phone down. "No use! I suppose he'll think I stood him up. Where were we?"

"Nadira," Eliza says, "can I ask you a question without you getting mad?"

Nadira bites her lip thoughtfully. "You know, it's really hard to promise that before knowing what the question is."

"Perhaps you wanted to steal the Necklace of Harmonia and sell it for extra money?"

She laughs. And not a fake laugh like Dr. Mandible—but a deep belly laugh. "Oh, that's a good one! You really think someone would be able to walk off this dig carrying the most valuable artifact in history? And then be able to sell it online?"

"Well, not online necessarily," Eliza says. "There's a secret market for this sort of thing."

Nadira shakes her head. "There's no market secret enough to contain one of this magnitude. Maybe you can get away with selling an artifact or two in a market like that. But if anyone on this dig thinks they're stealing and selling the Necklace of Harmonia, they're an idiot. I am no such idiot."

"Thank you," Eliza says, standing up. "I think that's all we need."

"No, it's not!" I say sharply. What is Eliza doing? "Ms. Nadeem, have you seen my mom?"

"Not for a while," she says without hesitation. "Do we have reason to be alarmed?"

"No, I'm sure it's okay," I say, but my voice is shaky and my throat wobbles. I'm convincing no one.

But we leave the tent anyway. Frank immediately runs to the bathroom. And then it's just Eliza and me. Standing out in the sun, I try hard not to feel as hot on the inside as I do on the outside. But I can't help it.

I'm confused. Really confused.

Here I thought we each had a role on our team. Eliza's the brains with puzzles and theories, Frank dives into all the small spots and finds all sorts of random clues, and I'm the one who talks to suspects and determines if we've gotten enough information out of them.

Eliza has been spending this whole case trying to go against every decision that I make, ending conversations before I'm ready to have them end, and refusing to help when I need her. She even stole the brochure from Dr. Mandible, which is usually Frank's job.

So why is Eliza trying to shake things up? Why fix

something that isn't broken? What is she trying to prove—that she can do all three jobs by herself?

Eliza puts a gentle hand on my back. "Are you okay, Carlos?"

TO LIE TO ELIZA, TURN TO PAGE 334.

←——→

TO TELL ELIZA THE TRUTH,
TURN TO PAGE 75.

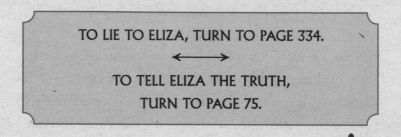

"ELIZA, WHAT DO you mean there's something actionable we can do? I don't know what to do with this!" My voice rises in panic. "I keep trying to see a message within a message, like you said, but I don't see anything!"

"We'll figure it out," Eliza says softly. "Together."

"Yeah!" Frank says. He pauses. "Wait, what are we doing?"

Eliza points to the end of the first line, then moves her finger down the page. "Look at this. I keep asking myself why the lines end where they do. The line breaks are very strange. What if . . . we only read the last word of each line?"

Dear Carlos,

There is nothing I can say that will make this any easier, but someone here knows the location of the missing artifacts and has been lying to you from the start. All I can say is that I am very taken with your detective skills, your determination, and your independent mind. Perhaps Eliza, Frank, and your mother don't appreciate your genius. But I do. I know you'll dive into danger. I know you'll do what's right to save the artifacts, help protect the catacombs, and save your mother—yes, don't be surprised. She needs your help. But there is no way I'm telling you where she is, in no universe can I write it down. Because I fear for my life. The years are flashing before my eyes: childhood, teen, adult years. But I'm doomed. The culprit is on to me. I have only minutes.

—A friend

ADD ONE HUNDRED TO THE NUMBER IN THE MESSAGE. THEN TURN TO THAT PAGE.

132

WE HAVE TO get to the exit! We have to get away!

Running as fast as we can, we reach the snakes in record time. We rub more garlic bread on our ankles and clear a path to a rope that Bones left dangling there.

We scurry out of the snake pit, run from the catacombs, and climb up the ladder of the excavation site. Then we weave through the tents, shrieking for help.

Suddenly my phone buzzes against my leg. Mom?

Nope—a text from a number I don't know. It's a picture of Bones, smiling, wearing the robe and the necklace.

Thanks for leaving the rope for me.

I turn to Eliza. "You didn't pull up the rope?"

"*You* were the last one out of the pit! I thought you were doing it!"

I get another text.

And thanks for my two treasures. Double or nothing!

"We have to catch him!" I say.

"How?" Eliza says. "He could be anywhere!"

My phone buzzes again. One last time.

I win. Game over.

CASE CLOSED.

"MR. BONES, HAVE you seen my mom?"

He chuckles humorlessly. "I guess my poker face isn't as good as I thought. That's exactly what I wanted to talk to you about." He pauses ominously, and it's like suddenly I forget how to breathe. "I saw your mom headed into the tunnels."

I instantly stand up. We have to go. We have to go *now* and get her.

Eliza puts a hand on my arm and slowly pulls me back to the table. When everything is telling me *go, go, go*, I have to remind myself to trust her hunches.

"When did you see her?"

"Yesterday."

"Yesterday?" I choke.

Frank wiggles his tooth back and forth like he didn't even register what Bones said.

But Eliza's eyes narrow. "Why didn't you tell us before?"

"Surely an accomplished professional detective doesn't need *me* to wait at the archway for her to emerge! She's supposed to be an ace." He adjusts his fedora and stares at me. "Look, when the chips are down, we find our courage. I figured you'd want to go after your mother, Mr. Serrano."

"Of course we do!" I say passionately. "But we need the disk."

Bones looks aghast. "No, you don't!"

"Yes, we do!" Frank says. "GIMME."

Eliza nods in agreement. "You found it on a podium inside the catacombs. It's *clearly* important—"

"You can go in without it. You really don't need it."

Why would he even show us the disk with the snakes and the Greek letters if he wasn't going to let us *use* it? I get that he's being protective of his artifacts, but this is my *mom*, and she's way more important.

There's no way that Bones will give it to us willingly. He's been clutching it like it's a life raft. But we need it. So we're going to have to get a little clever. . . .

The plan hinges on Frank. Somehow it always does.

Ten minutes after we leave, Bones gets up from the picnic tables.

"Go now!" I whisper to Frank, but he's already on his way. Just like we planned, Frank runs smack into Bones. Nearly bowls him over.

"Watch it!"

"WHOOPS!" Frank says.

"Shouldn't you be getting ready for the catacombs now?"

"Yup! Bye!"

Frank runs back to us . . . with Bones's phone in hand.

Perfectly executed.

Eliza takes the phone. "Nadira told us there are tensions between her and Bones—and we've already observed that on Bones's side. So all we have to do is place the perfect text. . . ."

> You skipped our meeting today. I'm not going to bankroll you if you're going to be irresponsible. You aren't getting paid for today. I'm doubling down on this.

She presses send and grins at me. "Let's hope it works."

Moments later, Nadira comes storming out of the bosses' tent. "Bones!" she fumes, marching over to the picnic tables. "I can't believe you would have the audacity to call *me* irresponsible, when *you're* the one who can never be reached."

"What are you talking about?"

Their commotion is gathering a crowd. I see our suspects: Dr. Mandible, Professor Worthington, Smarty Marty. They're all watching this spectacle gleefully.

"Your voicemail is always full—I can never get you. Are you punishing me for suggesting you take a sabbatical?"

"Why'd you say that in the first place? *You're* the

one who turned the dice cold!"

As much as I would love to hear them air all their grievances, we can't stay. We have to take advantage of this moment. We need to get the disk from Bones's desk.

We head toward the bosses' tent, but Frank starts running the opposite way.

"What are you doing?" I hiss at him.

"Potty!" he says, but he's running in the opposite direction from the bathrooms. . . .

"Carlos, we don't have time!" Eliza says, pulling me into the tent. We drop Bones's phone off at his desk. Then I turn to the cabinet with the disk.

My heart is pounding. I open the doors and . . . and there is a second door inside, which *of course* is protected with a digital lock. It's some kind of touch screen with a bunch of boxes and numbers.

"Oh, this is a nonogram!" Eliza says excitedly. "It's basically like a paint-by-number puzzle. See the numbers? They tell you how many boxes in that row or column are filled in. So, if it says ten above a column, it means that ten of the boxes going down are colored in."

"Why are there two or three numbers sometimes?"

"Because it's telling you there's a bunch in a row, then a gap, then another few. So the one at the bottom there—seven, one, seven. It means there are seven filled in. Then a gap. Then one filled in. Then a gap. Then seven."

"Uh-huh . . . ," I say, straining to hear Bones and Nadira's fight, very much aware that it could end at any second. "How do you know *which* box to color in?"

"You don't. Not at first glance. That's the puzzle of it! Sometimes it takes a little trial and error."

"And if we complete the nonogram correctly?"

Eliza smiles. "It'll reveal an image. And open up the cabinet—I'm sure of it."

								11	11	11		11	11	11					
			4	6	9	10	11	1	2	3	17	3	2	1	11	10	9	6	4
		1																	
		3																	
		5																	
		7																	
		9																	
		11																	
		13																	
		13																	
		15																	
		17																	
		17																	
		17																	
7	1	7																	
5	1	5																	
3	3	3																	
		5																	
		7																	

138

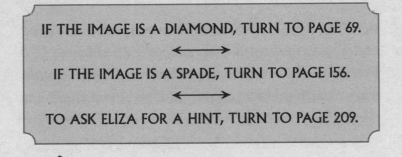

IF THE IMAGE IS A DIAMOND, TURN TO PAGE 69.

←——→

IF THE IMAGE IS A SPADE, TURN TO PAGE 156.

←——→

TO ASK ELIZA FOR A HINT, TURN TO PAGE 209.

139

WE CAN'T SNEAK around Zip's desk with Smarty Marty right here. I think it's safer to talk to her.

But when we walk up to her desk, she doesn't acknowledge us. She's staring straight at her computer.

"Smarty?" I ask.

She doesn't answer. Her headphone music must be *really* loud. We have to get her attention somehow.

I walk over to her phone and unplug her headphones. She looks up at me with a death glare—with fury and hatred stronger than the sun.

"I was in the zone!" she snaps. "Do you know how hard it is to get in the zone? How much concentration it takes?"

"Uh . . . no?"

"And do you know what happens to people who break me out of my zone before I'm ready?"

I gulp.

She reaches into her desk drawer and grabs a rope. She lunges at us. We scrap and roll around—next thing I know, she's tied me, Eliza, and Frank to the artifact shelf. We can't tug or struggle too hard, or we'll send a whole shelf of relics crashing to the ground.

"Let us go!" I shout.

"Ahhhh, sweet silence!" Smarty replies as she puts her headphones on and goes back to work.

CASE CLOSED.

"WHAT'S IN IT for you?" I say to Smarty Marty. "Let's see . . . if you let us borrow your car, we can get you a promotion."

Her face lights up for a second, but then she scowls even harder than before. "Wait a minute—you can't promise me that. You're not even an archaeologist!"

"I know," I say, "but we can always put in a good word for you with Mr. Bones and Ms. Nadeem."

"That won't go very far. I put in good words for myself all the time! They never listen." Smarty lets out an annoyed huff. "Okay, well, I have to finish compiling something for Mr. Bones."

Frank jumps. "Come on, Smarty! You can do it! Put a little power to it!"

She stares at Frank. "You can stop now."

"Be aggressive! B-E aggressive! B-E G-E-E-E-E-S-S-E-E-E!"

"That's not how you spell 'Be aggressive'!" Eliza whispers to me. "He just spelled 'Be geese'!"

I try—and fail—to contain my laughter.

Smarty looks annoyed now. She stands up from her desk and stomps her foot. "Seriously! This is *enough*."

"TWO, FOUR, SIX, EIGHT! WHO DO WE APPRECIATE?"

"He's just trying to cheer you on," Eliza says. "Since he has *nothing* better to do."

"Yeah, he could be in a car by now, far away from here."

"ONE, THREE, FIVE, NINE! WHO DO WE THINK IS MIGHTY FINE?"

"Will you leave me alone if I give you my keys?!" Smarty says.

"We'll get him as far away from you as possible," Mom promises.

"Wherever you're taking him . . . strand him there, would you?" She tosses Mom the keys.

I nearly sprint to the parking lot. When we started this case, I never dreamed that I'd be going on a literal treasure hunt. But here we are. The Las Pistas team: with a necklace, a translated message, a vehicle, and a mission.

All systems go!

DRIVE AWAY ON PAGE 31.

"ELIZA, HOW MANY times do we have to cross this river?"

"A thousand million billion," Frank says.

"It might help if we draw it out," she says. "You can't go first. Because then you will be on the other side of the river with the boat, and there will be no way to get the boat back to Frank and me. So Frank and I will have to go first."

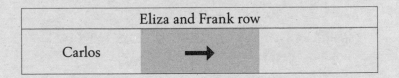

"Okay," I say. "Then one of you is going to have to bring the boat back to me."

"Me! Me! Me!" Frank volunteers.

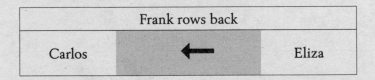

I already know the next step, without even discussing it; I have to go by myself.

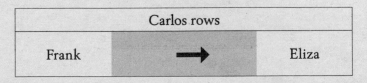

"Okay, so I'm across," I say. "How do we get Frank over here?"

"I have to go back and get him."

"And then?"

"Frank and I come back, and all of us are across. I know it's a pain to go back and forth like that, Carlos, but it's the only way."

ADD TWO HUNDRED TO THE
MINIMUM NUMBER OF TRIPS ACROSS THE RIVER.
THEN TURN TO THAT PAGE.

I YAWN. "FINE, Smarty, I'll take your lead."

"See that tent over there?" she says. "I overheard some nefarious activities going on while I was passing by. Real shady stuff. I think you should go and surprise whoever's inside."

"What kind of activities?"

"Definitely wheeling and dealing in artifacts. If you burst in, you can catch them in the act."

My brain is fuzzy. Something about this feels weird, but I don't know—maybe I'm too tired to judge what is good versus bad.

"Okay, we'll check it out," I say, heading over to the tent.

I don't hear anything, but Smarty nods encouragingly, so it might be right.

Three, two, one . . .

I burst inside and tackle the person lying on the bed. I don't realize until it's too late—I've attacked Mr. Bones! I woke him out of a dead sleep.

"WHAT IS GOING ON HERE?!"

Outside, Smarty Marty is laughing hysterically. "So much for knowing what you're doing!" she chortles as Bones fumes. "It was only too easy to get rid of you. Enjoy your flight home!"

CASE CLOSED.

145

I STRING A blue bead onto my side of the necklace.

Instantly Frank looks my way with laser eyes. "No!" he says. "No, no, no, no, NOOOOOOOOOOOOO!!!"

He smashes the clay. Then he destroys the gems. Then he spills the paint. Then he rips the twine. He's a one-man tornado. And when he's done with his tantrum, Eliza and I look at the wreckage in horror.

With no more materials to forge a fake necklace and no money left, there's no way to save Mom. I never thought one blue gem could make me feel so blue. . . .

CASE CLOSED.

WE HAVE TO trick Smarty.

"Smarty," I say, "I just wanted to talk to Zip about a rumor I heard."

Smarty looks at me suspiciously. "What rumor?"

"YEAH," Frank says. "Rumors, rumors are no fun, unless they're shared with *everyone*. And you can't spell everyone without F-R-A-N-K."

"Actually . . . ," Eliza starts to say, but then she trails off. Very softly, under her breath, she mumbles, "Never mind, it isn't worth it."

Smarty Marty glares at us. "I demand to know what's going on. Right. Now."

I look down at my toes, pretending to be sheepish. I'm just *praying* I'm a good enough actor to pull this off. "I mean . . . I wasn't supposed to say, but Ms. Nadeem is looking for an archaeologist for a dig she's supposed to work in three weeks, and she's interviewing—"

"Why haven't *I* heard about this?" Smarty roars. She grabs her blazer off the back of her chair and storms out of the tent.

"Clever!" Eliza says to me.

"Don't sound so surprised," I grumble.

Frank hops into Zip's chair and begins spinning around and around. "Wheeeeeee!" he squeals.

"So, I'm impressed," Zip says, folding their arms and leaning back against the desk. "You found me out."

147

"You mean—you stole the artifacts?"

"No, I'm talking about messing up the maps on purpose."

"So you *didn't* steal the artifacts?"

"I'm the one here trying to *save* them."

Eliza and I look at each other, confused.

"Explain," Eliza demands.

Zip opens the top drawer, digs under some messy papers, and pulls out a sticker with the letters AGDS on it.

"The Anti-Grave-Digging Society," Zip says with a touch of pride in their voice. "We're a group of activists who believe that archaeology is nothing more than glorified grave robbing. It's also detrimental to the local flora and fauna to excavate. It's our mission to stop all digs from going forward."

Wow. Okay. I wasn't expecting that. "Wait . . . so what are you doing working at a dig then?"

"Ohhh!" Eliza says. "I get it now."

"Get what?" I say.

"YEAH, GET WHAT?" Frank shouts as he spins another rotation on the desk chair.

"You are sabotaging the mission, aren't you, Zip?" Eliza says. "You don't want the Necklace of Harmonia to be found. You don't want *any* artifacts unearthed, not even the broken ones. You're making fake maps on purpose, so that no one gets to the treasure."

"But . . . there's no way this plan can last forever. Eventually Orlando Bones and Nadira Nadeem will catch on," I say.

"And fire you!" Frank adds gleefully.

"True," Zip says. "But I don't *have* to sabotage forever. I'm just buying time."

TO ASK ZIP WHY THEY'RE BUYING TIME,
TURN TO PAGE 100.

←——→

TO ASK ZIP FOR THE REAL MAPS,
TURN TO PAGE 323.

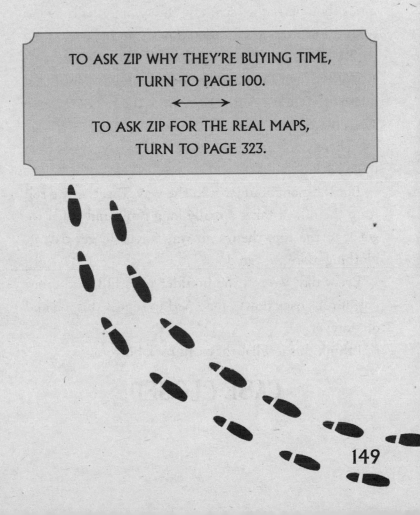

I PRESS B Δ Θ Λ Π Φ Σ, and the wall opens up. We did it! I run down this new pathway, excited. Eliza and Frank skip behind me. The path slopes downward, which further confirms that we're headed deeper underground.

"Do you hear that?" Eliza says.

I turn around to look at her, and scream. An enormous boulder—the size of the whole hallway—is rolling down the hill, headed *directly for us*.

"RUN!"

We run, run, run, and the boulder follows us. But it doesn't flatten us! At the bottom of the hill, it slows to a complete stop.

"There's nothing down here," Eliza says. "We have to go back."

But the giant boulder is in the way. Together we roll it up the hill. It takes a really long time, and when we get it to the top, there's no way for us to get past it. Nothing more we can do.

Every day, we roll the boulder up a hill, and every day, it rolls back down. Doomed to repeat this, on and on, forever.

I think this is what they call rock bottom.

CASE CLOSED.

"MS. NADEEM, CAN you tell us what happened to Keira? How did she end up in the hospital?"

Nadira frowns. "She went into the tunnels alone the evening the task force arrived, and she got trapped in some sort of ancient snare. It was quite a gruesome scene—she'd clearly broken several bones and had passed out from the pain. She was airlifted to Attikon University Hospital in Athens, where she had emergency surgery. She remains in recovery."

I shudder.

Nadira continues, "The funny thing is . . . we had walked right through that spot hours before, when Keira was showing the special task force around, and there was no booby trap there. Isn't that strange?"

"Well, we clearly didn't fall into the trap!" says Orlando Bones. "Since Keira was alone, we have no idea what triggered the snare she got caught in. It's all chance—a game of roulette!"

Nadira simply stares at him. The way she's looking at Bones—it's like she's rolling her eyes without actually doing it.

TO ASK ABOUT THE SUSPICIOUS MEMBERS OF THE SPECIAL TASK FORCE, TURN TO PAGE 295.

151

I REALLY WANT to go farther . . . but maybe Eliza's right. Maybe we should go back. "Fine," I say. "Let's go back."

We walk back out of the catacombs and nearly ram headfirst into someone at the entrance. Someone who's following us?

Before I can even catch a glimpse of who it is, they clonk me on the head. Next thing I know, I'm waking up on a rowboat in the middle of the Mediterranean. At least . . . I think it's the Mediterranean. There's no land in sight.

Eliza, Frank, and Mom are all with me, also stirring awake.

"I guess we just pick a direction and row?" I suggest.

This wasn't exactly how I wanted to *sea* the case through.

CASE CLOSED.

IF BONES WANTS to know what we've found, I'll give him a full suspect rundown.

"Right now, our prime suspect is Richard Leech. He's been hovering near the artifacts—and he even promised some of them to his museum donors."

Bones doesn't say anything.

I continue anyway. "We also found a flashlight that we think belongs to Nadira Nadeem." Eliza sighs heavily, and I talk louder so Bones doesn't hear her. "It was in an incriminating spot, near the entrance to the catacombs."

Bones blinks at me.

"And," Eliza adds, "we are planning to follow up on Zip and Smarty today."

Orlando Bones leans forward, pressing his lips against his tented hands. Frank also leans forward and begins a staring contest with our client. Neither one of them laughs or blinks for a solid thirty seconds—it's actually impressive.

Then, at last, Frank blows a puff of air at Orlando Bones, and Orlando's eyelids flutter shut. "I WIN!" Frank shouts.

But Bones doesn't even crack a smile. He's definitely not playing a game.

"Did you even," he says, his voice harder and sharper than the edge of a trowel, "talk to Professor Phineas Alistair Worthington yet?"

153

"No," I say. "Do you think we need to?"

"Yes!" He is exasperated. I can tell. I wonder if it's because of his phone call. His face flushes beneath a solid layer of grime.

This feels like one of those classic moments when the client is upset about something else but starts taking it out on us. But *why* is he so upset? Who was on the other end of that phone?

TO ASK ORLANDO ABOUT THE PHONE CALL,
TURN TO PAGE 211.

THE X HOLE is the right one. I'm certain.

"Okay, Frank, hop in!"

He nods and wiggles into the hole.

"Well?" I say.

"Aw, rats."

"What's wrong?"

"No, I mean, it's a room full of rats! And—AHHH! THEY GOT ME! YOU HAVE TO COME GET ME!"

How did our mission turn into a game of hide-and-squeak?

CASE CLOSED.

THE FINISHED NONOGRAM is a spade. I should have known, since a spade is both a card suit *and* an archaeology tool.

I open the cabinet with ease. The disk is lying there, along with a piece of paper. I snatch them both, put them in my backpack, and close the cabinet again. I'm ready to go after Mom.

I sneak out the back of the tent. It's empty outside—except for Eliza, who's guarding the entrance. "What happened to Bones?" I ask.

"He and Nadira stormed off into their sleeping tents."

Well, good. "And Frank?"

"Let's hope he's at the pit."

Luckily, there he is waiting for us, at the entrance to the catacombs. He waves wildly as I approach. "DID YOU GET THE DISK?"

"Shhhhhhhhh!" Eliza and I shush him.

"SORRY! BUT DID YOU?" he shouts.

"Yup."

"I got stuff too," Frank says, patting his backpack.

"What stuff?" I ask.

"NONE OF YOUR BEESWAX."

I pull the disk and the piece of paper out of my backpack. I think the paper is a translation of the Greek inscription along the side.

156

Deep in the catacombs where the necklace lies,
brave heroes seek its riches. Will they find it? It's
written in the stars above. Under the earth the
riches lie. Ophidian curses too.

"Ophidian?" I ask.

Eliza shrugs and starts typing into her phone. After a moment, she looks up. "It means 'pertaining to snakes.'"

"Creepy!" Frank says gleefully.

"Well, there are snakes on this disk."

"There are indeed."

"Okay. Here we go." I take a deep breath and cross into the catacombs. I'm expressly disobeying Mom now, but I also know I have to. Who knows what sort of horrible booby trap she fell into in these tunnels? I try to push the panic down. We're going to find her. And save her. Everything is going to be okay. "Hang on, Mom," I whisper into the dark. "I'm coming."

Almost instantly, it feels like we're headed into a black hole, where the light is getting swallowed up. We click on our flashlights and look around. There's a lot of empty walls and plain dirt beneath us. Thick spiderwebs hang from the ceiling.

"Do you see anything connected to our disk?" I ask.

"Nope!" says Frank. "Wait . . . nope!"

I shine my light on the translation again. "'It's written

in the stars above. Under the earth the riches lie.' Well, we have two directions. That must be on purpose—a clue to the riddle. So should we look up or down?"

"I don't know, Carlos," Eliza confesses. "Your guess is as good as mine."

TO SEARCH THE CEILING, TURN TO PAGE 315.

←—————→

TO SEARCH THE GROUND, TURN TO PAGE 236.

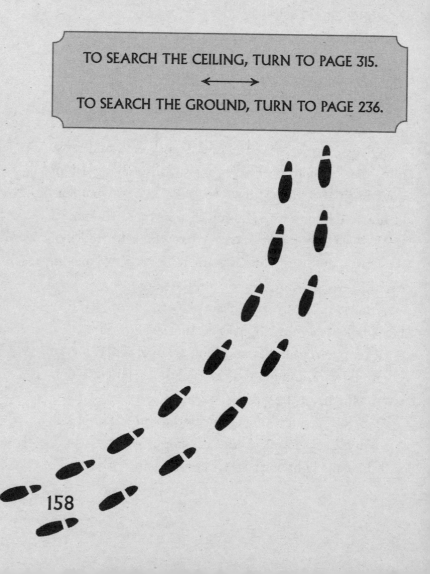

I'M SENDING FRANK down the hole with this letter: Ω.

"Bon voyage!" I say.

Frank crawls in. Almost immediately, I hear, "Uh . . . Carlos? Eliza? Detecto-Mom? I'm stuck."

No matter how hard we yank on him, he's really wedged in there. We're in a hole lot of trouble.

CASE CLOSED.

"THAT LIST OF ingredients—honey, green tea, char-coal. What are you making? And if it's so innocent, why would you keep it locked away in a drawer?"

"Carlos, honey, you're looking very flushed. Let me take your temperature." Dr. Mandible sticks a gadget in my ear.

"Are you avoiding our question?"

"Okay, ninety-eight point three. Good, that's normal. Now open your mouth."

"This isn't necess—"

"Of course it is!" she says. "Okay, now say ah!"

"Ahhh?" I say, as she presses my tongue down with an overlarge Popsicle stick. "Ahhh!"

"Excellent. There we go. Now . . ." She takes the tongue depressor out of my mouth. "Do you snore?"

"How am I supposed to know what I do when I'm sleeping?"

"Because I've noticed your tonsils are a bit on the larger side—"

"Thank you, but *no thank you*," I say firmly. "I don't need a checkup right now."

"Can you answer our question?" Eliza says. "Why do you need—"

"Oh, look at the time!" Dr. Mandible gathers up her papers and runs out of the tent. "I've got to go—very sorry—bye!"

160

She leaves.

"That was a waste of time," I complain.

"Was it?" Eliza says, her lips curling into a satisfied smile. She holds up a piece of paper. "Because while Dr. Amanda Mandible was busy examining you, I stole something from her pile. This looks like it will be of interest to us."

LOOK AT ELIZA'S CLUE ON 361.

161

I DECIDE TO look at Leech's notes. He's only taken one:

ARTIFACTS

- jade bird statue (Song dynasty)
- teacup set (Edo period)
- small silver bowl (Nara period)
- scarab amulet (ancient Egypt)
- four canopic jars (ancient Egypt)
- lekythos (Hellenistic period)
- bust (classical period)

I look up. "Wait a minute. Hellenistic. Classical. I recognize those words."

Eliza checks her notebook. "Those match up with the artifacts that have gone missing here."

"So Leech stole them!"

"Maybe. Or maybe these are just artifacts he's interested in getting for his museum. Perhaps his voicemail will give us some clarity."

TO LISTEN TO LEECH'S VOICEMAIL,
TURN TO PAGE 411.

"**TO BE HONEST,** Dr. Mandible, we found a piece of paper in your drawer that is really curious. It seems to be a list of ingredients. Can you tell us what those are for?"

"What *what* is for?" she says sweetly.

"The list of ingredients."

Her toothy smile gets even more stretched.

"I don't know what you're talking about."

"LIAR LIAR PANTS ON FIRE," Frank says. He enters the passcode again, pulls out her ingredient list, and hands it to her. "Explain."

She looks at the list and titters. It's a controlled laugh. Forced.

"It's my job to make sure the special task force remains healthy. This list contains things that are all part of a balanced diet."

"Really?" Eliza says skeptically. "The list includes bentonite clay, charcoal, and aloe vera—are you really proposing we should eat these things?"

Dr. Mandible chuckles again. To cover up her nerves? To distract us? I've never met a more giggly suspect.

"You're laughing a lot," I point out.

"Well, you know what they say: laughter is the best medicine."

"Actually, medicine is the best medicine," Eliza says.

"Actually, lollipops are the best medicine," Frank

says, grabbing three more and putting them into his mouth.

"Well, this has been fun," Amanda Mandible says, "but I really have to get back to work now."

"But—"

She walks us to the door flap. "Goodbye, kiddos. Please stop by if you're feeling under the weather."

"How about over the weather?" Frank says, staring into the clouds as he exits the tent. "Or what if I'm just feeling the weather?"

She laughs and closes the door flap behind us.

"Well, that was useless," Eliza says.

"Not really," I say. "She's clearly hiding something. And we got her ingredient list."

"Ingredients for what, though? And what does that have to do with the missing artifacts?"

I don't have an answer for that. But luckily, Frank comes to my rescue with a subject change. "Where to now? The tunnels? More tunnels? Please say the tunnels!"

"Maybe we should check in with Mr. Bones," I say, and Eliza gives a noncommittal shrug. "We should ask him what he knows about Dr. Mandible."

But when we arrive in the bosses' tent, it is empty. Another perfect opportunity to snoop. Two desks. One for Orlando Bones and one for Nadira Nadeem.

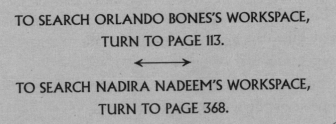

TO SEARCH ORLANDO BONES'S WORKSPACE,
TURN TO PAGE 113.

←→

TO SEARCH NADIRA NADEEM'S WORKSPACE,
TURN TO PAGE 368.

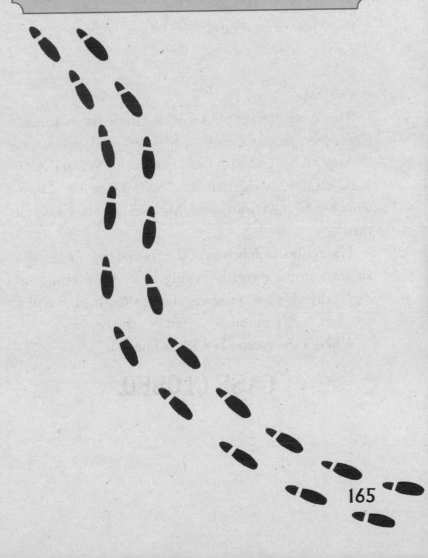

165

I ENTER IN the passcode X-Y-Z-P-D-Q, and Frank is literally dancing. "Told you, told you, told you!" he says. "Frank is always right!"

Suddenly the computer screen goes black. A skull appears on the screen. That *can't* be good.

Self-destruct initiated in five . . . four . . . three . . . two . . . one.

BOOM!

The computer explodes into hundreds of pieces. Computer keys all over the floor—and parts too. Smarty Marty looks up from her work. "WHAT ARE YOU DOING?" she bellows. "Nadira is going to have your heads! Just wait until Mr. Bones gets a load of this!"

The commotion brings in the special task force, who all start simultaneously yelling at us for messing up Zip's (already slow) progress. Their shouting lasts for a minute . . . five minutes . . . ten . . . thirty . . .

Where's the escape key when I need it?

CASE CLOSED.

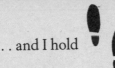

WE SEND FRANK through the Φ hole . . . and I hold my breath.

"Frank? You okay?" Eliza says.

The wall in front of us rotates, revealing a path forward now. And Frank stands there with a giant grin. "Holey moly, that was fun!"

I groan.

We step over the holes, and Eliza was right: only one went under the wall and back up on the other side. Who even knows where the other holes went? Glad we don't have to find out.

We continue down the path, and when I say down, I mean *down*. We're headed deeper underground. How far beneath the earth are we? And where are we going?

Frank runs up ahead, and Eliza skips after him to make sure he doesn't get into any trouble. Mom and I bring up the rear.

"Carlos, I couldn't help but overhear your discussion with Eliza. Small catacomb and all," Mom says quietly. "You know that I think you're brilliant, right?"

I snort. "Yeah, right."

"Yeah. Right," she says, dead serious. She puts a hand on my shoulder and squeezes. "Just because I compliment Eliza—or Frank, for that matter—doesn't mean I don't *also* think that good thing about you. Being good at something isn't a zero-sum game."

"Huh?"

"Oh, where's Mr. Bones to explain zero-sum games when I need him?" Mom jokes. "What I mean is . . . Eliza being smart doesn't make you any less smart. You and Eliza can both be smart at the same time. You both *are* smart. Eliza receiving praise doesn't take anything away from you. Got it?"

"Yeah." I think I do, now.

"Love you, mijo."

"Love you too, Mom."

We hear an excited gasp from farther down the tunnel, and we run to catch up with Eliza and Frank. They're standing beside a wall with painted words. The only problem? The words are in Greek, and none of us can read Greek.

Κάποτε απ' τους θεούς και στους θεούς ξανά.

Επιστρέψτε το δώρο.

Αυτό δεν είναι το τέλος μα το κλειδί για σπουδαιότερα πράγματα.

With three flashlights lighting up the words, I pull out my phone and take a picture.

"What's that for?" Eliza asks.

"We know two people who can read Greek: Nadira Nadeem and Professor Phineas Alistair Worthington. Maybe one of them can translate when we get out of here."

"*If* we get out of here," Frank says.

"When!" we all shout back at him.

We keep walking forward. At the end of the hall, there's another wall that swivels, and the room we stumble into is empty, except for one tall pedestal in the center.

"It has to have the necklace on it!" Eliza whispers.

"What makes you say that?" I ask.

"Just look at the stem of the platform!"

Carved snakes winding all the way up . . . with red gems for eyes. If this isn't a fancy platform for a fancy necklace, I don't know what is!

Because the podium is so tall—and so close to a gap in the ceiling—it makes me wonder: If we had taken another way through these catacombs, would we be able to reach down to grab the treasure instead of having to climb up for it? I guess we'll never know.

Frank hops over to the pedestal. Grabbing the snakes with his hands and using them as footholds for his feet, he scales the trunk of the podium easily. It might as well be a rock wall or a playground jungle gym.

"This seems too easy," I mumble.

"Don't forget," Eliza says, "we had to do a lot to get to this point."

"There's a necklace up here!" Frank calls as he reaches the top. "Shiny jewelry. It's got some gold snakes. Is this what we're looking for?"

"Yes!" Mom, Eliza, and I all yell.

"ONE SMALL STEP FOR FRANK," Frank says, holding his fist out dramatically. "ONE GIANT LEAP FOR FRANKKIND!"

He takes the necklace off the plinth.

Nothing happens. Thank goodness. I let out a sigh of relief as Frank climbs down with the prize and touches the ground.

But then.

The rumbling starts.

"What's that?" Mom says.

I point my flashlight all around. Then I see it—across the room. It looks like a wave coming toward us, only it's not water. It's black and twitchy and a little hairy. I am frozen in horror.

"ARE THOSE SPIDERS?" Eliza shrieks.

The rumbling has awakened an army of spiders. And I don't mean, like, ten spiders. I mean *thousands* of spiders. Ones that have been slumbering down here all their lives. They are fast. They are angry. And they are swiftly approaching.

170

"We have to get away!" Mom yells.

The spiders are so fast that if we run, they might overtake us. If we climb up and hold on to the stem of the podium, like Frank just did, we could wait them out. But I don't see an end to the arachnid parade. Holding on for dear life might require more stamina than we have.

"CARLOS, WHY ARE YOU JUST STANDING THERE?" Eliza roars.

TO HANG ON TO THE PEDESTAL UNTIL
THE SPIDERS PASS, TURN TO PAGE 96.

←——→

TO RUN BACK THROUGH THE CATACOMBS
TOWARD THE EXIT, TURN TO PAGE 253.

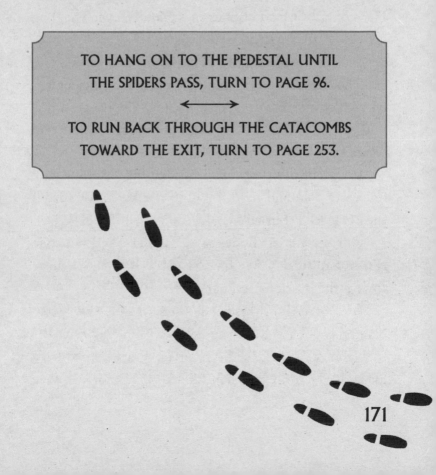

"WHAT'S IN THE catacombs that's so valuable?"

"Pizza!" Frank says. "Macaroni and cheese! Chicken nuggets!"

I turn to Frank. "You truly think *chicken nuggets* have been resting for thousands of years in an underground bunker, and they're still ready to be eaten?"

"That's what makes them so special," Frank says.

I snort.

"We think the catacombs house . . . the Necklace of Harmonia!" Orlando Bones says grandly, even wiggling his fingers for mystical emphasis.

"What's the Necklace of Harmonia?" Eliza asks.

"The Necklace of Harmonia is part of an ancient legend—it's an artifact made by the god Hephaestus. It is said to bring eternal youth and beauty to anyone who wears it."

"It also brings death and misfortune," Nadira says, her voice cold and hard. "We do not know for sure if the necklace is buried here—"

"Of course it is!" Bones says. "It's here, and someone is trying to steal it! We have to get to it first—we have to save the precious artifact!"

"I do not see how this pertains to our stolen artifacts," Nadira says. "We want the detectives to find out who took the relics off the drying rack and where they're located. The tunnels, the Necklace of Harmonia—none

172

of that is relevant. They should not even step foot near the catacombs, if they are doing their job properly."

Is it just me? Or does Nadira really *not* want us to go into the catacombs?

Bones frowns, and in the silence, Nadira looks at her watch. Time panic registers on her face. She stands up suddenly and says, "I know the catacombs sound exciting, but please do not forget why we hired you in the first place. And that is to *find the missing artifacts*. That's all. Now, if you'll excuse me—I really do have to run!" She leaves the tent.

I turn to Orlando Bones. "Are you suspicious of Nadira? Is that why you didn't want her in the room?"

He laughs. Very loudly. "Don't be preposterous! If Nadira were a playing card . . . why, she'd be the ace of spades! Most valuable card in the deck!"

"Also because archaeologists carry spades?" Eliza suggests.

"Sure, sure!" he says.

I squint at him, and I honestly can't tell if he's lying. Maybe he really doesn't suspect Nadira Nadeem. But then why were they fighting so much? And why was he so reluctant to bring her into the conversation? Like usual, I have more questions than answers.

Still, I think I've gotten all I can get out of Bones. "Thank you, Mr. Bones."

"No matter what Nadira says, the catacombs are a good bet." Bones dismisses us with a tip of his hat. "Best of luck!"

We file out of the tent, and I'm rearing to go.

But Eliza is wearing a deep frown. She consults her notebook, then looks at me. "Do you really think we got enough information out of that conversation, Carlos?" she says, and I can't believe she's being critical.

"Yes, I think that went great," I say coolly.

"It's just . . . I feel like the fighting really detracted from the evidence gathering."

I feel my good mood souring. "Look," I say softly to the huddled Las Pistas team, "I think we should check out the catacombs."

"Kitty combs!" Frank cheers. "Going on a treasure hunt . . . X marks the spot!"

Eliza lets out a deep sigh. "But we were hired to find the thief who stole the missing artifacts, not to explore an ancient tomb."

"But you heard Orlando—they're connected!"

"I think Nadira's right. Going into the tunnels won't get us any closer to figuring out who took the artifacts. Going to the crime scene will. I think we should examine the artifact shelves for clues."

Mom looks between us. "You both have excellent ideas. And you both make excellent points. Maybe we can take turns?"

174

"Well, it's two against one!" I tell Eliza, as I put my arm around Frank.

Her cheeks turn watermelon pink. Is that embarrassment on her face, or is she mad? Who even knows anymore? I mean . . . if I'm doing majority rules, then Frank and I outnumber her. On the other hand, maybe I should cave to what Eliza wants.

TO CHECK OUT THE CRIME SCENE,
TURN TO PAGE 63.

<——>

TO CHECK OUT THE CATACOMBS,
TURN TO PAGE 324.

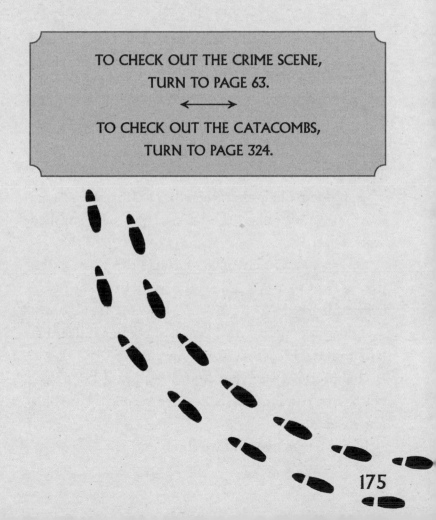

I PEEL A banana. Then I take the peel and wind up to lob it into the air as high as I can possibly throw it.

"Ooooh! I saw this on TV! Like a cartoon!" Frank says, excitedly yanking on my arm.

He changes the angle of my throw. *"Frank!"* I whisper-scold, as the banana peel arcs through the air like a glorious yellow football.

It lands *splat* on Smarty's head.

"Ewwwwwwww!!!!" she shrieks. She looks up into the sky, clearly thinking a bird has pooped on her. I guess that worked better than I thought! Thank you, Frank!

I grab Eliza and Frank by the hands. We duck and dash to Smarty's car, open the trunk, and climb in. There is barely enough room in this trunk for all three of us. It doesn't help that when the car finally *does* start moving, we all roll to the back, very much smushed against each other.

After an extremely uncomfortable fifteen minutes, the car finally stops. I unlock the trunk from the inside before Smarty locks us in, but I hold the trunk down so it doesn't pop up. After I've been holding it like that for a minute, Eliza breathes in my ear.

"I appreciate your caution, Carlos, but if I don't get out of this trunk in the next three seconds, I'm going to *scream.*"

I let the trunk go, and we climb out.

176

We're definitely in town. There are actually buildings here, instead of tents. There are lots of signs in Greek and people walking around. We walk down the strip until we find what we're looking for: a craft store.

The bell dings as we open the door and walk in. There are beads, gems, glitter, and cloth everywhere.

"This is *perfect*!" Eliza says as she runs her hands through a bin of some of the shiniest fake jewels I've ever seen—in greens, blues, purples, reds, and pinks.

We purchase clay, twine, jewels, and gold paint—as much as we can afford with our emergency euros. Then we walk to a taxi line. I don't speak the same language as the driver, so I hold up my phone and show him the address of the dig. He nods and starts driving.

In the back seat, we're exhausted. The sun is going down. It's been a long day, and it's about to be a long night. Physically, because we have to forge the Necklace of Harmonia. Also emotionally, because I can't stop thinking about Mom. Where is she? Who would kidnap her?

Which of our suspects is capable of artifact thievery *and* kidnapping? Now that we're assuming the letter we got is fake, I'm starting to question everything in this case. I mean . . . do we take Richard Leech's word for it when he says someone stole the artifacts before he could? Do we really trust Zip when they say sabotaging is their only agenda? Do we believe Orlando

Bones's explanation of his tense phone call? How much do I know about Nadira Nadeem—other than that she seemed very eager to point us toward other people? How much do I know about Smarty except that she is a huge thorn in everyone's side?

The taxi pulls into the parking lot. Once we pay, we have no more emergency funds left. Let's hope this works. . . .

Back in our tent, we lay out all the materials. I go to touch the clay, but Eliza swats my hand away.

"No, Carlos," she says. "Let the master work."

"And the master is . . . ?"

"ME!" Frank says, putting water on the clay and smushing it between his fingers.

"Um . . . Eliza, are you sure? This has to be convincing."

"That's why you came to *me*," Frank says. "The top professional in kindergarten clay art!"

"Frank, you're in first grade."

"I know that. I went pro *last* year. Now GRAPE ME!"

"What?"

"I want you to put a grape in my mouth."

"And where am I supposed to get grapes?"

"Fine," Frank says, pouty. "Chip me!"

I feed him a chip, and he begins to mold the clay.

"Is there something we can do to help?" I ask, after a

half hour of him *still* playing around with clay.

"Why don't we string the jewels, Carlos?" Eliza says. "With the gems we bought, we have enough to do twenty-three beads on each side. The pattern should be blue, green, green, red. I'll string this side. You pick up the pattern on the twenty-fourth bead in the sequence."

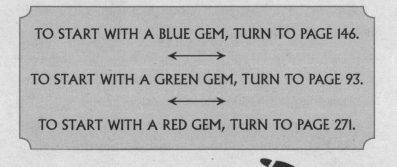

"Okay?" I say. "Which color should that be?"

Frank smashes the clay with his fist.

"Frankie, no! That snake was looking really good."

"No, no!" he says. "It looked like a worm. I am going for *snake*."

"Um . . . Eliza?"

"Can you figure it out, Carlos? Sometimes Frank has meltdowns when his vision doesn't match the final product, and I need to calm him down."

TO START WITH A BLUE GEM, TURN TO PAGE 146.

←→

TO START WITH A GREEN GEM, TURN TO PAGE 93.

←→

TO START WITH A RED GEM, TURN TO PAGE 271.

WE HAVE TO ambush whoever is in this tunnel. We absolutely cannot risk them running away. I turn off my phone light, and all we can see is the glow from their lantern.

"Frank," I whisper, quieter than a spider descending on its prey. "If you want to sneak attack, you have to be silent. The quieter you are, the better your sneak attack will be."

Frank nods. He doesn't say anything, which is honestly a marvel.

We tiptoe forward. *I* don't even hear us—that's how quiet we are. The person ahead definitely hasn't noticed us. It's not until we're ten feet away that I can tell who it is, and what they're doing: it's Zip, setting up a tripod.

"What are you doing here?" I ask.

Zip jumps and turns around. "You scared me!" They hold a hand over their heart. "I'm setting up my 3D laser!"

"To take pictures of the treasure?"

Zip laughs lightly. "No, it's to take scans of the tunnels. It's my job to make maps."

"Are you supposed to be in here alone?" I ask. I thought the whole team was supposed to go into the tunnels together. Everyone or no one.

"You think I'd really stop everyone from doing their work, just to watch me scan the catacombs with a laser? You know Nadira would panic if I threw her off schedule."

Hmmm . . . Zip's story *does* seem convincing.

"Let's say I believe you," I say.

"Why wouldn't you believe me?" Zip says. "I'm just here doing my job. Look, I'm the least suspicious person on the team. Ask me anything! I'm an open book."

TO ASK ZIP WHO THEY SUSPECT, TURN TO PAGE 66.

←——→

TO ASK ZIP ABOUT THEIR JOB, TURN TO PAGE 283.

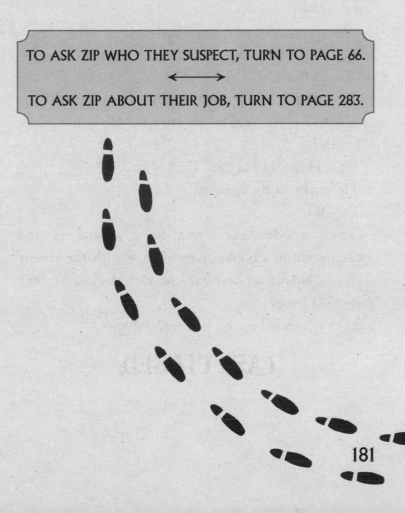

I JUST DON'T feel like talking with Eliza right now. "Frank, let's explore together."

"WOOHOO!"

Eliza looks disappointed, but she veers to the left side of the catacombs with Mom. Frank and I move through the tunnels, shining our flashlights across the cracked stone. I accidentally let my light fall, and I jump a mile.

There's a skeleton. A human one.

"COOL!" Frank says, gravitating toward it.

"Don't touch it, Frank!"

"But you let me get away with the most stuff!" he says with a pout. "You're my *favorite*." He blinks at me innocently.

Ugh. How can I say no? I'm his *favorite*!

He yanks on the skeleton.

BOOM!

Thick wooden spikes rain down around us, and we're caught in a booby-trapped cage with the creepy skeleton. No matter how hard we kick the beams, they just won't budge.

I really messed up, no bones about it.

CASE CLOSED.

"A FEW SLIDES?" I say to Professor Worthington. "Okay, sure, I'd love to see what else you have to say about Harmonia!"

The professor digs into his bag and sets up his tablet. "The story of Harmonia," he begins grandly, "actually starts five thousand years before she was born. I will commence by taking you through the detailed history of ancient—"

"Um, Professor?" Eliza interrupts. "How many slides are there?"

"Six hundred forty-three."

That's a few? We can't stay and listen to all that! "I'm sorry, but we have to—"

"Excuse me!" Professor Worthington says sharply. "It's extremely rude to talk during a professor's lecture. If you don't hush, I'm going to have to fail you."

"Fail?" Eliza squeaks.

"But we're not even in your class!"

"I will call every educator you have, and you'll receive a failing mark in every class in every grade if you talk again before my lecture concludes. Now. Where was I? Ah, yes. The story of Harmonia actually starts five thousand years before she was born. . . ."

CASE CLOSED.

NO MATTER HOW hard I try, I just can't figure out my way through this labyrinth. Now I know why it's famous for being unsolvable.

"Eliza, can you help?"

"I think if we go—yes! I think this'll work!" She traces a path that we should take through the labyrinth, once we go down the stairs.

"And now that we have our path," she says, "all we have to do is keep track of the ancient Greek numbers as we pass them."

Ancient Greek Number Chart

Alpha	Beta	Gamma	Delta	Epsilon	Digamma	Zeta	Eta	Theta
A	**B**	**Γ**	**Δ**	**E**	**Ϛ**	**Z**	**H**	**Θ**
1	2	3	4	5	6	7	8	9
Iota	Kappa	Lambda	Mu	Nu	Xi	Omicron	Pi	Koppa
I	**K**	**Λ**	**M**	**N**	**Ξ**	**O**	**Π**	**Ϟ**
10	20	30	40	50	60	70	80	90
Rho	Sigma	Tau	Upsilon	Phi	Chi	Psi	Omega	Sampi
P	**Σ**	**T**	**Y**	**Φ**	**X**	**Ψ**	**Ω**	**Ϡ**
100	200	300	400	500	600	700	800	900

ADD UP THE NUMBERS YOU PASS THROUGH, AND TURN TO THAT PAGE.

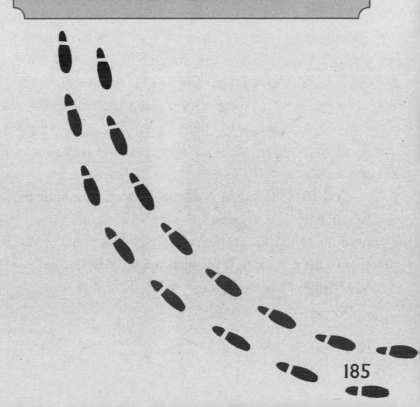

185

"SO, MR. LEECH . . . you didn't steal the artifacts because someone else did it first. Who beat you to the punch?"

Richard Leech scowls. "Who even knows? I thought it was your job to figure that out."

"We're working on it."

"And?" he says curtly. "What have you come up with?"

Frank pokes him in the stomach. "You! GUILTY!"

Leech frowns. "You're telling me I'm the *only* person you suspect? That can't be true."

I think long and hard. And then . . . ideas formulate. There's Smarty Marty, who is so eager to prove herself. Would staging a crime, then solving the crime, give her the praise and promotion she so desperately wants? And there's Zip, who has messed up five times on the same job, who looked pretty pleased with themself as they walked back to the tent.

We haven't even begun to dig into the professor or the doctor.

And there's Nadira Nadeem, whose flashlight we found near the catacombs, who was so effective in pointing us to Zip and Leech as suspects yesterday. Was that to keep us from investigating her? Was there more to Orlando Bones's hesitance when he didn't want her in the interrogation room?

"Actually, I have an idea."

"Me too," Eliza says.

"Zip!" I say, as she says, "Smarty!"

Two seconds later, Frank yells, "Frank!"

We stare at him.

"What? I just want to be included!"

I sigh as I turn back to Eliza. "We're really off sync today."

"You mean *out of* sync," she says quietly, correcting me.

Usually I would smile, but now I just feel tired. "So what do we do? Another coin toss?"

Eliza thinks for a moment. "Smarty and Zip work in the same tent. We'll go there and take an investigative opportunity as it arises."

"Can I have my phone back?" Leech complains.

"No," I say. "It's proof of your crimes."

"Hey—I didn't do any crimes. *Thinking* about stealing artifacts is not a crime."

I pocket the phone. He lunges at me. His hands close around the phone and we wrestle with it, but then Frank jumps into the fray, grabs Leech's phone, and puts it straight into his mouth.

"FRANK!" Eliza shrieks. "Spit that out! It has germs!"

Frank smiles and pulls it out of his mouth, making

sure to leave it drenched in saliva. "Still want it?"

"Yes."

"TOO BAD!" Frank shouts, running down the hill with his arms and legs flailing. "Last one back is a rotten egg!"

We run after Frank, leaving Richard Leech baffled and furious on the hillside. We finally catch up to Frank by the work tent, and he is grinning. "Rotten egg, rotten egg!"

I sigh. But at least Frank led us right where we needed to go.

We walk inside. In the back, Smarty Marty has her headphones on, and she is rocking out as she works. Closer to the front of the tent, Zip's workspace is empty, except for maps and diagrams lying on the table.

I want to look at Zip's maps. But . . . who knows how much time we'll have before Zip returns? And Smarty Marty is *right here.* If she catches us snooping through Zip's things, we're done. We would have to be extra sneaky, and . . .

I look at Frank, who is moving closer to Zip's spinny chair. Trusting Frank to keep quiet might be a losing battle. Is it worth trying? As Bones would say, high risk, high reward? Or should we play it safe and interrogate Smarty Marty?

TO EXAMINE ZIP'S WORKSPACE,
TURN TO PAGE 249.

←→

TO INTERRUPT SMARTY MARTY,
TURN TO PAGE 140.

189

I CAN'T EVEN believe I'm saying this, but I'm going to ask Frank for a hint.

"Frank, can you help me?"

"The long bone's connected to the . . . short bone. The short bone's connected to the . . . ear bone," he sings.

"Ears don't have bones," I say.

"The ear bone's connected to the . . . cheekbone!"

"Never mind, I'll do it myself," I grumble.

"The femur's connected to the . . . lemur! Okay, fine, I'll do it!"

He runs over to the chart, and I follow. I read out some of the harder clues to him, and he finds the bones on Dr. Mandible's poster. Then he spells the letters back to me. We're not half bad!

But we only get four done before he gets bored. Oh, well. At least I got his help with *some* of these. That's better than nothing, which is what I'm getting from Eliza!

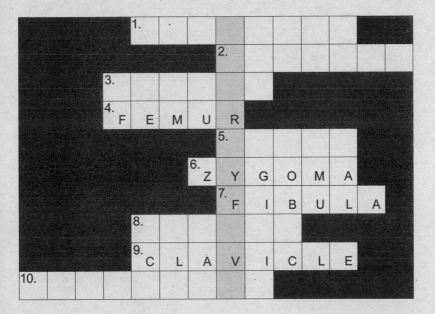

1. | | F | E | M | U | R |
4. F E M U R
6. Z Y G O M A
7. F I B U L A
9. C L A V I C L E

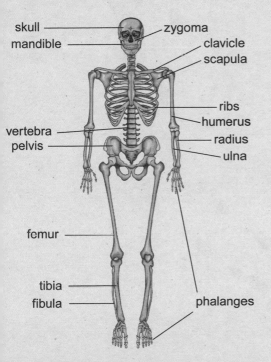

skull — zygoma
mandible — clavicle
— scapula
— ribs
— humerus
vertebra — radius
pelvis — ulna
femur
tibia
fibula — phalanges

1. On the spine
2. Upper arm
3. Hip
4. Longest
5. Part of shin
6. On the face
7. Calf
8. Part of forearm
9. Collarbone
10. Fingers and toes

191

192

I DON'T WANT to disappoint Eliza, but . . . I'd be disappointing myself if I didn't follow my own hunches.

"Eliza," I say, looking down at my shoes, "I think we should confront Nadira."

"Fine," she says coolly. "Lead the way."

We walk until we find Nadira, back at her desk. She looks up in surprise as we approach.

"I wish I could talk to you, detectives," she says, "but I'm totally swamped. I've got three meetings this afternoon, and I've got about seventy emails to answer. Plus we're taking Zip's map for a—"

I slam the flashlight on her desk. "Explain *this*," I say.

She looks confused. "It's called a flashlight?"

"I know that! But it's *your* flashlight." I show her the NN on the bottom.

She opens her desk drawer and pulls out a flashlight with no initials on it. "*This* is mine. I don't know whose that is."

"See?" Eliza says angrily. "Told you."

"You believe her, Eliza? She's a suspect!"

"Because it *makes sense*. I told you this was a foolish plan!"

"Foolish!" I say furiously. "Because you're the only one who can have thoughtful plans?"

"I never said that!" she roars.

Nadira stands up. "You know what? I'm not sure

what is going on between you two, but this is completely unprofessional behavior. When Mr. Bones said he was hiring child detectives, I didn't argue because I thought he knew what he was doing. But now I see that it was a mistake to hire people who are so . . . immature. Since Mr. Bones is out for the moment, I am in charge. And I think it's best you leave."

She snatches our badges from our backpacks. Security escorts us off the dig. And just like that, we lost this case in the speed of (flash)light.

CASE CLOSED.

NADIRA CAN HELP us translate the message in Greek. I know she can. "Ms. Nadeem," I say breathlessly, reaching into my pocket.

"Carlos?" Eliza warns.

"It's okay, Eliza," I say, pulling out my phone. I pull up the picture. "Ms. Nadeem, can you translate something for us?"

Nadira and Bones both crowd around the phone.

"Lady luck!" Bones says excitedly. He's like a puppy. "We hit the jackpot! You found this in there? I knew you were a good bet!"

Nadira zooms in closer to get a better look at the words. "We've never seen anything like this in there. Where was this message?"

"On the wall. *Obviously*," Frank says. So sassy!

Nadira mutters to herself for a minute as she puzzles it out. She clears her throat.

"Once from the gods, to the gods again. Return the gift. This is not the end but the key to greater things."

My heart thuds. Of course the message is about the necklace. But . . . is it saying what I think it's saying? This is not the end but the key to greater things? The necklace isn't the endgame. There's more treasure to find. Greater treasure. But what could that possibly be?

"Well? What does it mean?" Bones says eagerly,

looking back and forth between me, Eliza, Frank, and Mom.

"Heck if I know," I say with a shrug, but that's a lie. And judging from the flush in Eliza's face, she also recognizes that the message is significant.

Orlando Bones adjusts his fedora. He looks at us seriously. "I have to ask. Do you know where the Necklace of Harmonia is?"

My stomach flips. We *can't* give up the necklace—not until we know what this greater thing is. How do I get out of answering?

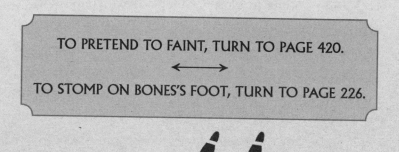

TO PRETEND TO FAINT, TURN TO PAGE 420.

TO STOMP ON BONES'S FOOT, TURN TO PAGE 226.

"YOU SAID YOU saw the tunnels?" I ask the professor.

"Oh yes," he says. "Dark, tiny things. I couldn't even fit. You three will do fine, but you"—he points at Mom—"might not."

Mom is small for an adult. How tiny *are* these tunnels anyway?

"Don't forget a flashlight," Professor Worthington says.

"If they're as small as you say, you must not have gone very far into the catacombs. Why are you so sure the necklace is there?"

"The imagery of the serpents. It ties Harmonia, the necklace, and the entranceway together."

"And Medusa," Eliza says.

"There are many serpents in Greek mythology, but only one that forms a necklace. If I had any doubt that the catacombs were connected to that fateful necklace, it was immediately quelled when we found that disk."

TO ASK THE PROFESSOR ABOUT THE DISK,
TURN TO PAGE 407.

I HOLD THE hammer, swing it over my shoulder, and smash the necklace.

Crunch!

It's in actual pieces. But I hear a *click!* from the back wall of the cave. We've clearly activated something.

"COOL!" Frank says. "Let me try!"

I hold the hammer away from him. But he keeps trying to swipe it. "Frank, no! Stop! We have to—"

"Hello there," says a voice from the mouth of the cave.

"Mom?" No, it's not Mom. The person is in shadow, so I can't see who it is, but the person is too tall and too muscular to be Mom. I don't know who it is—not for sure, anyway—until I see him take off a hat. A fedora.

"Orlando Bones!"

"What are you doing here?" Eliza asks.

"Collecting the necklace," he says cheerfully. "For the dig, of course. Thank you for retrieving it. Now give it here."

I'm so confused. What is he doing here—four and a half hours away from the dig? Was he the one following us in that silver car? But . . .

"How did you find us?"

He continues smiling, and shivers go up my spine. "When we get back to the dig, I'll cash you out," Bones says. "In fact, I'll sweeten the pot if you just hand the necklace over. . . ."

He doesn't realize we've already smashed it to pieces.

Everything about this is wrong. *Bones* being *here* is wrong. And suddenly, understanding zaps into my brain, like a lightning bolt from Zeus. "You're the artifact thief. And the wannabe necklace thief."

He doesn't say anything.

"But how, Mr. Bones?" Eliza asks. "Why?"

Finally, *finally*, his smile slips. "I bet the farm on you, and you failed me! I gave you simple directions. Go into the tunnel, retrieve the necklace. That's it. That's all I needed you to do."

"You hired us . . . to steal it for you?" Eliza says, aghast. "You wanted us to do your dirty work? You wanted to make us felons?"

"But why? For what reason?"

"For the money, okay?" he growls. "For the riches. For the chance to pay off my gambling debts." He laughs humorlessly. "It was either rob a bank or swipe a necklace that's been lost for millennia. I thought the odds were good that you'd be able to get it for me, since the catacombs are tiny. And the odds were even better that you'd give it to me right away, since you're just kids."

"*Just* kids?" I say furiously.

"I know you are but what am I?" Frank shouts.

"If that was your bet," Eliza says coolly, "now we know why you have gambling debts. You're really bad at this."

Bones shakes his head. "That's for sure. I never

would've taken a bet that you'd transport my necklace nearly *five hours away* from the dig."

"How did you find us here?" I ask.

"Please. I always have an ace up my sleeve! I have a tracking device on Smarty's car. Before you even got here, I ordered her to let you borrow her car whenever you needed it in the first place."

The wind whooshes outside, and I realize that Bones must have had to walk on the narrow ledge to get here. He must have overtaken . . . my breath catches.

"Where's my mom?"

"Oh, her? The die is cast."

My throat tightens. "MOM! *Mom!*" I call. But I hear no answer.

Bones takes a threatening step closer, blocking our exit. He holds out his hand. "My winnings."

"NO!" Frank shouts.

"I won't ask again."

He's closing in!

TO SWING HEPHAESTUS'S HAMMER AT BONES, TURN TO PAGE 395.

←——→

TO THROW THE NECKLACE PIECES OFF THE MOUNTAIN, TURN TO PAGE 84.

"MR. BONES!" I say, sitting on the picnic bench across from him. "Where have you been?"

"Where haven't I been?" he says. "Italy, Egypt, Russia, Germany, Thailand, Spain—oh, that was a lovely time—"

"No, I mean, where have you been *today*?"

He rubs his chin, which basically results in him spreading dirt from one side of his face to the other. When this case is over, maybe I'll use some of my salary to buy him some nice face wash. As a thank-you for hiring us.

"Here and there, all over."

"Why did you blow Nadira off?" Eliza asks.

"Huh?"

"You were supposed to meet with her," Eliza says. "And she was mad you stood her up."

He looks sheepish. Almost nervous. Like he has something he wants to tell us. But first . . . I need to ask about Mom.

TO ASK MR. BONES IF HE'S SEEN MOM,
TURN TO PAGE 134.

WE NEVER WOULD have found the key without the address from Professor Worthington. It's only fair we tell him about it.

"We found a key," I say. "We think it goes in the catacombs."

His eyes twinkle behind his glasses. "You actually found something? I've scoured that location multiple times, and—" He looks at us hungrily. "Are you going into the catacombs now? Perhaps you'd like me to accompany you?"

"No!" Eliza, Frank, Mom, and I say at the same time.

"I—I mean," I stammer, "we appreciate the offer, but we have it handled."

He looks affronted. "Well! I was only trying to help!" He storms out of the tent in a huff.

That went about as well as could be expected.

"So what now?" Mom asks.

"The tunnels!" Frank cries loudly.

And I'm so excited that at least *one* of the Thompsons is game for my original plan that I shout, "I second that!"

"I third," Eliza says to my surprise. She catches my look of shock and says, "What? Honestly, I don't think the clue I found us is connected to the disk at all. My hunch is that the keyhole is in the tunnels."

Mom holds up her hands. "Whoa there, team. We're not doing the tunnels now."

"We're not?" I say.

"Not even if I give you my puppy-dog eyes?" Frank says, pouting and batting his eyelashes.

Mom shakes her head. "Puppy-dog eyes don't work on cat people." That answer surprises me, since Mom's never seemed to like animals very much—and now she's a cat person? Then I laugh. Because when your name is Cat, you're a literal Cat person. "I'm glad you find me humorous, Carlos."

"Sorry, but that's such a corny joke."

She grins and ruffles my hair. "I'm excited to explore the catacombs with you three. But we're adjusting to a time difference. We've been up for hours. I know for a fact Frank didn't sleep on the plane."

"I watched three movies in a *row*!" Frank brags.

"I don't feel comfortable taking you into the tunnels in this condition—when we're on the brink of exhaustion. I have a feeling we'll need all our energy and strength for the catacombs. So we'll go first thing in the morning."

That makes sense to me. We all murmur in agreement.

"I'm glad we're united," she says, with a pointed glance at me and Eliza. "Now let's spend our final burst of energy today interviewing one last person."

"Well, before the professor came in," Eliza says, "we

had found a letter from Smarty to Bones, basically trashing Nadira Nadeem. We could confront Smarty about it."

"Or!" I say quickly. "We could ask Nadira if what Smarty said about her is true."

"I don't think that's a good idea," Eliza says.

"Well, I don't think talking to Smarty is a good idea."

"Are you serious?"

"Are you?"

Mom frowns, and Frank sighs heavily. Even *Frank*—who never gets annoyed at anything—is tired of us bickering.

TO CONFRONT SMARTY, TURN TO PAGE 331.

←——→

TO ASK NADIRA NADEEM ABOUT THE
ALLEGATIONS IN SMARTY'S EMAIL,
TURN TO PAGE 436.

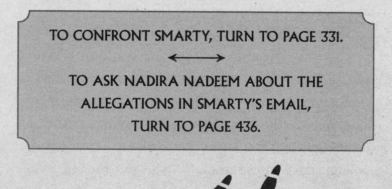

IT'S ANNOYING TO have to cross the river five times. And it eats up so many minutes—or maybe even hours. It's hard to tell down here, where the sun doesn't reach. It could be evening or the middle of the night, for all I know.

When we're all across, we can proceed. We shine our flashlights ahead, only to discover there's a wall blocking our path. The wall features the most enormous painting of a three-headed dog.

"Cerberus," Eliza says. "I knew we'd see this!"

"Huh?" Frank says, which is exactly how I feel.

"Cerberus is Hades's dog. You know . . . the three-headed hellhound that guards the gates of the underworld."

"How would I know that?" I ask. My stomach twists. "The River Styx, and now a hellhound. Are we going into the underworld?"

"We're already *here*! Mwahahahahahaha!" Frank cackles.

Eliza shrugs. "Well, technically, we are *under the world* right now."

There's a door in between the hellhound's legs, and I try it. But no surprise—it's locked. Above the knob, there are three ancient-looking dials that I can set to a single number. I bet if we had all three of those numbers . . .

5824 4582 2458 ????

3 7 12 18 25 ??

9 7 216 8 5
313 10 6 ???

206

"A three-digit code," I say. "Do you see anything like that?"

"Sort of," Eliza says. "At first I thought this was a painted collar, but . . . each of the dogs has a set of numbers scrawled across its neck. It looks like a number sequence. If we can figure out the next number in the pattern, we would know which digits to put into this ancient lock system!"

Eliza writes the sequences down in her notebook and shares it with me.

DOG 1

3   7   12   18   25   ??

DOG 2

5824   4582   2458   ????

DOG 3

9   7   216   8   5   313   10   6   ???

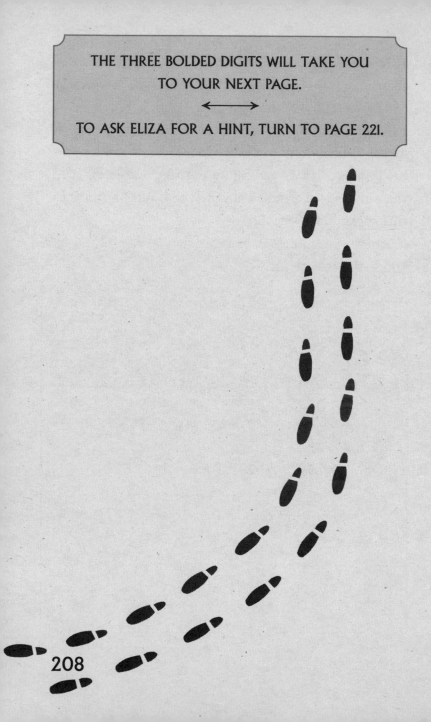

THE THREE BOLDED DIGITS WILL TAKE YOU
TO YOUR NEXT PAGE.
←——→

TO ASK ELIZA FOR A HINT, TURN TO PAGE 221.

208

THIS NONOGRAM PUZZLE is so intimidating. "Eliza," I say, "how do I do a nonogram?"

"It looks scarier than it is," Eliza says. "First, know that the grid is seventeen by seventeen. That means when we see the number seventeen in a column, then *all* the squares in that column should be filled in. And same thing when we see the number seventeen in the rows."

"Okay," I say. "I can handle that."

"And look at the numbers across the top. See how they mirror each other? There's seventeen in the middle, and then next to it on either side, there's eleven and three, and then eleven and two, and so on until the end? If I'm a betting person like Mr. Bones, then the chances are likely the left side of this image is going to be a complete and exact mirror of the right side of this image."

"So . . . that means . . . when looking at the numbers going down, we should probably center one, three, five, seven, and all the rest of them, right?"

Eliza beams at me. "Exactly! Here." She starts filling things in.

Suddenly there's silence from outside—have Nadira and Bones stopped fighting? Eliza turns to me. "I'll go distract Bones. Start with the seventeens and fill in every single box in any row or column with seventeen in it, like we talked about. Then go down the left side. Color seven in the middle, then eleven in the middle, then thirteen, and so on. I did some of the harder ones—I think the image will start to take form soon." And then she dashes away, leaving me all alone.

								11	11	11		11	11	11					
			4	6	9	10	11	1	2	3	17	3	2	1	11	10	9	6	4
		1																	
		3																	
		5																	
		7																	
		9																	
		11																	
		13																	
		13																	
		15																	
		17																	
		17																	
		17																	
7	1	7																	
5	1	5																	
3	3	3																	
		5																	
		7																	

IF THE IMAGE IS A DIAMOND, TURN TO PAGE 69.

←→

IF THE IMAGE IS A SPADE, TURN TO PAGE 156.

"WE, UM, OVERHEARD you on the phone, Mr. Bones, and you seemed very stressed out."

"Is that a question?" Bones says.

"Yes. What was that call about?"

"And who is Duff?" Eliza asks.

Bones sighs deeply. He takes off his hat and rests it on the desk. The hair underneath is matted with sweat. "I wasn't going to tell you because I didn't want to you to feel like I was dealing you a bad hand. But I was talking to Keira Skelberry's boss, the benefactor who is funding our research here."

"And?" Mom says.

"He upped the ante. He's going to shut down the dig."

"What? Why?" I ask.

"He says it's not worth the funding. Not unless I can retrieve the Necklace of Harmonia from its resting place. If I can't, I'll be sacked, and this will be a very bad blemish on my résumé. You haven't gone into the tunnels yet, have you?"

"Yes," I say, "we have."

"And?"

"It was dark. And tiny."

"How far did you go?"

"To infinity . . . and beyond!" Frank says, and I shake my head.

"What about the other artifacts?" Eliza asks. "Does Duff care that all of those have gone missing?"

"I haven't told him," Bones says. "I'm on a losing streak, and he's a bit of a wild card. Has a temper. I thought it would be best if he didn't know. But to lay my cards on the table, I know he's more interested in the Necklace of Harmonia than anything else. Do you think you'd be able to shift focus to the Necklace of Harmonia?"

TO AGREE TO FOCUS ON THE NECKLACE,
TURN TO PAGE 41.

←——————→

TO INSIST ON FINDING THE MISSING ARTIFACTS,
TURN TO PAGE 390.

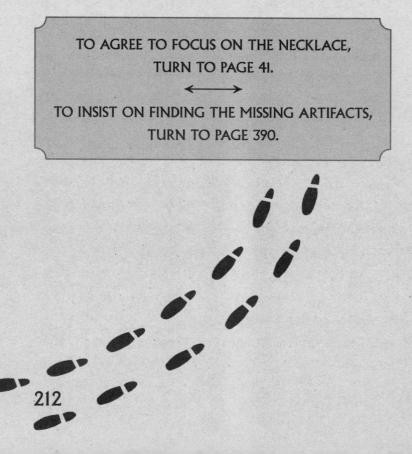

MAYBE I *CAN* just take Smarty's keys.

"If you want these," Smarty says, dangling her keys in front of us, "you're going to have to beg—HEY!"

I swipe the keys out of her hands and run, run, *run*! When we get to the parking lot, we jump into the car and drive off, leaving Smarty shaking her fist in our rearview window.

"I don't know, Carlos," Mom says. "This is wrong. We stole her car."

"We just borrowed it. It's fine."

But it isn't fine. Within fifteen minutes of driving, a cavalry of white cars with blue stripes are behind us— they flash their lights and blare their sirens.

Mom frowns deeply. "I guess Smarty reported us."

"STEP ON IT!" I shout to Mom. She speeds up, and so do the cop cars. They're catching up . . . then they're neck and neck . . . then they're in front of us. They brake hard.

"AHHHHHHHHH!" we scream as Mom is forced to slam on her brakes.

"The jig is up," Mom says as officers approach our car.

I guess the keys weren't the key after all.

CASE CLOSED.

WE HAVE TO run away—before Mr. Bones gets back to his tent.

"GO!" I cry, and we burst out of the exit. We sprint all the way across the dig until we're at the pit again. Safe!

There's still some light in the sky, but just barely. It's past sunset, and—I realize with a jolt—Mom should be back by now.

I dial her phone, but it goes to voicemail. I walk to the parking lot, and Eliza and Frank follow. I'm not sure what I'm looking for since I don't know which car Mom borrowed to go to the fire ruins. But Mom isn't in the parking lot.

We walk across the dig, only to find that she's not there either. And her bed hasn't been touched since this morning. I feel the panic start to rise in my chest, but I push it down. Maybe she's at dinner.

But when we get to the buffet line and the picnic tables, she's not there either. Where could she be? Is she in danger?

We sit down with our plates and wait for her to show up. I shuffle food around my plate; I have no appetite. Only dread.

"You have to eat, Carlos," Eliza says gently, though I clock that her appetite is less than usual too. I can tell she's also worried, but trying to keep it together for me. I appreciate that.

"Want me to help you eat?" Frank suggests.

"I don't see how you can—"

He drops a piece of pita into my open mouth, then moves my jaw up and down with his hands. "Now swallow," he says, rubbing my throat like I'm a dog taking a pill.

"Get off me!"

"We can try the bird method next," Frank says.

"You mean the one where the mama bird chews up food and spits it into the mouth of a baby bird?"

"That's the one!" Frank says.

"Uh, no thanks, I'll pass." I grab my fork and swirl some hummus around.

Let me retrace our steps. We split up this afternoon: us to the tunnels, Mom to the ruins of the fire. Did she come back? If not, did she get into an accident? Is she hurt? And if she did return, why didn't she find us? Did she . . . go to the tunnels searching for us? Did she reach a booby trap?

I wrestle all evening with what to do, but I don't come to any concrete answer. I just need Mom to show up out of the blue and shout, "Surprise!" But she doesn't.

I dial her phone over and over again, but I never get any answer. I leave messages until her voicemail is full.

I feel like I'm going to throw up.

By the time Eliza, Frank, and I are lying in our cots, I feel twisted and tangled with thoughts. I worry for hours after Eliza and Frank fall asleep. There's no sleep in my future . . . only a restless, fearful night.

THE NECKLACE OF Harmonia has wrapped itself once, twice, three times around my mom's neck . . . she's choking . . . she's cursed . . . the Greek gods are grabbing her by the ankles and pulling her away—

I wake up with a jolt.

"Mom?"

Her bed is still empty.

Something is definitely wrong.

I get up and start getting dressed. Eliza's sleeping, but Frank is awake. He's just sitting on the bed wiggling his tooth.

"Just let it come out naturally," I say. "It takes some time."

"Time I do not *have*."

"Um . . . why don't you have time?"

He sighs. "Because I want to exchange this tooth for money, and I want to exchange money for a souvenir."

"What souvenir are you going to buy with twenty-five cents? You can basically only afford a lollipop."

Frank grins excitedly, and he pushes his tooth with his tongue.

"Eliza," I say, walking over to her bed. "Wake up."

She nearly jumps out of bed. "Your mom?"

I shake my head.

"I'm sure she's okay. We can go find her."

"Go where? We're not even sure where she is!"

"We need to ask our suspects about your mom. I know we've been hired to find the artifacts, but she's way more important than the missing relics. She's even more important than the Necklace of Harmonia. And we should start with Dr. Mandible."

Frustration blossoms within me. Shouldn't *I* be calling the shots? It's my mom.

I think Eliza can read the frustration on my face. Her smile wavers. "Of course," she mumbles, sounding glum as she zips her backpack closed, "you can decide, since it's your mom."

Great, now I feel guilty, on top of irritated. But I'm also too tired and too worried to argue with her. So we walk to the medical tent.

"KNOCK KNOCK!" Frank says, in lieu of actually knocking on a door, since there is no door.

"Who's there?" a voice calls out.

"LOLLIPOPS!"

I groan.

"Lollipops who?"

"GIVE ME A SUCKER, SUCKER!"

218

"Frank!" Eliza scolds. "Be polite."

He nods. "Give me a sucker, sucker. *Please.*"

I put a palm on my forehead. There's just no hope with him.

Dr. Amanda Mandible opens the tent to let us in. I clock her checking her watch. She turns to us with that shiny, phony smile. Totally fake. Everything about her is *too* sweet, *too* smiley, *too* giggly. There's just something off about her. . . .

"I can spare you a minute. Then I must go."

Is it just me, or is she desperately trying not to spend any time with us?

TO ASK IF SHE'S SEEN MOM, TURN TO PAGE 33.

←——→

TO ASK ABOUT THE LIST OF INGREDIENTS AGAIN,
TURN TO PAGE 160.

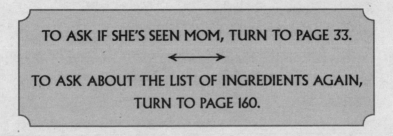

THE ALCHEMY RECIPE calls for gold, fire, earth, and salt. We put in the gold from Eliza's earring. Eliza lights an emergency match for fire. We grab earth from the dirt. And the salt comes from the potato chips in my bag.

A recipe for success!

Psssssss! Something white and gassy comes spitting out of the walls. It's making me really drowsy. I fall to my knees, and so do Eliza and Frank beside me.

"It's some kind of poison gas," Eliza chokes. "A sleeping powder."

Frank starts snoring immediately.

"Witchcraft?" I say, feeling light-headed, trying to hide my nose in my shirt.

"Alchemy," Eliza whispers as she falls asleep.

CASE CLOSED.

"ELIZA, THIS DOG puzzle is impossible."

"Im*paw*sible!" Frank says. "Get it? Because dogs have paws?"

I groan.

Eliza stops looking at the third dog and comes over to help me. "Let's go one at a time."

DOG 1

3   7   12   18   25   ??

"I always start these types of puzzles by trying to recognize a pattern between the first few numbers. If the numbers go from low to high, I usually start with addition. So what can you add to three to get to seven?"

"Four," I say.

"Right. And what can you add to seven to get to twelve?"

"Five."

"And what do you add to twelve to get to eighteen?"

3   7   12   18   25   ??
  +4   +5   +6

I grin. "I see it now!"

"Excellent!" she says as she shuffles over to the second dog.

DOG 2

5824 4582 2458 ???**?**

"Ugh! Should we still do addition with this one?" I ask.

"There doesn't seem to be any addition, subtraction, multiplication, or division that would make this pattern work."

"So . . . there's no pattern?"

"I didn't say that!" She hums. "It's very curious that all three of the numbers we have in this pattern have the same four digits in a different order. Do you see that? Each one has a five, an eight, a two, and a four."

"Hey—that's true! The numbers do repeat!" I take a closer look at the numbers. It seems like every number is moving one position to the right. And if that's the case . . .

I start filling in the last number. Now all I have left to do is place the four and the five.

5824 4582 2458 82?**?**

"Okay, Eliza. Next one!"

222

9   7   2|6   8   5   3|3   10   6   ???

"This, to me, is the trickiest one," she says. "No repeating numbers. And it's definitely not addition."

"So how do we solve it?"

She stares at the dog thoughtfully. After a few minutes, she laughs. "Okay, okay. Try subtraction, then addition."

I stare at the first three numbers. I try Eliza's suggestion: subtraction, then addition.

$$9 - 7 = 2$$
$$9 + 7 = 16$$

Put them together, and that's 216. I move on to the next three digits.

$$8 - 5 = 3$$
$$8 + 5 = 13$$

Put them together, and it's 313. "I got this one! Now all we have to do is take the highlighted digit—one from each dog—to unlock this door."

Frank sighs heavily. "*Finally*. These puzzles were ruff! Get it?"

"Unfortunately," I say, shaking my head.

> THE THREE BOLDED DIGITS WILL TAKE YOU
> TO YOUR NEXT PAGE.

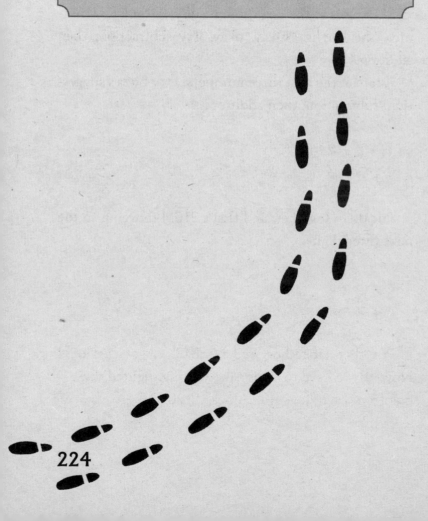

RICHARD LEECH LOOKS *terrifying.* We have to run away.

We turn on our heels and bolt.

Of course Leech follows us. He chases us across the dig, up a mountain, down again, through a valley, across the highway, beyond flatlands, across a beach.

And speaking of coasts . . . "Is the coast clear?" Eliza says, panting.

"YOU KIDS!" Leech bellows from a short distance behind us.

Nope! Gotta keep going, gotta keep running. Can't let him catch us. We run and run and run—through the days, through the nights. And when we're too exhausted to run anymore, we still stumble forward. We need to escape.

He's stuck with us longer than I thought he would, but I should have expected that from a man named Leech.

CASE CLOSED.

I'M GOING TO stomp on Bones's foot to distract him.

Bones searches me eagerly. "You have to tell me, if you know where—YOWCH!"

I jump on his foot. I feel terrible, but it works. It buys us time to hurry away while he's hopping on one foot and holding on to Nadira for support.

By the time he realizes we've bolted, we're halfway up the pit. "COME BACK!" he cries.

I guess he and Nadira must be putting two and two together, though. Neither one of them is stupid. If I'd rather trample Bones's poor toe than answer the question . . . and if I had a secret message to decode for them . . . and if we were running like mad from the catacombs . . .

I look back over my shoulder. Sure enough, Bones and Nadira are rushing into the tunnels.

Yup, they know something's up.

Outside the excavation pit, Eliza squeals. "We have to return the necklace to the gods!"

"To where, though?" I ask. "It's not like there's a Greek gods pop-up shop we can return the necklace to. Hello, Hephaestus? We'd like a refund."

"Well," Eliza says, an excited grin creeping across her face. "We're supposed to return it to the gods themselves, right? That leads us to one place in particular. The only place in the world where the gods are rumored to exist."

"In a pizza parlor!" Frank says confidently.

"No, Frankie! On top of Mount Olympus."

Mom scrunches up her face. "How far is Mount Olympus from here?"

I plug it into my phone. It's a four-and-a-half-hour drive. Good thing we got up ridiculously early today.

"We'll need a car," Mom says.

Eliza and I look at each other. Then we burst into a sprint. We don't stop running until we reach the work tent. We rush past Zip's desk (where they look thoroughly baffled) and slam our hands on Smarty's desk.

"We need to borrow your car!" Eliza and I say at the same time.

"Creepy. And no."

"No? Why not? You let us borrow it to go to the ruins yesterday!" I say as Frank and Mom catch up to us.

"Well, tell me what you need it for, and *maybe* I'll give it to you."

My mind is spinning. What sort of lie can I tell her? What sort of story can I spin?

Frank puts his elbows on her desk and says, "We need it to drive to Mount Olympus so we can return the Necklace of Harmonia to the god Hephaestus, in order to break the curse and exchange it for a bigger, better prize because that's what the inside of the

227

tunnels demanded we do." He collapses like he's run out of steam.

My mouth falls open. He told her *everything*. I search Smarty carefully for a reaction.

Finally she rolls her eyes. "You don't have to lie to me," she snaps. "Where are you *really* going?"

"Into town," Mom says. "We need a few supplies."

"There, was that so hard?" Smarty says, handing Mom the keys.

"Thank you," I say calmly, even though my heart is beating so fast. We try to maintain an even speed as we walk to the car. If we're too excited, we'll arouse suspicion.

But I don't think our plan works. Because as we pass by Professor Worthington's tent, he watches us curiously. I feel his eyes on us, all the way to the parking lot. . . .

When we get into Smarty's car, I let the excitement overtake me again. I'm practically bouncing in my seat. Mom is grinning. Eliza lets out a squeal. Frank leans forward, wedging his body between the driver's seat and the passenger seat; he slips the necklace around the rearview mirror. It dangles and spins, reflecting the sunlight.

I hope it doesn't curse Smarty's car.

DRIVE AWAY ON PAGE 31.

"WE'RE HERE!" I say breathlessly as we dash into Orlando Bones's tent, just like the loudspeaker told us to do. I don't know what I was expecting . . . but my stomach drops when I see Orlando Bones, Nadira Nadeem, Professor Worthington, Richard Leech, Dr. Mandible, and Smarty Marty all crowded around a tiny piece of paper.

They all look up at us, with pity, with worry. I'm not sure *what* is happening, but it feels ominous.

"Do you know where your mother is?" Bones says, and my chest suddenly feels tight.

"You sent her on an errand," I say.

"Yes, but I saw that she came back about an hour ago."

Where were we an hour ago? Probably talking to Richard Leech on that hilltop, on the far edge of the dig.

"What do you mean—where is she?" I say, my heart hammering. Eliza holds my hand and squeezes tight. Even Frank leans in to me, his version of a half hug.

We walk over to Orlando's desk and look at the paper that they're all staring at.

Dear Carlos,

There is nothing I can say that will make this any easier, but someone here knows the location of the missing artifacts and has been lying to you from the start. All I can say is that I am very taken with your detective skills, your determination, and your independent mind. Perhaps Eliza, Frank, and your mother don't appreciate your genius. But I do. I know you'll dive into danger. I know you'll do what's right to save the artifacts, help protect the catacombs, and save your mother—yes, don't be surprised. She needs your help. But there is no way I'm telling you where she is, in no universe can I write it down. Because I fear for my life. The years are flashing before my eyes: childhood, teen, adult years. But I'm doomed. The culprit is on to me. I have only minutes.

—A friend

"Is your mom in danger?" Nadira Nadeem says. "Can we help her? Do you want to take this?"

Somehow I grab the paper. I feel disconnected from my limbs, like I'm a marionette that someone is controlling from above.

"I . . . thank you," I croak. My throat is dry. My legs are shaking.

I don't even know what happens next—it's like I black out. The next thing I know, Eliza, Frank, and I are in our tent with the piece of paper addressed to me.

Eliza cups my face in her hands and whispers, "Carlos. Carlos . . . I know this is scary. I'm scared too. But we have to figure this out."

"Figure what out?" I say, my voice shaking. "There's nothing to figure out! My mom's in trouble, and I don't know where she is!"

Eliza twists her hair nervously. "I just can't help feeling like the spacing of this letter—the line breaks—are so awkward. It's like . . . there's a message within a message. Actually—I think I see a different way to read it. One that gives us something actionable to do—"

I grab the letter from her.

ADD ONE HUNDRED TO THE NUMBER IN THE MESSAGE. THEN TURN TO THAT PAGE.

←——————→

TO ASK ELIZA FOR A HINT, TURN TO PAGE 131.

I WANT TO get Professor Worthington to translate the message we got from inside the catacombs. I'm not sure I can trust Nadira Nadeem. For one thing, I don't love the way Nadira and Orlando are staring at me right now, like *I'm* a dig site that they just can't wait to excavate. . . .

Bones fires a hundred questions at me. "You were just in there . . . for how long? What direction did you take? Did you get close to the necklace? What were you running from? Did a booby trap stop you?"

"I'm so sorry, we have to go."

"Go where?"

"TO THE BATHROOM," Frank says, loud enough to make a few of the archaeologists from across the pit turn and stare at us. "It's an emergency!"

"You heard him," I say. "Potty emergency."

We run toward the ladder, and I'm acutely aware that Nadira and Orlando are both watching us the whole way up the pit. But we don't have time to be concerned about them.

"Professor Worthington!" I shout as we run through the tents.

"Here, kitty kitty kitty!" Frank says.

He's not at the picnic tables. He's not at the work tent. We find him in his sleeping tent, the one he shares with curator Richard Leech. "You are disrupting my

232

studies with that racket," he says, pulling the tent flap open angrily.

"Sorry," I say. "But we need your help. Can you translate this message for us?"

He sighs and lets us into his tent. His side is very neat. Mom sits on the cot next to Professor Worthington; Frank, Eliza, and I kneel on the floor. I hand him my phone, and his eyes get extremely wide. He grabs a piece of paper and a pen; then he starts jotting down the translation.

Once from the gods, to the gods again.
Return the gift.
This is not the end but the key to greater things.

My heart hammers. The key to greater things . . . does that mean that the necklace is just a cog in a larger machine? Is there a greater prize waiting for us? But what could be bigger than the Necklace of Harmonia?

"Ah, the monomyth," Professor Worthington says approvingly. "A classic hero's journey. Greek mythology is full of them. It seems you've received a call to adventure." For a moment, his eyes light up and he looks almost greedy. I try to take the paper with the translation from him, but he won't let go.

"Professor?" Eliza says.

"Huh?" His grip slackens just a bit, and I yank that paper out of his hands so fast that it's a wonder he doesn't get a paper cut.

"We have to go," I say. As we leave the tent, he tries to follow us, but Frank blocks his way. "NO. SIT. STAY. BAD DOGGIE."

Frank runs to catch up with us, and we duck behind the medical tent to hide from the professor, who's calling our names. We're all panting as we look at the translated message again.

"I know it sounds outlandish, but I think we're supposed to go to Mount Olympus, where the Greek gods live," Eliza whispers. "There must be something there that we're supposed to find—something the necklace reveals."

"That's a really interesting theory, Eliza," Mom says. Then she looks at me to make sure I'm okay with the compliment she's giving my best friend. I can't believe I was so jealous of Eliza before. Now, as I listen to her excitedly map out her plan, I couldn't be more proud.

"Mount Olympus." I check my phone. "It's far. A few hours away. We're going to need a car."

And that's how we find ourselves at Smarty Marty's desk, begging for her car. I hate being at the mercy of Smarty's generosity, since she has no mercy or generosity, but it's not like we have a choice.

"This is getting ridiculous," Smarty says, not looking up from her work. "Find someone else's car to borrow."

"Please, Smarty!" I say. "We really need it. And we need it quickly."

She stops typing. Then she looks at me suspiciously, from behind her fake glasses. "Why, what did you find?"

"Nothing," I say quickly.

"I don't see what's in it for me."

What's in it for her? I could offer her something she wants . . . but I'm tired of her bad attitude. I wish I could just take the keys!

TO PROMISE HER A PROMOTION,
TURN TO PAGE 141.

←——→

TO STEAL HER KEYS, TURN TO PAGE 213.

THE DISK SAYS, "Under the earth the riches lie." That couldn't be any clearer!

We walk along, searching the ground for any clues. Under the earth, the riches lie. But *where* under the earth are the riches?

Swoosh!

As we're looking down, a net drops from the ceiling. One of those booby traps we were warned about. And because we were looking down, not up, we don't realize it's happening until it's too late.

"Carlos, I'm stuck!" Eliza shouts.

"No, I'm stuck!" Frank says.

"No, I'm stuck!" Eliza argues.

"We're all stuck, okay?" I shout.

I guess that's what happens when my search didn't cast a wide enough net.

CASE CLOSED.

WE HAVE TO go into the catacombs. If Mom really is down there, I'll never forgive myself if we don't go after her. And if she isn't down there—if Eliza's right, and it *is* a trap—then we're just going to be prepared.

"I want you to know I respect your theory . . . ," I say to Eliza.

She laughs and shakes her head. "It's okay. I knew you'd pick the catacombs, Carlos. It's going to be dangerous."

"YAY!" Frank cheers.

"We don't know what we'll find down there. Booby traps."

"YAY!"

"And possibly an artifact thief."

"YAY YAY!"

I look seriously at Eliza. "I'm going to need you more than ever down there."

She nods.

"What about ME?" Frank says.

"Of course," I say. "No one can get into tiny spots like you can."

"True, I *am* the best!"

We all get off the bed and start gathering the items we need—flashlights, batteries, rope, a trowel, water, and snacks (including two big bags of chips, three bananas, and seven candy bars). Very quickly, we're all packed across two backpacks—one for Eliza, and one for me.

"Ready, Freddy?" Eliza asks.

"My name is *Frank*, not Freddy, remember?"

"Almost," I answer her. "We can't do anything until we get the real maps."

TO STEAL THE MAPS FROM ZIP'S TENT,
TURN TO PAGE 383.

←——→

TO BEG ZIP FOR THE MAPS,
TURN TO PAGE 119.

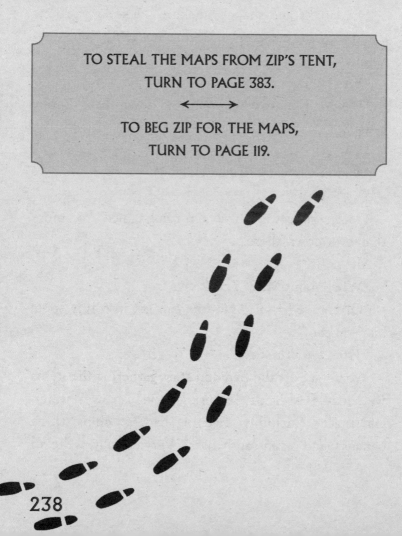

OKAY, IF A suspect is offering up free information on another suspect, I shouldn't turn it away. Even if the informant is the most arrogant human alive.

"Okay, Smarty Marty," I say. "What information do you have?"

She smiles. "Okay, so I don't usually love to gossip . . ." Lie. Instant lie. I know it, she knows it. She is taking *so much pleasure* in this gossip. "But I overheard a really incriminating conversation that Mr. Leech had on the phone."

"Okay, when? What did he say? What was incriminating about it?"

"It was a few days before I permanently kicked him out of the work tent and reported him to my direct supervisor, Ms. Nadeem. He clearly didn't realize I was nearby when he took the phone call. He was describing the dig here, and the artifacts we were finding."

"And?" I say, feeling like there's more to the story.

"And . . . he was promising artifacts to his donors. He was basically telling them what they could expect to see in his museum next month. But . . . he was talking about artifacts that he didn't have the authority to promise."

"Like the Necklace of Harmonia?"

Smarty Marty's eyes bulge behind her glasses. "You know about the Necklace of Harmonia? Yes, the necklace. But other things too."

"Any of the things that have gone missing?"

Smarty hums noncommittally. "I'm not sure. But I would keep a close eye on him if I were you."

Hmm. I don't know what to think. Is it possible that Smarty Marty is really being helpful? With no agenda or ulterior motive?

"By the way, if Richard Leech is the thief, you have to give me credit in front of everyone else for pointing you in the right direction."

Okay, *there's* the ulterior motive.

Eliza and Mom shuffle out from the artifact storage shelves, notebooks in hand. Frank runs over to his sister and tugs on her sleeve. "Eliza, Eliza, look at *this*!" He blows air in and out of his mouth, and his tooth wiggles on its own. "Isn't that amazing?"

"We have a very low bar for *amazing*, I see," Smarty says.

Eliza smiles at her brother, then says, "Okay, I compiled a list of all the missing artifacts so far, along with their value, date of origin, and the date they were cataloged."

"Great," I say dully. "My conversation with Smarty Marty was fruitful. She was telling us all about how suspicious Leech is, and—"

"Oh, really?" Eliza says. "That's excellent! Let's go talk to Richard Leech now!"

"Or maybe we can go to the tunnels. I know you

don't think it has anything to do with finding the missing artifacts—and maybe you're right!" *But maybe you're wrong*, I don't say. "Eliza, please. I have a really good feeling the catacombs are where we need to be."

Eliza hesitates. "You did my thing—going to check out the crime scene. I guess it's only fair that I do your thing now."

"Hopefully, one of these days, we'll be on the same page again." I expect to make Eliza smile with that, but it actually makes her frown. I don't know how to bridge the gap between her and me. I'm not even sure *why* there's a gap.

As we head to the excavation site, there's a whole line of archaeologists, waiting for a buffet-style lunch. Frank somehow cuts the line without anyone noticing. He grabs a roll for each of us, and we eat as we walk. I guess I'm hungry? But I'm also extremely tired. Jet lag is pulling me under, and I'm not sure how much longer I'm going to last without a big nap.

We go down into the excavation site and walk toward the covered part of the pit. That's when we spot Zip, going the opposite way. They have their laser mapmaking tool in hand.

"Hi there," they say. "Wish I could stay and chat, but I've got another map to make."

Then Zip scampers away. I'll have to talk to Zip later. Is it suspicious they were in the catacombs alone?

Under the tarp roof, the air is hot and sticky. We take half a lap around the perimeter before I'm staring at a doorway with a sign next to it marked *Dangerous: Special Task Force Only.*

The entrance to the catacombs is much smaller than I thought it would be. It's actually the perfect size for Mom, but I imagine it would be a tight squeeze for broad-shouldered Orlando Bones and exceedingly tall Professor Phineas Alistair Worthington. The doorway is more of an archway, painted with snakes. At the top, there's a snake around a woman's neck—I guess this is supposed to be a depiction of the Necklace of Harmonia?

"It's an ouroboros!" Eliza says, her gray eyes wide in excitement.

"Bora Bora?" Frank says.

"Ouroboros," Eliza repeats, much slower. "See the snake around the painted lady's neck? It's biting its own tail. That's called an ouroboros."

"And what is it exactly?"

"It's a very popular symbol in alchemy."

"Okay, and what is *that* exactly?"

She sighs and then draws upon her encyclopedic knowledge. "Alchemy is an ancient study . . . it's basically what would happen if chemistry, witchcraft, and philosophy had a mind meld. And the serpent eating itself is a symbol of infinity."

"How?"

In the air, she mimes drawing an O. "A circle with no beginning and no ending."

"But it has a beginning—the mouth. And an ending—the tail."

"But the end becomes part of the beginning again."

Already alchemy is going over my head. But at least Eliza understands it. "Shall we go in?" I say.

And without even answering, Frank bounds forward.

Inside, the catacombs are so dark that I can't even see my hand when I hold it in front of my face. My mom puts her phone's flashlight on.

"I think we're unprepared to advance," Mom says. "We need a better light source."

"Maybe your mom is right, Carlos," Eliza says. "It's really creepy down here."

The air is dry and cold, and the shadows are spooky. It feels like we've walked into someplace sacred, and maybe even sinister. Someplace that definitely does not want to be disturbed.

"Come on, we just got here! We'll turn back in a minute. Just a little farther . . ."

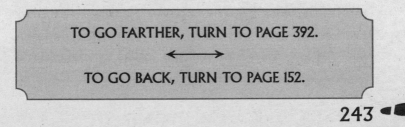

TO GO FARTHER, TURN TO PAGE 392.

TO GO BACK, TURN TO PAGE 152.

I CAN'T BELIEVE we solved an unsolvable maze, but *we did it*! And now we're here. At the center. There's another staircase leading deeper underground. This is the third level down. I wonder how far we're descending, and how close we're going to get to the earth's core.

Eliza gestures to the stairwell. "Shall we go down again?"

"Shhhhh!" For some reason, I thought I heard footsteps. But it can't be. "Mom?" I shout, and my voice echoes around and around the maze. I don't hear a reply, and I also don't hear any more footsteps.

Maybe it was the Minotaur. I shudder.

Eliza goes first, then Frank, then me. And I swear—*I swear*—I hear a footstep again just before I descend.

At the bottom of the staircase, a short hall leads to a circular room with a faint blue light, which is coming from glowworms on the ceiling. I guess it's an improvement on snakes! The floor is made of tile, and there's one in the middle with a very strange marking. Around the room are columns. In front of each column is a different statue, crumbling and broken.

"Are these Greek gods?" I ask, shining my flashlight on the statue of a woman with a crescent on her head.

Eliza thumbs through the pages of her book with her flashlight wedged between her cheek and her shoulder. "Ah! I think they're Titans, the parents of the Greek

244

gods. That's Okeanos . . . the ocean." She consults her book. Then she spins around the room and points them out, one by one. "Uranus, the sky. Astraeus, the stars. Gaia, the earth—"

"There's an earth Titan?" Something sparks in me. My whole body is buzzing. "'Under the earth the riches lie!'"

Eliza gasps. We move to the statue of Gaia. She has a carved crown of leaves and twigs. But we have to look under her, like the disk said.

As funny as it is, Eliza and I are the muscle so that Frank can reach under. "One, two, *three*!" We tilt the statue back. Gaia must be made of fifteen tons of solid steel, because she is ridiculously heavy. My arms start shaking . . . I can't keep holding this much weight.

"Watch out!" Eliza cries. Frank wiggles out just in time, and the statue hits the tile with a thump.

Frank lays out a long black cloth, and we all crouch over it. I expect the necklace to be wrapped up inside. But . . .

Eliza and I pat the cloth down. We find dust and dirt and the smell of old musty laundry, but no Necklace of Harmonia.

Eliza has a sharp intake of breath. "Oh—this is Harmonia's robe! The cursed robe that Cadmus gave to her on her wedding night!"

"How many curses *are* there?" Frank says. And then he starts rattling off a string of curse words, counting them as he goes. "I can think of ten." Of course, one of the ten is *doodoo brain*, so technically, I don't think that counts.

"I'm not saying the robe isn't an important relic," I say, "but where's the necklace?"

"Here," says a deep voice behind us. I scramble for my flashlight and shine it on someone in the center of the room. He's swiping blood from his hand onto a tile. There's a grinding sound, and the person looks up at me. His grimy, sweaty face breaks into a wide grin. And as a podium rises in the center of the room—with a shining, glittering necklace on it—he tips his fedora hat to me.

"Orlando Bones!" we all shout.

"I owe you my thanks."

My eyes dart between the podium and Mr. Bones. I could grab the necklace and run, but I need to be careful. I need to time this exactly right. . . .

"What are you doing here?" I ask.

"Isn't it obvious?" Bones says lightly, gesturing to the necklace. "I have to thank you three. See, I hired you to go straight into the catacombs. If you had just kept following the path, there's a spot too small for adults to fit. But instead you stole my disk and found another way in. You discovered a path I never knew about. You clever kids!" He slow claps for us. "And in doing so, you opened up the floor wide enough that an adult could fit. And now? You're as useful to me as a pair of twos."

I shiver. "How did you get past the snakes?"

"I walked," he said. "I don't know what you did, but after you, they were spooked."

"And you followed us here . . . why, to steal the Necklace of Harmonia?"

"To *sell* the Necklace of Harmonia. To the highest bidder on the dark web."

"Why?" Eliza says, horror-struck. "I thought you were an archaeologist! I thought you appreciated artifacts and history!"

"I am. And I do. But when Keira Skelberry called me to do this job, it was like opportunity knocking at the perfect moment. It was in the cards."

"What made it the perfect moment?" I ask.

"I got into a bit of a sticky situation gambling. Lost a bit too much money and took out a *questionable* loan. Now I have mobsters hounding me for money I don't have, threatening to break my kneecaps if I don't deliver. So I must deliver."

"And where's my mom?"

He laughs. Full-on guffaws. "Kids are so gullible. So easily tricked. She's not down here. She never was. I detained her yesterday, at the ruins she investigated all by herself. I kept her alive in case I needed to use her to manipulate you somehow. But when I'm done here, let's just say . . . all bets are off."

"You must have no intention of letting us go," Eliza says, "if you showed us all your cards."

He grins at Eliza's use of the gambling term. "Well, the house always wins. Enjoy your tomb."

We have to get out of here! Do we grab the necklace before he does, so we can take the upper hand? Or do we throw the robe over his head? We could deter him for a few seconds, just long enough to run for dear life toward the exit. But then we'd lose both treasures.

TO GRAB THE NECKLACE BEFORE HE DOES, TURN TO PAGE 416.

←——→

TO THROW HARMONIA'S ROBE ON HIS HEAD, TURN TO PAGE 109.

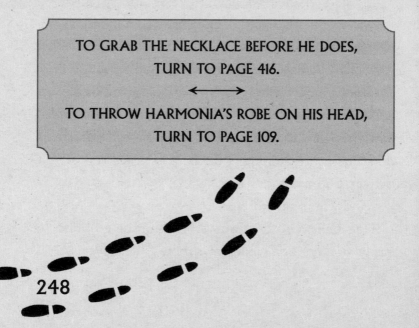

I WANT TO search through Zip's workspace. Sure, it's a risk with Smarty in the room, but she looks absorbed in her work, with her back to us. Besides, her music is so loud that I can hear it from across the tent.

I tap Frank on the shoulder and put my finger to my lips. I try to look as stern as possible, and I think it works, because he nods at me, eyes wide. The three of us slink to the desk and look at the maps.

"What are we looking at?" Eliza whispers.

I lean in closer. "I dunno. It's all Greek to me."

Eliza smiles and shakes her head at the same time. "Good one."

Frank reaches up and wiggles the mouse. The computer is passcode protected.

"Try X-Y-Z-P-D-Q," Frank says.

"I'm not trying that," I say.

"Try one."

"Why?"

"Try two. Try three. Try four."

I sigh.

Eliza clicks *Forgot Password*.

Suddenly the computer starts freaking out—spitting out a whole bunch of zeros and ones right in a row.

I gasp. "You broke it!"

01110000 01100001 01110011 01110011 01100011
01101111 01100100 01100101 01100001 01101110
01110011 01110111 01100101 01110010 01101001
01110011 01110001 01110111 01100101 01110010
01110100 01111001

"Ooooooh, someone's in trouble!" Frank says, a bit too loudly.

"Shhhhhhhh!" Eliza and I hiss. Smarty Marty shifts in her seat, and we all freeze—but then she goes back to doing her work.

"It's not broken," Eliza explains to Frank. "It's binary code. Computer language. I bet if we translated the code, we'd be able to get into Zip's computer."

"But none of us knows binary code," I say.

Eliza pulls up a key from the internet. "There. Now we do."

a 01100001	b 01100010	c 01100011
d 01100100	e 01100101	f 01100110
g 01100111	h 01101000	i 01101001
j 01101010	k 01101011	l 01101100
m 01101101	n 01101110	o 01101111
p 01110000	q 01110001	r 01110010
s 01110011	t 01110100	u 01110101
v 01110110	w 01110111	x 01111000
y 01111001	z 01111010	

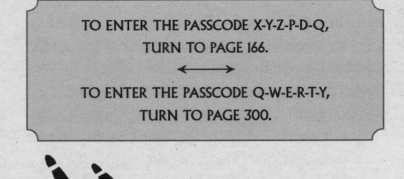

TO ENTER THE PASSCODE X-Y-Z-P-D-Q,
TURN TO PAGE 166.

←——————→

TO ENTER THE PASSCODE Q-W-E-R-T-Y,
TURN TO PAGE 300.

251

MAYBE ELIZA'S RIGHT . . . maybe we should preserve the necklace. I put the hammer down, and Eliza clutches the necklace in her hands.

"It's so pretty," she whispers. "So exquisite."

Uh . . . I don't love the way she's looking at the necklace. Her expression is greedy. And her usually alert eyes are glazed over. She looks almost like she's in a trance.

She puts the necklace around her neck and secures the clasp.

"Maybe you should take that off," I suggest.

"It's *mine*!" she growls at me.

"Are you cursed?" Frank says, poking his sister.

Eliza breaks into a wide-eyed smile. "No, I'm enlightened." Then she turns and bolts out of the cave, still wearing the necklace.

"Where are you going?!" I cry, running after her. But she disappears around the ledge.

I spend weeks trying to find her, but she's gone. Overtaken by the power of Hephaestus's curse. Talk about a pain in the neck!

CASE CLOSED.

I DON'T KNOW if we can outrun the spiders, but we have to try.

"GO, GO, GO!" I shout as Mom, Eliza, Frank, and I bolt toward the exit.

Through the tunnel, out the door with the keyhole, through the main hall—running faster than I ever have in my life. I turn around. The spiders are still coming. We're slowing down, and they're—if possible—speeding up.

We're not going to make it. My side is splitting. Eliza is out of breath. Mom is wheezing.

"Last one to the exit is a rotten egg!" Frank shouts from somewhere way ahead of the rest of us. We have to keep going. The archway's up ahead—light shines in! Just one last push.

We fly out of the catacombs.

Smack!

We slam right into Orlando Bones and Nadira Nadeem, who are thrown backward onto their butts. We fall on top of them. Their clipboard and notes go flying into the air. Behind us, there are no spiders. Safe!

"Mr. Bones!" Mom says, flustered, as she climbs off him. I don't think she's used to looking so unprofessional. She rushes around their feet, collecting their papers.

Nadira Nadeem stands up. She brushes off her pants,

her shirt, and her hijab. But it's no use—the excavation dirt won't wipe off without water . . . and probably soap. "This was certainly unexpected. What on earth were you running from?"

"And what game are you playing at?" Orlando Bones says. "The way you were running . . . what did you see?"

"I spy with my little eye," Frank says, "something brown."

"Is it dirt?" Eliza asks.

"Yup!"

"But did you find anything *in the catacombs*?" Bones asks.

"We spied with our little eyes . . . ," Frank begins.

I silently beg. Frank, please don't tell them about the necklace, *please* don't tell.

"Something black!" he finishes.

"Is it darkness?" Eliza guesses.

"Yup!"

Orlando Bones sighs.

Nadira Nadeem looks between us. Her eyebrows inch closer to each other in a confused expression. "You mean to tell me that you were running like that for no reason at all?"

"You're really not going to reveal your cards to me? Your *client*?" Bones says incredulously.

"Sorry, we really—" I cut off. I was about to find an excuse to get away from this conversation, but then I remember the writing on the wall. The one I took a picture of. Nadira Nadeem is standing right here. She could translate the Greek for us!

Do we trust her with this ginormous clue? Or do we go find Professor Phineas Alistair Worthington to translate instead?

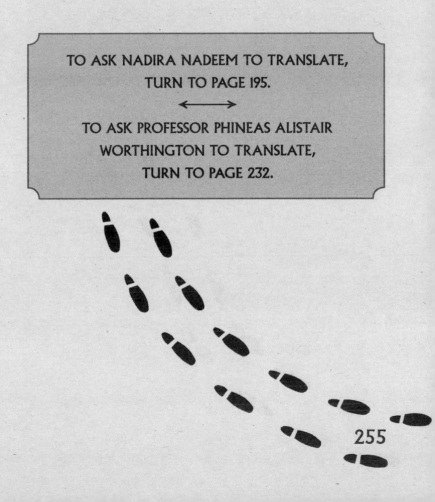

TO ASK NADIRA NADEEM TO TRANSLATE,
TURN TO PAGE 195.

←→

TO ASK PROFESSOR PHINEAS ALISTAIR
WORTHINGTON TO TRANSLATE,
TURN TO PAGE 232.

ORLANDO BONES'S WINNING blackjack hand is two, five, six, and eight of hearts. I type those numbers and suit, press enter, and bingo—we're in.

He's got two windows open. One is his email, and the other is a spreadsheet.

"Well? This was *your* idea," Eliza says.

TO LOOK AT ORLANDO BONES'S EMAIL, TURN TO PAGE 430.

←→

TO LOOK AT ORLANDO BONES'S SPREADSHEET, TURN TO PAGE 98.

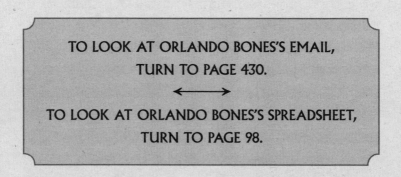

"SMARTY, ARE YOU trying to find the Necklace of Harmonia on your own?"

"Of course I am," she says.

My eyes get wide. "You are?"

"Sure. It's not like I can trust *you* to find and protect it."

"And . . . do you want the necklace for personal gain?" Eliza asks.

"Of course I do," she says.

I nearly choke. I didn't expect such an easy confession.

Smarty's rabbity nose twitches. "Do you know how many awards and job offers will come my way if I find it? My career will be *made*."

I wonder if that also applies to finding a whole handful of extremely valuable artifacts that just so happened to have gone missing. . . .

TO ASK SMARTY IF SHE STOLE THE ARTIFACTS, TURN TO PAGE 53.

257

"YOU WERE THE one who kicked Richard Leech out of this tent, right? Great work, by the way." I figure the extra flattery will butter her up, and I'm right: she turns to me smugly.

"Absolutely, it was me! Leech was being super suspicious, always hanging around the artifacts. I even saw him open the plastic baggie and take out one of the plates. *With his bare hands.*"

"And that's . . . bad?"

"Of course! The oils on his fingers could deteriorate some of the paint!"

"So . . . he should have been wearing gloves?" I ask.

She pushes her glasses up her nose. "Absolutely not! He should not have taken the artifact out of the baggie at all. Once it's in the baggie, it is not to be touched until the dig is over."

"So what was Leech doing with the artifacts? And did Zip see Leech cozying up to the artifact shelf too?"

She stops typing and squints at me. "It's *sooooo* annoying that Mr. Bones wouldn't let me be a detective, you know that?"

I know. She says it every two seconds.

"But," she says, dropping her voice to a whisper. "If you're going to do the job right, then I have a piece of information for you."

"Okay . . . but I'm not done asking you questions yet."

258

She blows the bangs away from her face, clearly annoyed. "You'd rather ask me a question than hear my super-important piece of investigative information? Mr. Bones *really* should have let me handle this case!"

TO ASK SMARTY MARTY ABOUT ZIP,
TURN TO PAGE 423.

←——————→

TO HEAR SMARTY MARTY'S INFORMATION,
TURN TO PAGE 239.

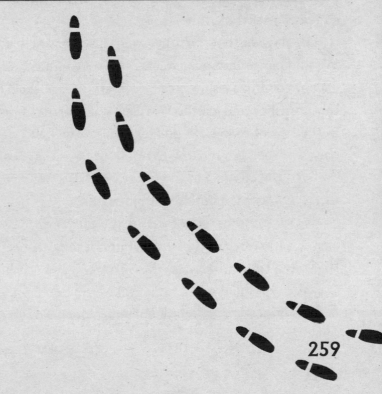

259

I'M NO GOOD to Mr. Bones if I am too tired to lift my head, let alone analyze clues. It's time to call it a night. And if Smarty Marty really has a lead for us, then we can always get it out of her tomorrow, when we're all thinking more clearly.

"Sorry, Smarty, but we're off the clock right now. We'll resume in the morning, and I hope you'll share your lead with us then."

"Don't count on it," she says before marching off.

We climb into our tent. All four of us have our own cot, in each corner. There's really nothing else here— no furniture, no decorations. We'll be living out of our suitcases the whole time.

The day was hot, but the night is surprisingly cold. We all change into our sweats, and we're totally silent except for Eliza's shivering. As a group, we grab our toothbrushes and paste. We each take a porta-potty in the row of toilets, do our nightly routine, and travel back together. I'm starting to miss the cases that I could do from the comfort of my own home or a hotel room (even if one of the hotels was haunted).

Usually at the end of an investigative day, I feel chatty with my Las Pistas team, but not today. The long flight, the time difference, the unspoken awkwardness between Eliza and me . . . it all takes too much energy. I crawl into bed, and I'm asleep before my head hits the pillow.

260

I **WAKE UP** to a flurry of activity outside the tent. Archaeologists getting ready for the day, eating breakfast, calling out to each other. I yawn and roll over to see that Mom and Frank are gone. Having slept over at Eliza's too many times to count, I know Frank *always* wakes up at the crack of dawn and isn't satisfied until he wakes everyone else up too. I have to thank Mom later for taking one for the team. I definitely need the sleep, and so must Eliza. Her back is to me, and she's curled up on her cot.

I sit up in bed. Wait a second—Eliza is awake! She's on her side, reading a book.

"What are you reading?" I ask.

She flips around, startled. Then she holds up the cover for me to see. "It's a book about forensic science. This chapter is about fingerprinting. Every fingerprint makes a unique pattern. Like a snowflake, no two are alike."

"Eliza, you've been studying detective work?"

She looks scandalized. "Well, of course, Carlos! I thought it might come in handy one day on a case."

"But you learn on the job!"

"There's *always* more to learn," she insists. "I like learning on the job, but I thought if I studied more . . ." Suddenly she looks flushed. Then she shakes her head and says, "Are you a loop, whorl, or arch?"

"Huh?"

"Fingerprints!" she says. "I'm a whorl. So is Frank. Let me see your hand." I hop onto her bed and let her examine my pointer. She compares it to a page of fingerprint pictures in her book. At last she looks up and says, "Interesting. Classic arch."

"Is that good, or is that bad?"

She lets go of my hand. "Neither. It just is."

The flap to the tent opens, and Mom and Frank come bounding in.

Frank is like a fly, flitting around the room and buzzing about his morning. "Detecto-Mom and I took a walk all the way up a *mountain*!" Frank says. "And I caught a caterpillar, but then I let him go. Then I picked some grass. Then we came back here, and I had a muffin. And my tooth is even looser than yesterday— watch *this*!" He waggles his tooth back and forth.

"Sounds like you had a fun morning," I say to Mom.

She groans and collapses onto her cot. "Gone are the days when I used to work cases alone!"

"You love us!" I say.

"Claro," she responds. Then she adds in the softest

of whispers, "Pero necesito dormir."

"You'll get excellent sleep tonight," I promise. "After we solve the case."

"Speaking of," Eliza says, "we should probably check in with Orlando Bones."

For once, I agree with her. So we pack up, tie our laces, and head over to Bones's tent. When we arrive, he's outside, whispering into his phone. It seems like a very intense conversation. I pull Eliza and Frank against the tent so we can listen.

"Just a few more days!" Bones says with a tense laugh. "I swear I'll get it. I'm so close." There's a brief silence. And suddenly he looks sweaty and sickly. "No, no, no—that's not necessary!" Another pause. "Come on, come on! I swear I'm not hedging my bets. I'm cashing my chips. You know me, Duff. We go way ba—" He clears his throat. "Mmm. Yes," he says stiffly. "Got it."

He hangs up the phone. He's definitely in a bad mood—all brooding and miserable. Then he storms into the tent.

"Shall we?" I say, gesturing to the tent's entrance.

Bones whips around as we walk in. He tries to smile, but it's definitely strained. "Ah! If it isn't my favorite detectives! What are the odds?"

"Probably high, since you hired us," Eliza points out.

"We wanted to check in with you," I say.

He sits down in his desk chair and tents his hands. "Excellent—I'd love to hear it. What have you found?"

I want to answer his question . . . but I have a question of my own. About that phone call we just overheard.

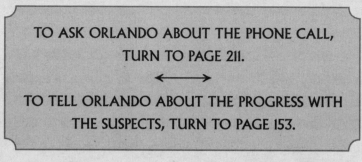

TO ASK ORLANDO ABOUT THE PHONE CALL,
TURN TO PAGE 211.

←——→

TO TELL ORLANDO ABOUT THE PROGRESS WITH
THE SUSPECTS, TURN TO PAGE 153.

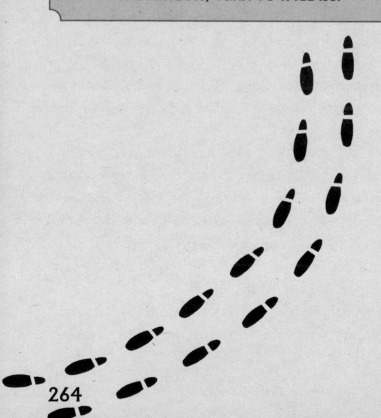

ELIZA REALLY WANTS to explore the catacombs with me. I can tell from her voice that she's anxious about it too.

"Come on," I say, taking her hand and going to the left side with her.

"Finally," Mom whispers. "I mean . . . we'll be over here. Don't mind us!"

Eliza and I scour the left wall for any signs of a key-hole, but so far, I don't see anything but stone with a few jagged cracks. She's silent, except for an occasional deep sigh. After five minutes or so, she finally says something.

"I know you're upset."

"I'm not—"

"Don't you dare try to lie to me. Don't insult my intelligence like that."

Does she always have to bring up how smart she is? "You're sounding more and more like Smarty."

She stops in her tracks. "What? What do you mean by that?"

"Nothing. I didn't mean that."

There's a silence between us. On the other side of the tunnel, I hear Mom cry, "Frank! Don't eat that!" I don't even *want* to know.

"Clearly you meant something by it."

"Right, I forgot. You can read people like a pro now. You can be the lead detective, and I won't contribute anything. I know you're better than me."

"I'm not better than you."

"It feels like it."

Our lights sweep across the wall. Nothing, nothing, and more nothing.

Finally Eliza says, "Have you ever thought about how I feel? I have the same detective ambitions as you, and I am just as excited as you are to make choices and talk to suspects." She sighs. "Carlos, I don't want to be your sidekick. I want to be your equal."

"How can we be equals when you're so much better than me at everything?"

Eliza makes a noise like she's upset. I wonder if she's crying . . . but I don't want to shine the flashlight on her face. I think it's easier to be honest in the dark. "Carlos, I don't know how else to tell you . . . we're not competing! We're a team! My successes are your successes, and your successes are my successes."

I never thought about it like that. That actually sounds . . . nice. And if we're graded together—if her successes *are* my successes—then I'd have to admit we're doing pretty well. Even if I, individually, didn't add much.

"Our friendship will never survive if we're frenemies or rivals," Eliza says. "It's so important to support each other—not just when we're feeling low, but also when we're doing well. It's probably harder to do that. But we have to learn."

266

I swallow the lump in my throat. "I've never heard my mom compliment anyone so much."

Eliza laughs, and it rings throughout the tunnels. "She knows I feel undervalued—that's why she keeps pointing out the good things I'm doing and keeps trying to get you to compliment me."

I think really hard about today and yesterday. "She is?"

"She's been trying to mend our friendship, not put you down."

"So much for being good at reading people—I totally missed that!" I say with a laugh. At first it's a small chuckle, but it grows and grows. And then we're both hysterical, for some weird reason, as we swing our flashlights around.

"ARE YOU DONE FIGHTING?" Frank hollers from across the room.

"Yeah," I say. "We're done."

"Good. Because I found something!"

We cross over to the other side of the catacombs, climbing over a few pieces of debris that have lodged in the dirt. Mom and Frank both have their flashlights aimed at a hole in the middle of the wall, between two cracks that run from ceiling to floor. The hole would be easy to miss if we weren't looking for it. The cracks look just like all the others in the catacombs, and the hole looks like . . . well . . . a hole. It's not fancy or decorated in any way, shape, or form.

I fetch the key so that Eliza doesn't have to take off her backpack. Then I press it up to the hole.

The key fits perfectly. I shiver.

"You do the honors," I say to Eliza.

"Together," she replies.

We turn the key.

The wall swings open like it's on a hinge. The path before us is even smaller. Poor Mom has to hunch to step in, and the ceiling brushes my hair.

The more we walk, the breezier the tunnel gets, until I feel like we're fighting a full-on windstorm to get to the end. At last when we reach the end, there seem to be five holes in the ground. Beside each hole is a small metal disk with a different symbol per pathway. I run my hands above each hole and feel a cold breeze whooshing back at me. So *this* is where the wind was coming from.

I look at Eliza, and to my surprise, she is shining her flashlight *up*. At a stone wall with those same symbols on it. No, not symbols—Greek letters.

"Look at that square, Carlos," Eliza says, pointing to a stone in the second column, third row that seems much darker than the others. The letter on it has completely faded away.

"Do you think that stone is important?" I ask.

Eliza hums. "I think so, yes. Something about it feels intentional. Like it's showing us what hole to climb through to get to the other side of the wall."

Frank pumps his fist in the air. "I get to go in it, right?"

"Frank," I say, "you're literally the only person who can."

"Hang on there," Mom says. "Your parents are trusting me, and I'm not sure I want to send Frank into a random hole, especially if it might be dangerous."

"It won't be dangerous by the time I'm done with it. No . . ." Eliza links elbows with me. "By the time *we're* done with it. I'm certain that this darker stone is the answer—telling us which hole Frank has to crawl through."

"How do we figure it out, though?"

"It's like a Greek sudoku, right?" Mom says.

Eliza twists her hair thoughtfully. "If that's true, then I guess normal sudoku rules apply. Which means we can't repeat any of the Greek letters in any row, any column, or any section, and we'll be fine."

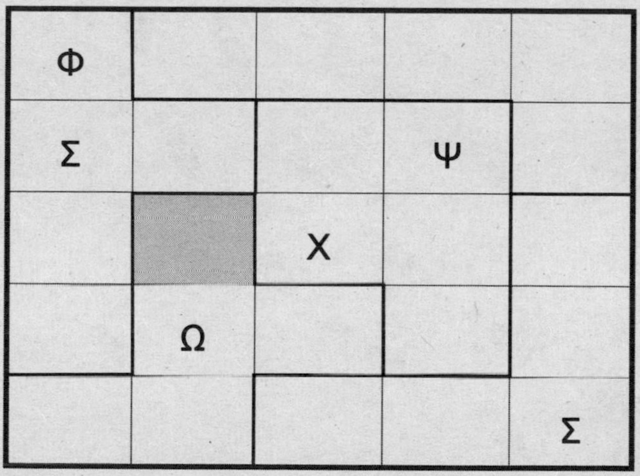

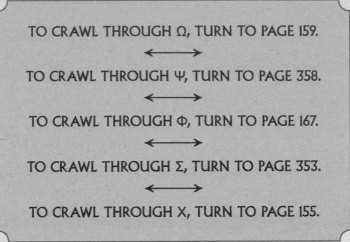

TO CRAWL THROUGH Ω, TURN TO PAGE 159.

←——————→

TO CRAWL THROUGH Ψ, TURN TO PAGE 358.

←——————→

TO CRAWL THROUGH Φ, TURN TO PAGE 167.

←——————→

TO CRAWL THROUGH Σ, TURN TO PAGE 353.

←——————→

TO CRAWL THROUGH Χ, TURN TO PAGE 155.

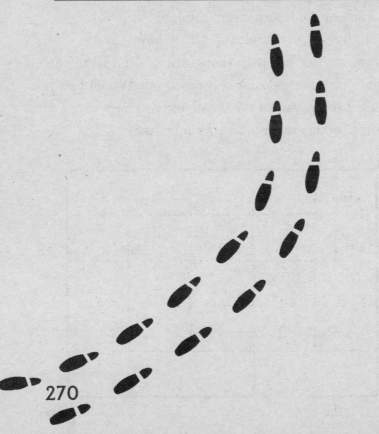

270

I PUT A red gem on, and the rest of the pattern goes seamlessly.

When Eliza, Frank, and I are all done, we put our individual pieces together. I have to admit—our forgery looks good. *Really* good. I can't believe that Frank is a little Michelangelo, and I never even knew!

Eliza paints a topcoat on the fake necklace, takes a really nice picture of it, and puts a filter on the photo. Then we set the necklace aside. Without a kiln, it'll get all dry and crumbly, but we got the picture we needed.

"We have the forgery," Eliza says, "but now we have to sell the lie."

"What do you mean?" I ask.

"We need to go to the tunnel and leave footprints and evidence. Basically, we have to make it look convincing that we were really there . . . without actually going in."

We head over to the tunnels at about two in the morning. The dig is so quiet. There's no sound at all except for the chirping crickets. At the entrance to the catacombs, I shine my flashlight on the painted necklace again, and I have to admit—ours really does look the part.

We trample and stamp our footprints all over the entrance. On the way back, we're all yawning. Frank leans on me, pulling at my shirt, so that he can keep

271

walking, even with his eyes closed. I lean down to grab his hand, so I can guide him to our tent without my shirt fully stretching out, and that's when I see he's barefoot.

"Uh . . . Frank? Where are your shoes?"

"I left them," he says sleepily, "by the entrance."

"Why?"

"I thought we were leaving foots behind."

"Foot*prints*," I whisper.

"Ooops."

It's okay, though. I imagine in the morning, *someone* is going to find his shoes there and believe our fake story. We only need to trick one person. Let's hope, I think as we walk into our tent, that it's the right person.

DAY THREE

I WAKE UP with a jolt.

"Mom!" I say, but her bed is still empty. I don't know what I was expecting—that her captor would magically release her?

I'm glad we have a plan ready to go. Every moment Mom is missing feels like another minute where she's closer and closer to danger.

I wake Eliza and Frank. It's the first time I've ever been up before Frank, and probably the last time too. We're all a little somber. I think it's the nerves.

Outside, the ground is damp, and it smells like rain. A few archaeologists are up, having a quiet morning with their phones and coffee.

With the fake necklace in my backpack, we move to the work tent. No one is inside, but I know Smarty has a schedule on her wall. And there it is—"Morning meeting at eight a.m. in front of the bosses' tent." That means we only have seventeen minutes to wait.

Of course, these seventeen minutes are the longest of my *life*. I've never seen a clock tick more slowly. We walk around the dig, just taking in the sights of the pit,

273

the columns, the distant mountains.

At eight o'clock, we start heading to the bosses' tent, making our (very planned) fashionably late arrival.

"Perhaps we can have a modified map by this afternoon, Zip? Dr. Mandible, are you ready with a medical kit, just in case—oh, and Professor, how many books are you able to carry down into the excavation pit? I'll have you posted outside the catacombs in case we need your knowle—"

Nadira Nadeem stops talking when she sees us approach.

"Good morning! Good morning! To you, and you, and you, and you!" Frank sings.

"Oh, I'm so sorry, detectives," Nadira says. "We have a lot to do today, and our schedule doesn't permit time for interruptions, unfortunately."

"We'll only take a minute," Eliza says, holding up her phone. "Take a look—we found the Necklace of Harmonia."

"You did *not*." Smarty snorts indignantly.

But they all gather around the phone, snatching it from Eliza's hands and zooming in closer. Orlando Bones's jaw drops so wide that I can basically see his tonsils.

"No way, *no way*!" Smarty says.

Nadira squints at us. "I don't understand—how?"

"We went last night," I lie. "After midnight. Looking for *my mom*, remember? By the way, thanks for making it your priority to find her."

Everyone shuffles uncomfortably.

"So we went into the catacombs, searching for her. Guess who we didn't find? But we did stumble upon this. It's even more beautiful in person. You guys should really see it."

"It's a MASTERPIECE," Frank agrees. "Created by a master sculptor!"

I nearly elbow him. He's not great at being discreet.

"So where is it?" Richard Leech says greedily.

"Where's what?"

"The necklace," he says, nearly salivating. That's when I notice that just about everybody—except Zip—looks hungry for the relic.

"Here's the thing," Eliza says. "We're going to set up an exchange. The Necklace of Harmonia for the missing artifacts."

Nadira Nadeem splutters. "You—you can't do that! The Necklace of Harmonia is the most prized legendary artifact in the world! It's worth a hundred times what the other artifacts are worth. You can't just *give it* to a thief."

"I don't know what to tell you," Eliza says. "We were hired to find missing artifacts, not the Necklace of

Harmonia. And that's exactly what we're going to find. After that, we wash our hands of this whole deal."

"You're sweetening the pot for the thief?" Bones wails, throwing his fedora to the ground and stomping on it. "They get rewarded with the jackpot? What I've worked my whole career for?"

"Sorry, Mr. Bones, but we're finding the artifacts you asked us to find," I say, and he looks *miserable*.

"You really went down there?" Smarty says skeptically, grabbing the phone to look at the picture of our forgery again.

"We really did," I confirm. "You underestimated us."

She opens and closes her mouth wordlessly.

"Here's how this is going to work," Eliza says. "Between now and noon, one of you will leave the bag of stolen artifacts in—"

"THE BATHROOM," Frank says.

"Er . . . sure, the bathroom," Eliza says.

"Once we get the artifacts," I continue, "we will call everyone together again to announce the next handoff: the necklace, in exchange for my mom's location."

There's a collective mumble.

Eliza raises her hand for silence. "In essence, we're trading one artifact for all the others *and* Detective Serrano unharmed. You'll be able to take the necklace and escape, so long as we have the information about where to find Cat Serrano. Whoever the thief is among you, we hope you find this deal amenable. We think it's more than fair."

"Makes me wish I *had* stolen the artifacts," Professor Worthington mutters. "If this is how one gets rewarded for thievery."

Frank claps the professor on the back. "I guess it goes to show you that CRIME ALWAYS PAYS."

If waiting seventeen minutes was painful earlier, waiting nearly three hours is even worse. We try to stand watch around the porta-potties, but it seems like a lot of people are going in and out, and no one with a bag—at least not that I can see.

We snack nervously on bread that Frank takes from the food table, and all the while I'm trying really hard not to think of Mom. How frightened she must be—and whether we really can trust the culprit to release her.

At last the clock strikes noon. Time to check out the porta-potties.

We open door after door. In front of each new stall, my heart races faster—but each door I open leads to an empty porta-potty.

It has to be here.

It *has to*.

But it's not.

Our plan failed.

My throat feels tight, and I know I'm going to cry, even in front of all our suspects who have come to the porta-potties to witness part one of the hostage exchanges. But it was all for nothing.

"It's okay, Carlos," Eliza whispers, rubbing my back gently. "We'll figure it out."

A long shadow appears on the ground. Someone is walking toward us holding a giant trash bag. One of the archaeologists who's not on the special task force.

"Does this belong to someone here?" she says. "Someone left it at my tent with instructions to bring it to the porta-potties at noon. Oh, are you those detectives? Nice to meet you. Thanks for trying to find our missing artifacts."

"We aren't trying," Eliza says. "We are succeeding. Can you put that bag down, please?"

She places it on the ground. "Okay, well, I don't know what this is, but I did my duty—I have to get back to excavating." She scurries away.

Eliza puts on gloves before reaching into the bag. She pulls out artifact after artifact—three vases, the bust, the golden armband, the coins, the hair ornament. It's all here.

Now that we've got the artifacts, it's time to set up the second exchange. "Okay, we will be putting the necklace—"

278

"Hold on a second, Carlos," Eliza says.

What is she doing, deviating from the plan? She's looking very intently at a vase, and she slowly slips into a grin. I lean down next to her, and she whispers, "You know how I've been studying fingerprinting? I think if we dust the artifacts, we could compare the fingerprints on the artifacts to those of our suspects. And then—"

"BLAMMO!" Frank shouts in my other ear.

"Yes, blammo, we have our culprit."

"But that wasn't the plan," I say softly.

"I know," she whispers. "But I think the fingerprints thing is better. I have my kit in my backpack."

"But—"

"Our necklace has served its purpose already—we got the artifacts back. And didn't you say you were going to try to be more flexible?"

TO SET UP THE NEXT EXCHANGE,
TURN TO PAGE 108.

←——→

TO FINGERPRINT THE ARTIFACTS AND SUSPECTS,
TURN TO PAGE 434.

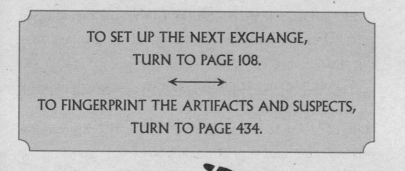

279

I'VE UNTANGLED THE snakes on the disk . . . or at least I think so. I press N K Σ Ψ Γ E O.

Crack! The floor splits open beneath us, and we fall.

"AHHHHHHHHHHHH!" we scream as we drop down.

We land on a sand dune. There's a weird hissing sound, but I didn't break a bone or twist a limb. I breathe a sigh of relief. Unexpected bone fractures would really mess up my day.

I wonder if Mom even came through this way, or did we just get stuck in a part of the catacombs where she's never been? The ground we fell through is about ten feet above us. "How do we get back up later?"

"That's the least of our worries," Eliza says, her voice trembling.

I look where her flashlight's shining. And suddenly I understand what the hissing is.

There are snakes.

Hundreds, maybe *thousands*, of them. Tangled up in each other like some giant rat king. Hissing and slithering and spitting.

"Cool! Are they friendly?" Frank says, as one lets out an angry *sssssss*.

I gulp. "Are these the kind of snakes that are venomous? Or the kind that strangle you?"

"Red touches black, venom lack. Yellow touches red,

280

soon you'll be dead," Eliza recites.

"That doesn't help us at all! All these snakes are tan!"

"I don't know!" Eliza says. "I'm not a walking snake encyclopedia!"

Snakes. Something horrible pops into my head, and I start to groan. "Oh no . . ."

"Carlos, you're scaring me. What is it?"

"I just remembered. 'Under the earth the riches lie. Ophidian curses too.'"

"Well, this is clearly an ophidian curse!" Eliza shrieks as she kicks sand at a snake crawling ever nearer.

"This is the catacomb part, Eliza. This is where the bodies are."

I see her expression in the faint light of my flashlight beam. She looks confused. "What do you mean?"

"Harmonia and Cadmus got turned into serpents, remember? What if this room is the resting place for all humans turned into serpents?"

"Carlos, there's no way Harmonia and Cadmus survived thousands of years down here, not even as snakes."

"Maybe these are their snake descendants." Fifteen slither toward me with evil gleams in their eyes. "We can't stay here. The snakes are getting closer, and they look hungry."

"Do you think they like garlic bread?" Frank asks. "I don't mind sharing mine."

"Frank? Explain."

"I saw they were about to serve garlic bread for dinner, so I stole some."

"*That's* where you ran off to while we were working on the nonogram?" Eliza says.

"I stole a whole backpack full of garlic bread. That's the special thing I brought. You're welcome!"

"Frankie, I don't think they'll eat garlic bread. They like mice and frogs. . . ."

"Things that are alive," I say with a shiver.

"Humph! Well you never know until you *invite them to dinner*!"

The serpents are closing in. Inching closer and closer. The only thing we have is sand. Maybe we can throw it in their eyes and stun them. I know I can't do *anything* when I get sand in my eyes.

"Garlic bread! Garlic bread!" Frank chants.

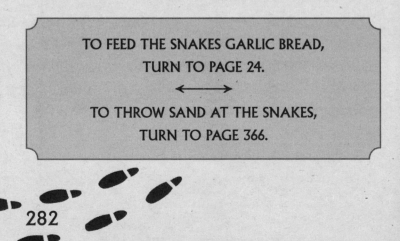

TO FEED THE SNAKES GARLIC BREAD,
TURN TO PAGE 24.

←——→

TO THROW SAND AT THE SNAKES,
TURN TO PAGE 366.

"CAN YOU TELL us more about your job, Zip?" I ask.

"Sure. My job is to take laser imaging scans of the interior of the catacombs, then provide 3D maps that will allow everyone to head underground safely."

"And everyone's waiting on you to get the job done?"

"Zip," Eliza says, cutting in with her own line of questioning, "you work where all the artifacts are. Nadira seems to think that you would have the easiest time taking an artifact."

I want to groan—why would Eliza think accusing Zip is a good idea? Especially when they were being so cooperative?

"She thinks *I* stole them?" Zip is really riled up now, just like I knew they would be. They wring their hands together. "Why would I do that?"

"YOU TELL ME!" Frank says, waggling a finger at Zip.

"Money?" Mom says. "Spite?"

Zip takes a deep breath, and the angry energy seeps out of them. Suddenly, they're cool, calm, and collected again. "I don't have a motive," Zip says evenly. "This is all speculation and conjecture."

"If not you, then *who*?" Frank shouts.

"Right now, you're our lead suspect," Mom lies, and a little pink comes into her cheeks.

"Me?" Zip says incredulously. "I don't see how you can possibly come to that conclusion—and so fast too. Are you sure you looked at everybody thoroughly?"

"Sounds like you have some suspects in mind. Would you like to help us out with our investigation, Zip? If you can give us other leads, perhaps our investigation would be fundamentally altered, away from you."

TO ASK WHO ZIP SUSPECTS, TURN TO PAGE 66.

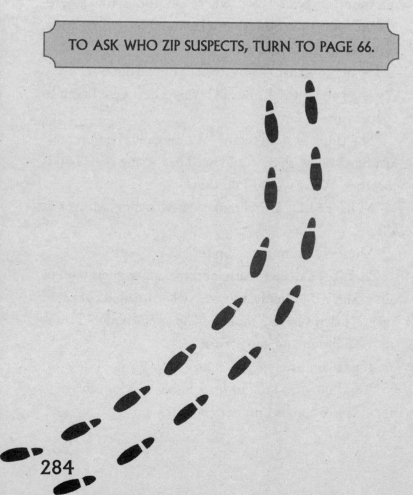

WE TRACE 285 across the clock's face, and it pops open to reveal a hollow interior. I reach in and grab a long L-shaped object . . . only, the bottom of the L looks like a comb. I've never seen anything like this before.

"Um, Eliza?"

"It's a key," she says as she turns the object over in her hands. "An ancient key. This is what they used to look like, thousands of years ago."

"A key to *what*, though?" I ask.

"To the Necklace of Harmonia," Mom says in awe. "There has to be a reason why someone would have left *this* key at *this* site. For anyone who bothered to learn the history . . . this is a bread-crumb trail."

"YAY, ELIZA! MY SMARTY SISTER!"

"Yes, this was an excellent detective instinct, Eliza. I'm so proud of you."

Eliza looks smug, and for a second, annoyance jolts through me. If we had gone the way I wanted to go, maybe we would have found something in the tunnels, and Mom would be looking at *me* with wonder and respect.

"So there is a keyhole somewhere in the tunnels?" I ask. "And this will open up, well, whatever needs to be opened?"

"Possibly," Eliza says, slipping the key into her back-pack.

"Do you think it has something to do with the disk

Mr. Bones showed us this morning?"

Eliza half shrugs. "Maybe," she says, like she doesn't think it's likely at all. She's clearly just trying to be nice. "I didn't see any keyholes on it, but we could . . . um, go back and ask Mr. Bones to see it again?" She sounds skeptical.

We hop into the car and drive back to the dig. The drive back seems so much longer than the drive there—I think because I am so eager to get back. I can't wait to see the look on Mr. Bones's face when we tell him what we've found. And hear his barking laughter . . .

But to our surprise, Orlando Bones is not in his tent. No one is. It's completely empty.

I walk over to his desk, hoping to leave a note. There are a bunch of playing cards scattered across his desk, along with pictures of him grinning at different casinos. And then there's his computer. Sitting there. Waiting for us.

I look up at the tent flap. We could risk it . . . I think we have enough time. . . .

"What are you doing?" Eliza says.

"Breaking into his computer."

"Why?"

"Why not?"

Eliza frowns. "I don't see how this could be productive for our case. It's not like we suspect Mr. Bones . . . do we?"

I shrug. "You never know what we'll find on his computer. Maybe about him, or maybe about someone else. I wouldn't discount anything. It's all relevant to our case." I stare at the playing cards again. "This could be crucial, for all you know. If only we can break in. . . ."

"Aren't you the one always saying we shouldn't anger the client? If Bones catches us, we're *done* for."

"Well, I think it's only fair you do what I want since I did what *you* wanted this morning. Fair is fair."

"Don't talk to me about fair!" Eliza cries.

Mom looks between Eliza and me, concerned. "Okay, well, why don't Carlos and Eliza do that, while Frank and I . . . um . . . keep guard up front?" Mom says, in a thinly veiled attempt to give Eliza and me alone time to work out our issues. Mom drags Frank outside, and I can hear him protesting through the flap.

Eliza sighs and puts her elbows on Bones's desk. "For the record, I think this is a terrible idea."

"Noted," I say, rolling my eyes. And thanks for the confidence in me, I almost add. But I don't.

Bones's computer is password protected. I click on the password hint, and it tells me:

The blackjack hand closest to your heart, four cards, low to high, no faces, no aces, we're off to the races.

Well, that doesn't help us. Unless . . . I look at the

pictures around Mr. Bones's desk, the ones of him at gambling tables. One of them *must* be his favorite winning hand, if he has a picture of it in his office. Every card I see in the pictures, I take out of his deck of cards and lay it on his desk.

"Eliza, what's blackjack?"

"It's a game where you have to get your cards as close to twenty-one as possible without going over. But if you get twenty-one exactly, it's a winning hand. Face cards are ten. Aces can be one or eleven, depending on what you need. It's an interesting game."

Twenty-one exactly, huh? I think Bones gave us enough clues to figure out his password.

THE FIRST THREE PLAYING CARDS ARE
THE DIGITS OF YOUR NEXT PAGE.

←——————→

TO ASK ELIZA FOR A HINT, TURN TO PAGE 307.

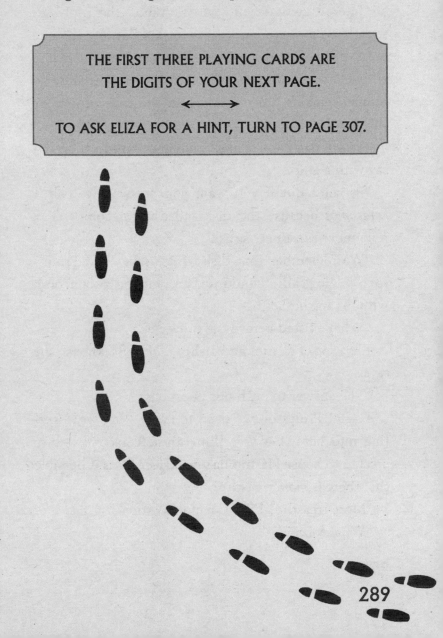

"WHY DOES EVERYONE keep calling the tunnels *catacombs*? Are there bones or bodies down there?"

"Interesting question, Mr. Serrano," the professor says, like I'm a student in one of his classes. "If there are, we have not discovered them yet. But . . . if it is truly Harmonia's resting place, then there would be no human remains, since she was turned into a snake by the gods."

"So are there . . . snake bones and skins in there?" I say with a gulp.

"Perhaps. But if you want your answer, we call it *catacombs* because the disk called it catacombs. You remember Mr. Bones's disk?"

"We remember that disk," Eliza says. "But Professor . . . logically, would a catacomb be a catacomb without any bodies?"

"What existed before the universe?"

Eliza looks at me, and I shrug. "I don't know," she says.

"The answer to both our questions."

I sigh. "Professor, we need to know what we're getting into here. Do you think these catacombs were created to house Harmonia's necklace? Or is it possible that there is *more* treasure?"

"More treasure? Like Harmonia's robe?"

"What robe?"

"Surely I told you about the robe. The robe that Cadmus presented to Harmonia along with the ill-fated necklace!"

"The *terry-cloth* robe," Frank reminds me.

It's coming back to me now. "Oh, right! The robe! Did that disappear too?"

"Indeed," the professor says, pushing his glasses up his nose.

"I was talking about other treasure, though."

"Explain."

Eliza jumps in, totally stealing my thunder. "I think what Carlos means is if the tunnels were created before Harmonia's necklace ended up down there, then maybe this underground bunker was the home of other treasures first."

"I cannot confirm, since I seem to be too large in stature for these catacombs. But anything is possible, I suppose."

I look at my phone. I really have to go—Mom needs me, and I can't justify spending any more time here. "Thank you so much for answering my questions, Professor Worthington. I have to run."

"Perhaps you would do me the honor of finding me privately, before Mr. Bones or anyone else, if you find anything . . . anything of *note*," he says pointedly. He looks hungry. "This is my life's work. And I wouldn't want it getting into the wrong hands."

"We have to run," I repeat. And I brush past the professor and charge into Nadira Nadeem's tent. I'll make Eliza follow *me* this time.

Nadira is the only one in the tent at the moment. She's sitting at her desk, and I know I should be focused on her, but I can only think of Mom. Did Mom get too close to the answer of the missing artifacts by going to the ruins? Is her disappearance innocent or sinister? Why did I think it was a good idea for Las Pistas to split up?

Nadira looks up. "Can I help you? I'm sorry—I'm very busy and don't have much time."

We sit down on the chairs in front of her. "We have a confession to make to you, Ms. Nadeem. And then we'll need yours."

Nadira searches the tent like she's looking for a hidden camera. "What are you kids talking about? By the way, you have three minutes before I have to meet with Bones—"

"What we mean," I say, "is that we snuck onto your computer yesterday."

"But it's password protected!"

"That doesn't stop *us*!" Frank crows. "Yesterday's password was two days before the day after the day before the day after tomorrow. In other words . . . SATURDAY!"

She blanches and nervously twists the bottom of her hijab. "You didn't," she whispers.

"We saw that you were selling things online for a lot of money."

"There's nothing wrong with that," she protests.

"There is if the items are stolen artifacts," Eliza says.

Nadira Nadeem laughs dryly. Then she opens up her computer, clicks on a few things, and the printer whirs to life. She lays the printed paper in front of us. "This is an itemized list of everything I have been selling."

Diamond-encrusted blue-sapphire engagement ring
Emerald and diamond V-bar necklace
Ruby tennis bracelet
Rose gold pearl-drop earrings

TO ASK NADIRA WHERE THE ITEMS CAME FROM,
TURN TO PAGE 94.

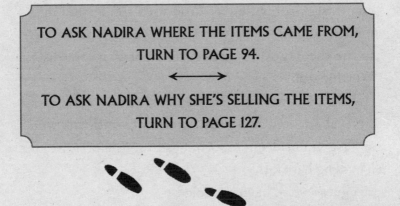

←→

TO ASK NADIRA WHY SHE'S SELLING THE ITEMS,
TURN TO PAGE 127.

"WE DIDN'T FIND anything in the ruins, Professor!"

He adjusts his glasses and squints at us. "Hmm." Then he stares at Eliza, who is turning red in the face. She is the world's *worst* liar, even when she doesn't have to say anything! "Is there something you would like to tell me, young lady?"

Eliza squeaks and shakes her head no.

"I believe you are lying to me."

"She's not," I say.

"Then why is she so red?"

"Oh, silly me!" Eliza says. "I forgot to put on sunscreen this morning. I must be flushed from a burn—I'm not used to all the sun in Greece!"

The professor sniffs. "I have been teaching for thirty-some years, and I know when a pupil is lying to me." He starts to storm off, but then he turns around to deliver one final, crushing blow. "You used me for my information, and now you won't share yours. You will live to rue the day you spurned Professor Phineas Alistair Worthington!"

I did, indeed, rue the day. I guess he made up a story about how we were interfering with his work, and Nadira Nadeem escorted us from the premises for harassing her staff.

I guess we've been schooled.

CASE CLOSED.

"MS. NADEEM, YOU said you thought some people on your team were acting suspiciously. Can you elaborate on that?"

"Absolutely," she says. "Let us start with the most pressing: Richard Leech. He has been skulking around the artifacts. It is so common an occurrence that my intern, Smarty—she picked you up at the airport, yes?—well, she had to chase Mr. Leech away from the work tent."

Eliza and I look at each other.

Suspicious? I say with my eyes.

She nods.

"Did he ever say why he was so interested in the artifact shelf?" Eliza asks.

"He *claims* he is just examining the objects as potential 'gets' for his museum. But I am not so sure. With artifacts disappearing . . . I simply do not trust him."

"Well, I do," Orlando Bones says firmly.

Nadira frowns like she wants to say something else about Richard Leech, but she swallows it down. The silence is awkward.

"Okay," I say, trying to break the tension. "Who else on your team is acting suspiciously?"

"I am also not sure I trust Zip, if I am being frank."

"Frank?" Frank perks up.

"Not you," I mumble.

"What has Zip done?" Mom asks.

295

"Well, it is not what Zip has or has not done. In fact, I am not sure if Zip has a motive, but they certainly have means and opportunity. They work all day in the same tent where artifacts are stored. How hard would it be for Zip to slip artifacts into their bag? Relatively easy, I would think."

Bones snorts. "I trust Zip! They're more reliable than pocket aces!"

Nadira throws her hands up, exasperated. Orlando just shoots down all of Nadira's suspect ideas, without throwing any of his own into the ring. So I have to ask, "Well, is there anyone you don't trust, Mr. Bones?"

"Smarty Marty."

"So, *my* only hire," Nadira says, frustration rising in her voice.

"I'm sorry," Bones says. "But she's constantly asking for a raise. She's looking to make a name for herself—and seeking glory. Bet your bottom dollar she'd steal the treasure in the catacombs."

Nadira clicks her tongue. "What are you talking about? There has been no theft in the catacombs!"

"Yes, but there probably will be!"

"That makes no sense," Nadira says. "And this has nothing to do with why we hired Las Pistas Detective Agency—for the missing artifacts."

"But the artifact thefts and the catacombs *connect*,

though, don't they?" he says passionately. "Whoever is taking the insignificant artifacts off our shelves will certainly go after the winning hand in the catacombs next!"

"Those artifacts that were stolen are hardly insignificant," Nadira says. "They're worth hundreds of thousands."

"But the treasure in the catacombs is worth millions!"

"Yes, but *there has been no theft in the catacombs*," Nadira says, frustrated to the breaking point.

"We found evidence that someone has been down there alone—without the rest of the team. If that doesn't make you worried about the safety of the world's most valuable object, Nadira, I don't know what will."

TO ASK ABOUT THE WORLD'S MOST VALUABLE OBJECT, TURN TO PAGE 172.

←——→

TO ASK ABOUT EVIDENCE THAT SOMEONE'S BEEN IN THE TUNNELS, TURN TO PAGE 396.

WE HAVE TO ask Bones about the missing artifacts. After all, if we're going to figure out who's taking them, we need details and clues. "Can you tell us about the missing artifacts?" I ask.

Bones blinks at me. "The what?"

"The artifacts that have gone missing out of the work tent."

"That's a great idea—let's start an itemized list," Eliza says, pen at the ready. "Which artifacts do you need us to find?"

"Oh!" Bones says. "Um . . . let's see. There were three vases from the archaic period that have gone missing. Very valuable. A bust from the classical period. Coins from the Hellenistic period. One classical-period hair ornament. We also found a gold armband near the mouth of the catacombs that was in the process of being cleaned and hadn't been categorized yet. Also missing now."

"Don't worry," I say confidently. "We'll recover all your missing artifacts."

"To lay my cards on the table," he says as he theatrically spreads a deck of playing cards on his desk in a quick and practiced motion, "I'm less worried about these past thefts, and much more worried about the *future* theft."

"What's a future theft?" Eliza asks. Somehow,

thankfully, she doesn't roll her eyes. But I can tell she thinks it's extraordinarily silly to pre-investigate a crime that hasn't happened yet.

Even Mom has her eyebrows raised. She looks just as skeptical.

"I know how it sounds," Orlando Bones says, leaning forward and whispering, "but you have no idea how enticing . . ." He pauses, considering his words carefully. Then he finally says, "The item in the catacombs is *priceless.*"

TO ASK ABOUT THE TREASURE
IN THE CATACOMBS, TURN TO PAGE 27.

"WHAT'S Q-W-E-R-T-Y?" I ask Eliza as I type it into Zip's computer.

"It's the name for a keyboard design," she whispers back. "You ever notice how keys on a standard computer aren't arranged alphabetically? That's a qwerty design."

I press enter, and—we're in!

Up pops a whole bunch of maps and a red flashing exclamation point.

"Click that!" Frank says.

"Shhhhhhh!" Eliza and I hiss.

Smarty stiffens in her chair. She starts to turn. We immediately duck down behind Zip's desk. We stay frozen for a tense minute.

"Think it's safe?" Eliza mouths.

I peek over the desk, very slowly. Smarty is back to work. Man, that was a close call!

I grab the computer mouse and click the flashing exclamation point. A window pops up.

Map error!

So the computer program tells Zip when there's an error? Then how did Zip mess up so many times? Or . . . the better question: *Why* did Zip mess up so many times? Because Zip's mistakes were clearly not an accident.

300

Is it connected to stealing the artifacts?

Suddenly I gasp.

"What?" Eliza says.

"If Zip gives the special task force bad maps and keeps the good ones, then Zip is the only one with access to the proper maps. Zip can explore down there all alone, and no one else can go."

"It's a ruse," Eliza says. "But why—"

"Enjoying yourselves?" says a cool voice behind us. We all whip around, and Zip is standing behind us. I thought they'd be mad, but no—they're mildly irritated, at best. Confused, mostly.

"What are these?" I say, picking the maps off the table and shaking them at Zip.

"Maps."

"You got them wrong on purpose!" I say loudly.

Zip's eyes dart over to Smarty, who takes off her headphones and turns around. "Excuse me," she says. "I'm working *extremely hard* over here. And I can't do promotion-worthy work with all this racket."

"Sorry, Smarty," Zip says softly. "Do you mind if we have the tent for a second?"

Her eyes narrow. She stands up and smooths out her pencil skirt. "Why? Is there something I need to hear? As your supervisor, I demand you tell me!"

"You're not my supervisor."

"Well, I should be."

"Never mind," I say. "We'll just go. Come on, Zip."

"I'm going to follow!" Smarty says stubbornly.

We have to get Smarty away from us. I bet if we pushed her work off her desk, she'd stay to clean things up while we made a break for it . . . but maybe it's too cruel to mess with something she worked so hard on. We could try to trick her out of the tent somehow, maybe by baiting her with the thing she wants most in the world.

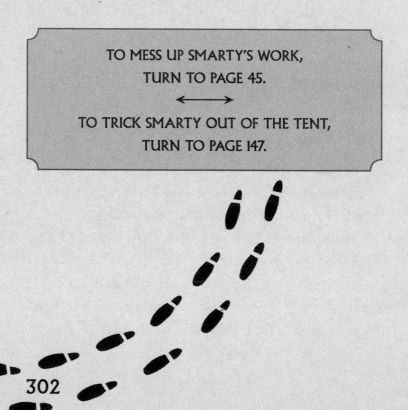

TO MESS UP SMARTY'S WORK,
TURN TO PAGE 45.

←——→

TO TRICK SMARTY OUT OF THE TENT,
TURN TO PAGE 147.

"YOU DON'T WANT to find the necklace?" I say to Professor Phineas Alistair Worthington. "But I don't get it . . . you seemed really excited about the possibility of studying it, when you were fighting with Richard Leech earlier."

"Do not mistake me," the professor says. "I would love to find and study the necklace. But I fear that the relic will end up in the hands of people—like Mr. Leech—who might want to wear it. And *that*, I would advise against."

"You don't truly believe that it's cursed, do you?" Eliza asks. "It's just a necklace."

"I do indeed believe it's cursed. How could I not with its . . . history?"

"You mean what happened to Harmonia?" Mom asks. "Or others after her?"

"Both. All of the above."

I guess it's time to ask who Harmonia is. Her connection to the necklace seems crucial.

TO ASK ABOUT HARMONIA, TURN TO PAGE 90.

THERE'S NO DOUBT about it. The loop finger-print belongs to . . .

"Orlando Bones," I say, looking up at him. My head is spinning. How are his fingerprints on the artifacts? How is he the artifact thief? This has to be a mistake. It makes no sense—he's the one who hired us. He hired us to find himself?

He laughs boisterously. "You've got to be joking. That must be an old fingerprint—from before the artifacts got stolen."

"No," Smarty says, looking at him in disgust. "No. We wear gloves when we catalog artifacts. There's no way a fingerprint would be on it unless . . ."

"*You're* the artifact thief!" I accuse. "And you kidnapped my mom!"

There's an outcry from his teammates.

"Really, Mr. Bones?" Nadira says. "I thought we were a team! What am I running ragged for every day?"

"You stole the relics?" Richard Leech says incredulously to his old work buddy. *"You?"*

Orlando Bones's mouth slides into a scowl.

"Where is the necklace?" he says sharply.

"Now see here, Bones!" Professor Phineas Alistair Worthington says in his pompous British accent. "You can't think that we'll possibly let you take that most precious artifact for . . . for what, personal gain?"

"To save my skin!" Orlando Bones says. "Have you ever met a loan shark?"

"I've never met *any* shark," Frank says. "Period! But if I did ever meet a shark, I would want it to be a hammerhead. Those are funny. Or a saw shark. Why are all sharks named after tools?"

"What's a loan shark?" I ask Eliza.

"It's someone who offers loans at extremely high interest rates . . . and if you can't pay up, they often resort to violence."

"You're in trouble with a loan shark?" And then it suddenly hits me. "*That's* who you were really talking to on the phone—your loan shark! You're a big gambler. You used a loan shark to pay off your gambling debts, and now you need the necklace money to pay off your loan shark debts. . . ."

"Where is the necklace?" he says again.

"It's definitely NOT in Carlos's backpack!" Frank says cheerfully.

"Well, gotta go for broke!" Bones snatches my backpack and sprints through the ruins. All six of our former suspects start running after him.

Eliza, Frank, and I sprint past the rest of the adults. Bones is fast, but we're faster. We need to stop him somehow!

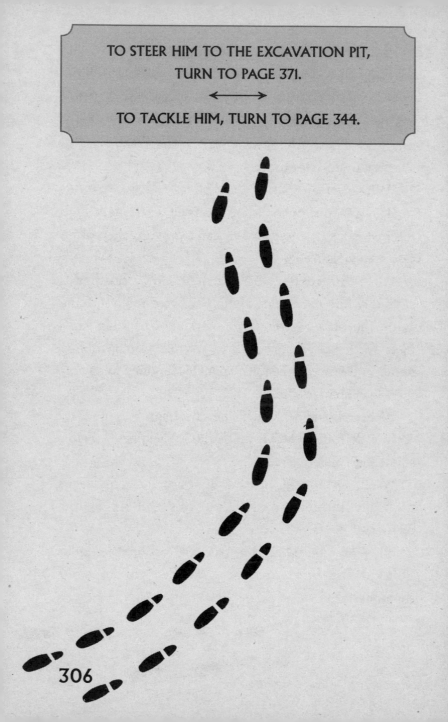

TO STEER HIM TO THE EXCAVATION PIT,
TURN TO PAGE 371.

TO TACKLE HIM, TURN TO PAGE 344.

306

I AM THOROUGHLY stumped by Orlando Bones's playing cards password. But I don't want to ask Eliza. Not when she's being like this.

Eliza laughs dryly. "Going to ask me for puzzle help?"

"No," I say, too quickly.

"Liar." She leans a little closer. Then she glances back at Orlando Bones's password hint and gives me the smuggest look. "You're not using enough of Bones's hints, Carlos."

> The blackjack hand closest to your heart, four cards, low to high, no faces, no aces, we're off to the races.

I don't say anything. I feel my face getting hot. I get the point—Eliza's the smartest detective in the world, and I'm nothing in comparison. Mom pretty much already made that clear earlier, when she was fawning over Eliza.

"The first clue is: the blackjack hand closest to your heart."

"I know, I know," I say irritably. "That tells us we're playing blackjack."

"*And* it's a super-sneaky way to tell you to use heart cards."

I look at it again . . . I see what she's saying. "No clubs at all?"

"Correct. None of the clovers. Next, you need four

cards, so even if you can make twenty-one work with fewer, that's a no go. You have to arrange the cards from the lowest number to the highest."

"And 'no faces' means we're not using the cards with people on them."

Eliza sighs. "Yes. That's what that means. And no aces either."

"Don't tell me! I've got it!" I say.

When we eliminate all the cards I can't use, I have the two, five, six, seven, eight, and ten of hearts to choose from. Now all I have to do is figure out which four of those cards add up to be twenty-one, and arrange them from low to high.

You're not the only smart one, Eliza.

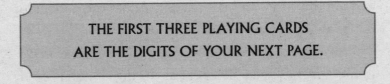

THE FIRST THREE PLAYING CARDS
ARE THE DIGITS OF YOUR NEXT PAGE.

"FLOOR IT, MOM! We have to lose this car behind us!"

She slams her foot on the gas, and our car speeds up. The acceleration wakes Frank, who puts his hands in the air like he's on a roller coaster. Eliza holds on to the grab handle for dear life.

The silver car behind us speeds up too. We weave in and out of traffic, and the silver car does the same. No doubt about it: they're following us!

I turn to get a closer look, but I still can't see who's in the car. Did I see a silver car at the dig? I wish I could remember.

A car honks at us, and I face front again. We're going way too fast—I can barely breathe. But as long as this silver car is stalking us, we have no choice but to fly.

Shoot! Up ahead—a pothole in the road.

"MOM, LOOK OUT!"

She's going too fast to stop, and there's a car beside us—she can't swerve. She runs right into the pothole.

BOOM!

The car jerks and veers to the right. Mom grips the wheel tightly and grits her teeth. "Hold on, kids!" she says as she steps lightly on the gas. The car rights itself. Then slows. Then we stop on the side of the road and check the damage.

We don't just have a flat tire—we have a *completely*

exploded tire. Bits of it are littered all over the road. The silver car drives past us. And keeps going.

There's nothing around for miles. We can't even get a cell signal out here. We must be in the middle of nowhere. There's nothing we can do except walk along the side of the road for miles and miles and miles. . . .

Who knew one lousy tire could make us so *tired*?

CASE CLOSED.

WE HAVE TO investigate Richard Leech's tent, especially if he refuses to talk to us. This could be the only way to get information out of him.

"Let's go to Leech's tent," I say.

"DO WE FINALLY GET TO SNEAK?" Frank shouts so loudly that a random archaeologist on his way back from the bathroom yelps and starts running in fright. Mom snickers.

"Well, it's not sneaky if you yell like that," I say.

"I'm just SO EXCITED. It's about time we sneaked! Snuck? Snook!"

Quietly, we slip inside the tent that Richard Leech shares with Professor Phineas Alistair Worthington. It's easy to tell whose side of the tent is whose. There's a whole library of books that belong to the professor, and Leech's side is full of clay busts, tiny models, and pottery.

"These aren't the stolen artifacts, are they?" I ask.

Eliza shakes her head as she flips one of the busts over. "They seem to be collectibles. Just ornamental figurines to decorate his space."

"Frank?" I say. "You have to be *very careful*. Don't break anything."

"Break everything," Frank says.

"No! Break nothing."

"Break something."

"Frank, are you *really* not hearing me? Or are you purposely not hearing me?"

312

He grins.

Mom steps in. "Frank, if you break anything, then we won't go on our morning walk tomorrow. Instead I'll make you sit in the tent and read a book."

"Noooooooooooooooo!" Frank wails. "NOT READ-ING! Anything but that!"

"It's really not *that* horrible," I mumble.

"It's not horrible at all!" Eliza replies. "It's delightful!"

But it seems to work on Frank, who is shockingly careful as he goes through Leech's suitcase. Mom sifts with him while Eliza and I check under his mattress. It's really difficult to ransack someone's place without actually ransacking it. Everything has to go back in its proper place. Leech can't know we were here.

"Catalina Serrano, Catalina Serrano, please report to Orlando Bones!" blares a loudspeaker. Mom sighs. "I wonder what he wants from me now. Will you be okay without me for a little while? I don't know how long this is going to take."

"All good, Mom," I say.

She leaves, and I sift through Leech's statues. Nothing, nothing, nothing.

Wait a second.

I pick up a figurine that is significantly lighter than the others. I flip it over and realize why—it's hollow. It's got a rubber bottom, like a piggy bank, which I peel off. Inside is one thing: a cell phone. But . . . I'm certain

313

that I saw Leech earlier with a phone. So what's he doing with a *second* phone?

I show Eliza and Frank. "Two phones . . . that's pretty shady, right?"

"One phone, two phone, three phones, four," Frank sings softly. "Five phones, six phones, seven phones, more!"

"Yes," Eliza says. "A second phone is suspicious."

There's something weird about this phone . . . it's not password protected and it barely has any apps. Just texts, calls, and notes. I immediately open the text messages, and . . . nothing. It's been wiped clean.

Eliza points to the bottom left corner. "It looks like Mr. Leech has a new voicemail since he last looked at this phone. Should we check it out?"

"Sure," I say. "Or we can check out his notes. It's not like there's that much to explore on this phone anyway."

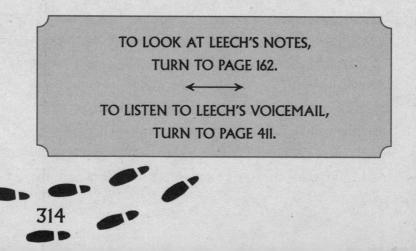

TO LOOK AT LEECH'S NOTES,
TURN TO PAGE 162.

←——→

TO LISTEN TO LEECH'S VOICEMAIL,
TURN TO PAGE 411.

THE CLUE ON the disk says, "It's written in the stars above. Under the earth the riches lie." I feel so confident that we need to look up to go down.

"Everyone, shine your light on the ceiling!"

We walk slowly down the path. There seems to be nothing above but spiders and spiderwebs. And a web that looks particularly solid. . . .

"LOOK OUT!" I shout as a net comes flying down from above. It misses us, just barely.

"Good thing you were looking up," Eliza says, holding her heart and panting.

We brush ourselves off and continue heading forward. Eventually the path veers off leftward and downward, and if you weren't paying attention, it would look like one road, just going to one place. But for a good ten feet, the wall on the right side sits a little farther back before curving and following the trajectory of the left wall. In this pocket of space, there's a circle on the floor, made of tile instead of dirt.

I move closer. My light moves around the ceiling, but there are too many cobwebs.

I reach up. The ceiling is low, but I'm still not tall enough. I need Frank.

"Climb on my back and brush the spiderwebs away," I tell him.

"Okay!" he says without hesitation.

Eliza stands back, for fear of raining spiders. And that's

a good call, because one definitely drops into my hair.

"Ooooh!" Frank says. "Buttons!"

"Don't press anything!" I say, sliding him off my back before he can do any real damage.

They aren't buttons above—there are tiles. It seems pretty clear that I can press them. Each one has a different Greek letter on it—the same Greek letters that are on our puzzle disk.

I think I know what to do with the disk! "We have to figure out all the letters the snakes are pointing to, put them in order, and press the tiles."

"Well, let's not waste any time," Eliza says, shining her flashlight on the disk.

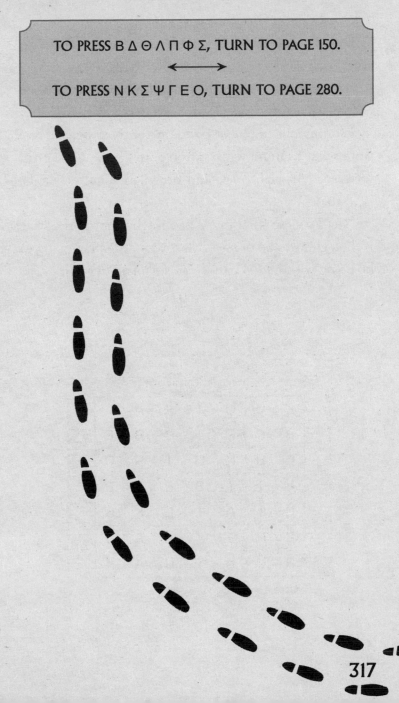

TO PRESS B Δ Θ Λ Π Φ Σ, TURN TO PAGE 150.

←——————→

TO PRESS N K Σ Ψ Γ E O, TURN TO PAGE 280.

317

"I DON'T UNDERSTAND how to turn off the electricity!"

"Here," Eliza says, and she starts to find a pathway. "We just have to find C-I-R-C-U-I-T-B-R-E-A-K-E-R in a continuous line! I've fixed one of these before, and from what I can remember, the path can be backward, forward, left, right, up, and down. But *no* diagonals. And then—"

"No, I can do it!" I say, elbowing her out of the way. If she's going to be bossy with my job, then I'm going to be bossy with hers. I can do this *without* her help!

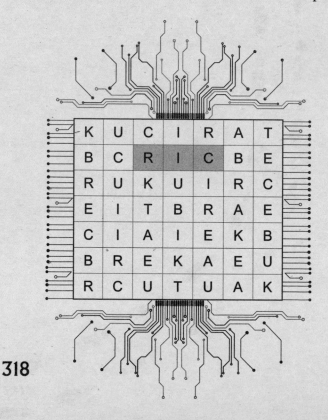

THE PATHWAY FORMS A NUMBER.
ADD ONE HUNDRED TO THE NUMBER
AND TURN TO THAT PAGE.

319

BONES IS STANDING between us and the exit, but we can get past him. We have to run between his legs.

"Go, Frank!" I shout.

"CHAAAAAARRRRGGGE!" he bellows as he runs forward. He slides between Bones's legs—he's going to make it!

Bones squeezes his legs tight and traps Frank.

"Thanks," Bones says. He snatches the necklace from around Frank's neck, while Frank is squirming between Bones's shins. "You hand delivered just what I needed. Now I'm leaving. And to keep you from following suit . . ."

He escapes through the door and seals it shut behind him. We're stuck here . . . just us and the river. And we're in deep water.

CASE CLOSED.

WE'VE SOLVED NADIRA Nadeem's calendar riddle, and we're in! Her computer opens to a website where people can sell things to others online. This must have been what she was doing before she went to go meet Professor Worthington.

I scroll through Nadira's profile, and my jaw drops. Nadira Nadeem is flush with cash. She has *tens of thousands* of euros in her account, ready to be transferred to a bank.

"What is she selling," I say, "that could be worth that much?"

"Priceless artifacts?" Eliza takes over the mouse. "Do you see any indication that she's selling things from the dig? Because if so . . ."

She clicks on the transaction history just as the tent flap opens.

We quickly X out of the window. Smarty Marty comes barging in.

"What are you doing?" Smarty says. Her eyes narrow.

"Nothing," I say quickly.

"Were you spying on my boss?"

"No, we—"

"You're not supposed to be in this tent. This is off-limits to everyone!"

"Then what are you doing here?" Eliza asks.

Smarty scowls. "Mr. Bones would be *livid* if he knew you were in here. Don't make me call him."

"You wouldn't—"

"MR. BONES!" Smarty shouts. "OH, MR. BONES!"

"Run!" I yell.

"Hide!" Eliza cries.

"Can't you agree on *anything* anymore?" Frank groans.

TO RUN, TURN TO PAGE 214.

←→

TO HIDE, TURN TO PAGE 398.

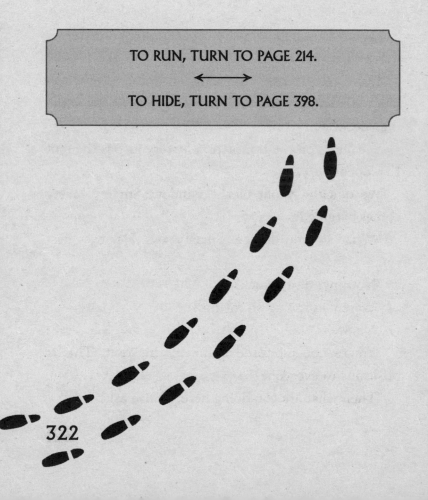

"ZIP, CAN WE have the real maps?"

Zip looks at us suspiciously. "Why? You're just going to help the task force find the treasure."

"No, we are trying to protect the treasure, just like you," I say. "We want to catch the person who's going to take it."

"So then catch them without my maps. You don't need to find the Necklace of Harmonia to do that."

"But—"

"I'm sorry, Carlos," Zip says, sounding kind but firm. "My answer is no."

Ugh! I'm just about to argue some more—when the loudspeaker screeches, and a crackly voice rings out.

"Attention! Attention! Las Pistas Detective Agency, please report to Orlando Bones in his tent immediately. This is urgent."

What could possibly be so urgent that they needed to call us on the loudspeaker?

Eliza's face is ghostly white. "Do you think . . ."

"What?"

She puts a hand on my shoulder and squeezes. Her gray eyes look fearful. "Do you think this is an emergency?"

REPORT TO BONES ON PAGE 229.

I HATE DISAGREEING with Eliza, but we have to go into the catacombs—I just know it.

"Please, Eliza. Trust me on this. The catacombs are where we have to go."

She scowls, then nods.

As she follows me to the excavation area, though, I get the sense that she's feeling glum. Usually, at this point in a case, she's nearly giddy with excitement, but her frown is prominent, and she shuffles slowly to the tunnel entrance.

I don't understand what's the matter. It's *always* been this way on cases—I make gut decisions about clues and leads, and she supports me. Then she makes headway on puzzles and riddles, and I support her. We each have our roles to play on the team, and it's worked like clockwork . . . until that mock case Mom made for us last month.

We twist through the excavation site and lower ourselves into the pit. We pass a cluster of archaeologists with their hats and trowels, digging in the sun. When we arrive at the covered area, it's clear the archaeologists have abandoned this side. I guess no one else on Keira Skelberry's team wants to end up in the hospital.

The mild breeze that we felt outside does not reach the tented area. In fact, I feel sticky and sweaty. Eliza rolls up her sleeves, and Frank fans himself with the used plane ticket in his back pocket.

"Look," Mom says, and that's when I see the entrance in the curve of the wall. It's smaller than I imagined it would be. It's slightly taller than Mom, and she's a fairly short adult. I imagine that tall and reedy Professor Phineas Alistair Worthington would have an especially hard time fitting inside, and I'm sure even Orlando Bones has to hunch to get in here.

The archway is full of painted, intertwined snakes. At the top of the arch there's a snake around a woman's neck, and it's eating its own tail.

"Cool!" Frank says, pointing. Then he starts trying to pull his foot off the ground and toward his mouth.

"Frank, don't do that," Mom says. "Your feet are full of dirt."

"Dirt won't hurt!"

"Ouroboros," Eliza whispers. "The serpent eating its own tail—it's called an ouroboros. It symbolizes eternity. It's an alchemical symbol."

"A what?" I ask.

"Alchemy. It's like an early precursor to chemistry, but with elements of philosophy and witchcraft thrown in. It's the art and practice of transforming matter. And the ouroboros is a way to show the idea that everything in the universe is infinite. The end is the beginning, and the beginning is the end again."

Goose bumps appear on my arm. Something about this doorway, this ouroboros, and the hot, sticky silence of this pit gives me the shivers.

"Well," Eliza says, "you wanted to go in, Carlos. Shall we proceed?"

Now that I'm here, I'm not sure I want to go in . . . but after I made Eliza go with my plan, I can't stop now.

It's dark inside, and the air becomes cool and dry. It smells like something old and musty. I pull my phone out and use the flashlight. The walls are bare tiles—I wonder if this thing is going to collapse. Every time I shine a spot on the wall, I think I see a shadow on the other side, and so I keep switching from left to right as we follow the pathway farther.

"Carlos, this is making me dizzy," Mom says.

"Sorry, I—wait! Quiet!"

The path slopes downward ahead, and there's a light. A lantern. *Someone* is in here right now, without the rest of the group. Is this it—are we about to catch our thief in action? And set the record for the quickest case ever solved?

Should we call out to them? It's definitely safer to keep our distance. Or should we ambush them from behind? If we surprise them up close, we can see what they're doing.

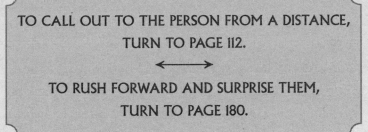

TO CALL OUT TO THE PERSON FROM A DISTANCE,
TURN TO PAGE 112.

←——————→

TO RUSH FORWARD AND SURPRISE THEM,
TURN TO PAGE 180.

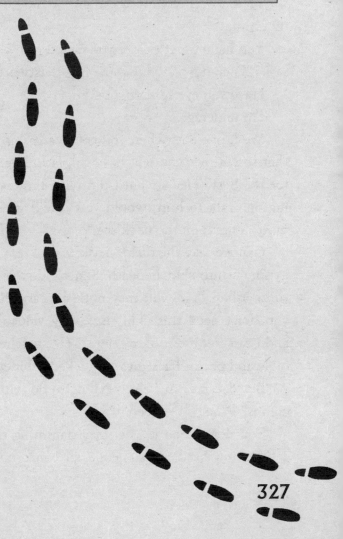

327

"CAN YOU TELL us more about the Necklace of Harmonia?" I ask Bones.

"I cannot," he says cheerfully. "I believe that's something you ought to ask Professor Phineas Alistair Worthington. He's the expert on the matter, and that's the reason I called him to the dig, without ever having met him."

"You hadn't met before you called him here?" Eliza says. "Then how do you know he's trustworthy?"

"Have you ever placed a bet?"

"I'm underage."

"Well, one day, when you get to a casino, you'll see that sometimes you just have to place a bet and hope for the best. That's what I did with Professor Worthington. Talk to him, would you? He'll give you a lot more context on the necklace."

"Can we take the disk?" I ask.

The white skin beneath Bones's dirt-covered face turns ashen. "No, you may not!" he says. "I—I mean, you don't need this. This is a very valuable artifact, and I can't let it out of my sight!" He snatches it off the table and puts it back into his locked cabinet.

"But doesn't it have something to do with the catacombs? What if we need it?"

"You don't need it," he says, slamming the cabinet a little too hard for someone so concerned about a

328

delicate artifact inside. "If you go into the tunnels, you just . . . go into the tunnels!" He waves us off. This is a definite dismissal.

We leave the tent.

"I think we should go talk to Professor Worthington," Eliza says the moment we step outside.

"Well, I think we should check out the tunnels, just like our client told us to do," I say.

"Fight! Fight! Fight!" Frank shouts.

Mom looks between us warily. "You both have good instincts, and the professor and the tunnels are equally pressing," she says diplomatically.

I can tell Mom doesn't want to intervene—she wants us to work it out. Eliza folds her arms. There's no way we're going to agree.

"How about Frank chooses for once?" Mom says.

I pull a candy bar out of my pocket. "Frank, if you choose me, this is yours."

Just as he starts walking over to me, Eliza quickly says, "Frank, if you choose me, I'll let you read my diary."

"I'm listening," he says.

"And you can have the good seat on the couch next movie night."

"And?"

"You can choose the movie on my next turn."

"ELIZA! ELIZA!" he shouts, hugging his sister. Eliza looks obnoxiously proud of herself.

TO TALK TO PROFESSOR PHINEAS ALISTAIR WORTHINGTON, TURN TO PAGE 386.

ELIZA REALLY WANTS to confront Smarty . . . *fine*.

We find Smarty in the work tent at her desk, typing quicker than I've ever seen anyone type.

"Um, excuse me?" Eliza says.

Smarty looks at us, then looks down again at whatever she's typing. She's choosing to ignore us.

Eliza continues, in a louder voice this time. "We saw the email you sent to Orlando Bones."

Smarty stops typing. She juts her jaw forward. It's a gesture of stubbornness. She's about to dig her heels in so deep they might as well be trowels. "So what? It's not a crime to think my boss is incompetent."

"*Is* she incompetent?" I ask.

"I thought you said you read the letter."

"We did. We're just trying to determine if the letter is *true*."

Smarty smirks. "What is *truth*, anyway?" She peers at us over her glasses, which—I've just noticed—don't even have prescription lenses in them. They're just ordinary glass.

"Well, your glasses sure aren't," I say. "Do you even need them?"

Smarty smiles. "Well, well, well. Looks like I've underestimated you." She takes off her glasses. "I have perfect twenty-twenty vision. Glasses make me look

331

smarter. And when you look smarter, people take you more seriously. And people *will* take me seriously."

"So you're willing to lie if it's beneficial to you?" Eliza says. "Would you lie for a promotion?"

Smarty says nothing, but her eyebrows rise and lower quickly. The involuntary gesture speaks for itself. She would lie for just about any reason.

"The email you wrote Bones is a lie," I say.

"Or at least, seriously embellished," Eliza adds. "You want Nadira Nadeem to be fired so you can have her job."

"*Obviously.*" Smarty rolls her eyes. "I basically told you I had high ambitions from the first minute I met you. I know you're trying to make me feel guilty, but I have no remorse whatsoever. You don't get to accomplish your life goals before the age of thirty without cutting a few people down along the way. This is a dog-eat-dog world."

"Dogs eat dogs?" Frank gasps, turning to his sister with wide eyes.

"It's just an expression," Eliza says. "It means that Smarty will do whatever it takes to have her way, even if it means hurting other people."

"That's rude!" Frank says. "You shouldn't eat dogs."

"No one's eating dogs!" I say.

If Smarty is willing to lie and cheat her way to her

goals, would she steal too? She has so much motive, but did she have means or opportunity?

I want to ask her outright if she stole the artifacts, but I also want to know more about her relationship with the Necklace of Harmonia. After all, finding the long-lost necklace would be just as fruitful for her career as finding the missing artifacts. . . .

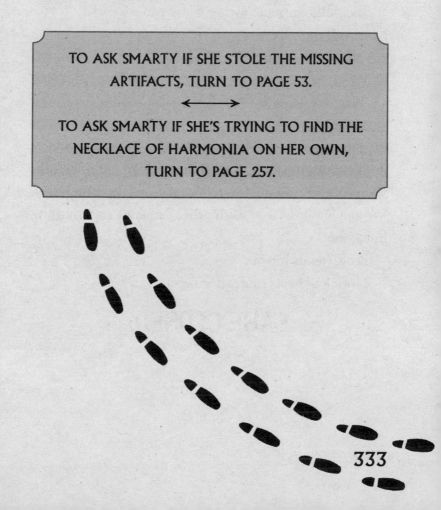

TO ASK SMARTY IF SHE STOLE THE MISSING ARTIFACTS, TURN TO PAGE 53.

←——→

TO ASK SMARTY IF SHE'S TRYING TO FIND THE NECKLACE OF HARMONIA ON HER OWN, TURN TO PAGE 257.

HOW CAN I possibly tell Eliza all my bottled-up feelings? I just have to shove them down and make sure they never come back up again.

"I'm fine, Eliza."

She squeezes my hand. "No, you're not. I know you're not."

"I said I'm *fine*."

She pulls her hand away. "How can we fix this if you won't tell me what's wrong?"

"Nothing's wrong! I'm FINE."

"Well, fine!"

"Fine!"

"Fine!"

"Fine!'

We shout it back and forth until we're out of breath. Turns out, this fined down our relationship completely. We can barely look at each other, let alone say anything but "Fine!"

Best friends forever?

More like best friends for *never*.

CASE CLOSED.

I HATE TO disappoint Eliza, but I *know* I'm on to something with the disk puzzle, and that means we have to go into the tunnels. But it doesn't make disappointing Eliza any easier.

"I'm sorry," I say to Eliza. "But I really think—"

"Fine," she snaps. "Whatever."

I turn to Mom, and she sighs heavily. Does that mean she thinks I chose wrong?

"Eliza," Mom says, putting a gentle hand on her shoulder, "we can split up and do both. You and Carlos can look at the tunnels while Frank and I go investigate the ruins of the fire. We can meet back up and share clues. Does that sound okay?"

Eliza thinks for a moment. Then she nods.

"Wait, wait, wait!" Frank says. "I WANT ELIZA AND CARLOS." He grabs me around the waist and squeezes.

"Maybe we should let them, er . . . have some space?" Mom says. "Come with me, Frank."

He hugs me tighter. "No!"

"Why doesn't Frank stay with Carlos, and I go with you?" Eliza says, perking up.

"No!" Mom says. As Mom looks between Eliza and me, I suddenly realize what she's doing—she's trying to get us alone so we can talk things out and make up. That is some master-level manipulation right there.

"It's fine," I say. "Mom, you go. The three of us will investigate here."

Mom hesitates. "Okay. But I don't want to worry about your safety. Remember, Keira Skelberry ended up in the hospital from these booby traps! Promise me you won't go deep into the tunnels until I get back. You can go in only as far as the natural light reaches. The moment you need a flashlight to see, get out."

I sigh. If that's what it takes to go check out the tunnels, then fine. "I promise, Mom."

She ruffles my hair. "Thank you, kiddo." And she takes off for the parking lot.

We start walking toward the tunnels.

There's a tarp—or tented roof—over one side of the pit. No one is in the pit right now—not on the light side or the dark side. It's a ghost town. All except for the fifteen trowels left in the dirt, gleaming in the sunlight. I wonder if the main dig had to go on pause, now that their lead archaeologist is in the hospital.

Then again, it seems like the treasure-hunting special task force isn't pausing for any reason. Orlando Bones is full steam ahead.

"Look!" Frank says excitedly.

The archway that leads to the catacombs is impossible to miss. It's a relatively small arch—about two feet taller than me—but it's got a million serpents engraved on it, just like the disk in Bones's office. At the top of the archway is a very faded painting of a girl. Around her neck are two serpents whose mouths form a clasp. Their tails entwine around a few gemstones. I can see now why everyone is so convinced that the necklace is down there.

"Shall we?" I say.

Frank links arms with me and practically yanks me inside. He's even more excited than I am.

The catacombs are just as dark as Professor Worthington warned us they would be. We click on our flashlights for extra light, even though we're just inside the mouth of the tomb. I don't see anything here, though.

"Should we go deeper in?"

"I don't know, Carlos. We promised your mom we'd only stay where the natural light shines until she can go with us," says Eliza.

This is so frustrating. We wouldn't even have had to separate from Mom if Eliza hadn't been so stubborn about her own idea. And then I would have been able to thoroughly investigate these tunnels. It's like we compromised, and neither of us is getting what we want.

I sigh and shine my flashlight deeper in, hoping to get a glimpse of something helpful from our spot.

Wait a second . . .

Up ahead, a large woman in a white lab coat kneels on the ground. She scoops up some dirt and puts it into a jar.

"Hey!" I shout. "What are you doing? No one's supposed to be in here!"

She turns around.

It's Dr. Amanda Mandible.

"Eh . . . what's up, Doc?" Frank calls.

She yelps. Then, faster than a blink, she scoops up the jar in her hands and bolts. Amanda Mandible runs into the tunnels, farther away from the exit.

Frank starts to run after her, but I grab his shirt and pull him back. Because as much as I want to go explore the catacombs, Eliza's right—we *did* promise Mom we wouldn't. And after some of the previous trust issues Mom and I had on earlier cases, keeping my word—and her trust—is the most important thing right now.

So we go wait for Dr. Mandible at her medical tent. But after twenty minutes of waiting, I'm starting to wonder if she's even coming.

"Bored, bored, I am so bored," Frank groans, lying upside down on a chair.

"Me too," I say. Then I grin. "Maybe we should look around."

"Isn't that risky, Carlos? What if she returns?"

"Don't be a party pooper, Eliza!"

"But . . ."

"Let's check her computer, drawers, cabinets—*don't!*" I shout at Frank, who's about to yank all the tongue depressors out of a jar. "We have to be careful. She can never know we poked around."

We go to the cabinets, then check the drawers. The very bottom one looks like it's the perfect size for holding files, but the drawer is locked with a two-digit padlock. Rats!

"What exactly are you looking for?" Eliza asks. "If Dr. Mandible stole the artifacts, it's not like she would have hidden them here!"

"You never know," I say. "And besides, maybe there's some clue that will help us. Something incriminating."

We move to her papers, and at last I find what I'm searching for. One of her papers has REMEMBER PASSCODE scribbled on the top. And there's a whole crossword-looking thing underneath.

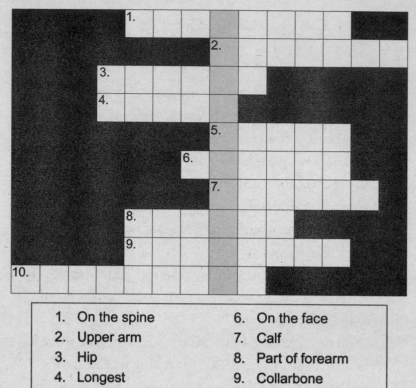

1. On the spine
2. Upper arm
3. Hip
4. Longest
5. Part of shin
6. On the face
7. Calf
8. Part of forearm
9. Collarbone
10. Fingers and toes

"How are we supposed to solve this?" I ask Eliza.

Eliza folds her arms.

"Come on," I beg. "Please help?"

She points to the wall, where Dr. Mandible has a bunch of posters hanging: the digestive tract, the muscular system, and—

"Oh! The skeletal system!" I say. "You think we're looking for bones and stuff?"

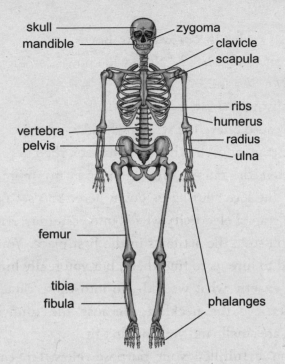

skull — zygoma
mandible — clavicle
scapula
ribs
humerus
vertebra — radius
pelvis — ulna
femur
tibia
fibula — phalanges

Eliza ignores me. She pulls a book out of her bag and kicks back in Dr. Mandible's chair. This isn't like her—she doesn't seem to care about solving this puzzle at all, and I've never met a puzzle Eliza doesn't love.

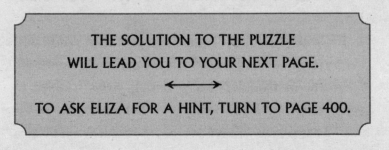

THE SOLUTION TO THE PUZZLE
WILL LEAD YOU TO YOUR NEXT PAGE.

←→

TO ASK ELIZA FOR A HINT, TURN TO PAGE 400.

"GET OUT OF our way, Mr. Bones," I say.

He shakes his head. "Now, you know I can't fold like that, Mr. Serrano."

"Why not?" I say.

"Because I have the winning hand."

We stare at each other. My stomach flips.

"*You're* the culprit. You kidnapped my mom. You wrote the letter luring us down here. You set up the booby trap of electricity we fell into yesterday. And . . . and you stole the artifacts in the first place. You pretended to hire us to find them, but you really hired us to do exactly what we did—go into these catacombs and retrieve the necklace. Because the tunnels up ahead are small, and you couldn't fit."

"You've fulfilled your purpose. Now I'm cashing in my chips." He snaps his fingers at the necklace. "Gimme."

"What are you going to do with it?" Eliza asks. "Wear it?"

"It's cursed!" Frank chimes in. "You should know that."

"I'm going to sell it. To the highest bidder. And I will take that money and pay off all my gambling debts."

"You're in trouble," I say, noticing the trickles of sweat sliding out from beneath his fedora and down his face. "That phone call we overheard—that wasn't Keira

342

Skelberry's boss wanting to shut down the dig, was it? Someone was threatening you because you owe them money."

"Neither a borrower nor a lender be."

"Shakespeare said that," Eliza says. "And you must have borrowed money. Now that it's time to pay up, you don't have it?"

"Well," he says, eyeing the necklace hungrily. "I do now."

My heart hammers. We have seconds to act.

TO THROW THE NECKLACE INTO THE WATER,
TURN TO PAGE 78.

←——→

TO RUN BETWEEN HIS LEGS,
TURN TO PAGE 320.

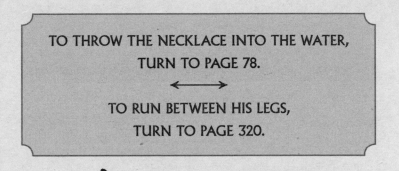

343

IF WE TACKLE him, we can stop him.

"TACKLE!" I shout.

Eliza, Frank, and I all dive at Bones, but Frank is the only one who makes contact. He hops right onto Orlando's back, piggyback style, and Bones doesn't even skip a beat. He keeps running.

"Byeeeeeeeeeee!" Frank calls to us as Bones makes a clean getaway.

CASE CLOSED.

WE HAVE TO hide in the maze. I grab Eliza's and Frank's hands and pull them down the wrong path. Eliza resists, but I squeeze her palm. *Trust me.*

"Hello?" Bones shouts, shining his flashlight down our pathway. We stand against the wall, completely silent, even as Frank starts clawing at my closed hand for the tooth I definitely don't have.

We stay tight against the wall until Bones's voice and footsteps get farther and farther away. At last it's safe to whisper.

"What did you do, Carlos?" Eliza says. "Now he's going to escape with the necklace and the robe—and probably find some way to trap us down here."

"Where's my tooth?" Frank asks.

"You'll get it up above," I say. Then I address Eliza. "And no. You're usually right, but this time, I think you're wrong."

Eliza guides us back to the main path and through the maze. When we reach the bottom of the stairs, Eliza goes to get the garlic bread out of Frank's bag.

"Don't," I say. We start climbing the stairs, and I explain. "Remember when Bones surprised us after we found the robe? He said he didn't know what we did to the snakes, but they stayed away from him."

"Yes?" Eliza says as we reach the top step.

"Enough time has passed that the garlic smell should

have worn off. So I thought I'd let Mr. Bones take the lead on this one."

I shine my flashlight into the snake room, where Orlando Bones is on the ground, a hundred snakes wrapped around his writhing body. They're like ropes that have tied themselves around him. He looks at us with wide eyes. "Help! Me!" he begs.

"Carlos!" Eliza says proudly. "You had an ace up your sleeve!"

"Okay, okay, but where's my tooth?!"

We take out slices of the garlic bread and rub them on our ankles. We walk around the perimeter of the room, making sure to stay far away from Orlando Bones and the snakes in his vicinity. We get to the rope Bones used to climb down. I send Eliza and Frank up first. I see something glint in the sand. I swoop down and grab it.

"Carlos?"

"Coming!" I shout.

Twenty minutes later.

A rescue team is here to retrieve Orlando Bones from the snake pit. As much as I would have loved to let him squirm a little longer, he *is* the only person with information about Mom's location. So of course we have to retrieve him.

346

We're waiting for him at the mouth of the catacombs, along with the whole rest of the dig—special treasure-hunting task force and regular archaeologists alike.

First, someone carries up the robe, which Smarty Marty snatches with glee. "I'll catalog this! Important artifact coming through!" she says snottily.

Then comes Bones, on a stretcher. He suffered a few snakebites that swelled his ankles to the size of softballs. He's slightly delirious as he's carried away. "I rolled snake eyes!" he whispers hoarsely. "My treasure! Get the snake!"

Eliza looks at me with wide eyes.

But to my surprise, one of the rescuers carries out—after Bones—a thick, sandy-colored serpent on a long, skinny stretcher.

"RUMPLESNAKESKIN!" Frank cries. "What happened to you, buddy?"

"He seems to have swallowed a necklace. You can feel it in his body. Don't worry—we're taking him to the vet. They'll save the necklace *and* the snake."

Eliza turns to me, confused. "Wait a second. I thought I saw you reach down and grab something. That wasn't the necklace?"

I grin. "Nope. It was Frank's tooth." I open my palm and show him a snake's fang that I picked out of the sand for him. He blinks at it, and for a second, I'm

terrified he's going to be mad at me for lying to him—
or, even worse, make me go back into the labyrinth to
search for his real tooth.

But instead he reaches forward and says, "Whaaaaat?
This was in *my* mouth?" Then he turns to the archae-
ologists proudly. "EVERYONE! LOOK AT MY
TOOTH! It's an important artifact!"

Eliza and I burst out laughing. But the laughter
dies quickly. I see, across the pit, a local detective and
Nadira Nadeem coming over to the rest of the group,
walking away from where Bones is being lifted out of
the pit. They both look serious.

"Carlos?" Nadira says as she approaches. My stomach flips. "We found your mom."

Nadira takes me, Eliza, and Frank to Dr. Amanda
Mandible's medical tent, where she's tending to Mom.
Mom looks a little worse for wear—she's disheveled,
with eye bags and a bruise on her arm. But she lights
up when we walk in.

"You look . . . ," I say. I can't even lie and tell her she
looks good.

"Lousy," Frank finishes for me.

Dr. Mandible hands Mom a brochure for Harmonia
Clay. "Use our green tea mask as part of your nightly
beauty regimen, and you'll be back to a hundred percent in no time."

348

"Mijo! Would you believe me if I told you I took a really, really, really long bathroom break?"

"Bones trapped her in a porta-potty at the edge of the dig," Nadira explains.

"I think it'll take years to get the stench out of my nose. Let me smell your head." I walk over and she breathes me in, even though I probably smell sweaty and gross myself. "Much better."

I really want to be happy, but guilt twists inside me. I hang my head low. "We disobeyed your orders. We went into the tunnels when you asked us not to."

But she laughs and kisses my cheek. "The important thing is that you, Eliza, and Frank—"

"AND ME!" Frank says, brandishing his snake fang.

"—knew how to come together and work as a team. You listened to each other and strengthened your communication. That's all I wanted when I designed that mock case to begin with. I didn't mean to derail your teamwork."

"You didn't," Eliza says, squeezing my mom's hand. "We're stronger than ever now."

I turn to Nadira. "What will happen with the robe and necklace?"

She smiles. "Catalog, appraisal, museum. The usual track. You did a great thing, rescuing *two* priceless relics from the catacombs. And the other artifacts, as well—we'll be able to get them back from Bones. All is harmonious with Harmonia, thanks to Las Pistas Detective Agency."

I look around the room at my favorite team: Mom, Eliza, and Frank. No matter what case we take next, as long as I'm with them, I've hit the jackpot.

CASE CLOSED.

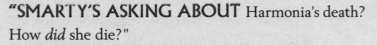

"SMARTY'S ASKING ABOUT Harmonia's death? How *did* she die?"

"I'm certain I told you," the professor says.

Eliza shakes her head. "You told us how Harmonia came to get the necklace—as a wedding present. And why Hephaestus cursed it—to get back at Aphrodite for cheating on him and having a child with Ares. But you never told us how Harmonia died."

His long face quirks into a curious expression. "She and her husband were turned into snakes."

"Awessssssssssome!" Frank says with a hiss.

Eliza and I look at each other.

"Why?" I ask.

"Before Cadmus—that's Harmonia's husband— married Harmonia and became the king of Thebes, he was Ares's servant for eight years. It was Cadmus's punishment for slaying a dragon that was protected by the gods. After that, as you know, he married Harmonia, and her cursed necklace brought ill luck and disease to their family. Near the end, Cadmus was so exhausted with his lot in life that he wished to become a snake. And the gods granted this wish."

"Well, that stinks! Why would he wish for that?"

Professor Worthington raises one eyebrow at me.

I continue. "I mean . . . if you're unhappy with your life, turning into a snake isn't going to solve your problems. I'm pretty sure that only makes things worse."

The professor laughs. "Indeed. Well, Harmonia was so distraught that she begged to join her husband, and so she became a serpent as well."

Eliza shudders.

"That's a really bad way to go," I say. But then I wonder: If Harmonia lived out her life as a snake, was she really buried when she died? And if not, why is everyone calling this her catacomb?

"Is there a reason," the professor says, "that you have a sudden interest in Harmonia? Because I would love to show you a few slides I have on her. I think it would further illuminate Harmonia's importance."

TO ASK TO SEE THE PROFESSOR'S SLIDES,
TURN TO PAGE 183.

←——————→

TO ASK WHY EVERYONE KEEPS CALLING
THE TUNNELS THE "CATACOMBS,"
TURN TO PAGE 290.

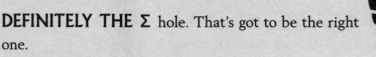

DEFINITELY THE Σ hole. That's got to be the right one.

We send Frank through.

Suddenly, water pours into the hall, and the dirt turns to mud—super-sinkable mud! It pulls us down. And down. And down . . .

CASE CLOSED.

WE ENTER 354 into the ancient lock. I hear a *click* that lets me know that we got it. I open the door, which is heavier than I thought it'd be.

Inside the door is the world's smallest tunnel. It's barely tall enough for me, and it's definitely not wide enough—I have to go in sideways. Same with Eliza. Frank fits just fine, sandwiched between the two of us.

"Um," Eliza whispers, as we shuffle along the tunnel, "this is a claustrophobic person's worst nightmare."

"Are you claustrophobic?" I ask.

She just whimpers in response.

"And here I thought you were arachnophobic!"

"People can have more than one fear, Carlos!"

"She's also scared of dogs!" Frank says. "And natural disasters! And the inside of black holes! And viruses! And seaweed!"

"Seaweed?" I say, trying not to laugh.

"My sister's a scaredy-cat. Oh yeah, she's also scared of cats!"

Eliza tries to shove her brother, but in this narrow tunnel, she can't quite reach him. "Frank, that's private!"

"Not anymore!" he says gleefully.

The tunnel is getting colder. I don't know how much farther it goes on, or how much more of this I can take. I start to think about the person who built this elaborate underworld setting. At first, I thought maybe these puzzles and tricks were here so that only the worthy could reach the necklace.

But I'm beginning to suspect that the person who built this didn't want *anyone* to find the necklace. At all.

At last I see a soft blue light up ahead, and I blink rapidly. Why is there *light* in this tiny underground cave that hasn't been visited for a thousand years or more?

"Hurry," I say, speeding up my side shuffles until I spill out of the tunnel into a tiny, circular room.

I don't know what I was expecting—a lavish space full of gold, gems, and treasures, maybe? But the room is made of tan stone and lined with columns, cracked and weathered from time. The light, I realize, is coming from a colony of glowworms on the ceiling, bathing us in neon blue.

The perimeter of the floor has a snake inlay pattern—another ouroboros. Someone really went in hard on the alchemy theme.

"Mom?" I shout. "MOM!"

Nothing.

I'm starting to think Eliza's right—Mom's really not here. I look to Eliza, trying to blink back tears.

She looks nervous, but her voice is steady. "Don't panic yet. We'll find her."

"Eliza! Carlos! Look at this!" Frank is on the floor—exactly in the middle of the room—and he's wiggling one of the tan stones on the ground. "It's loose! Like my tooth!"

"Is it . . . supposed to be loose?" I ask him. "Or did you break it?"

He shrugs. "It had a picture on it."

"We've seen that before," Eliza says excitedly, flipping open her book of alchemy symbols. "There! It's iron."

"So the necklace is made of iron?" I ask.

Eliza hums as Frank continues to jiggle the stone. I get on the floor next to him to see what we're dealing with.

"It's kind of stuck, Frank. There's no way you can get that loose with just your fingers. We have to stomp on it."

"Or perhaps . . . ," Eliza finally says. She sounds measured, like she always does when testing the waters of a new theory. "We should *feed* the stone, like we did the last time we saw alchemical symbols in these tunnels."

"Feed it . . . iron? I knew I should've packed a skillet in our bag," I say sarcastically.

"We do have iron with us."

"Where?"

Eliza looks at me seriously. "In our blood."

There's a pause as what she says sinks in. "That sounds dangerous. I can't let us do that."

"We've come this far," Eliza offers.

"All the more reason to stop before we go *too* far."

TO STOMP ON THE STONE, TURN TO PAGE 70.

←——————→

TO GIVE THE STONE A DROP OF BLOOD,
TURN TO PAGE 425.

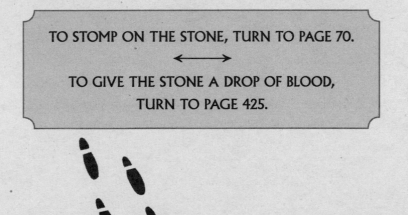

I POINT TO the hole with this Greek letter: Ψ. Frank salutes me and inches in.

"How's it looking in there, Frank?" I ask.

No answer.

"Frank?"

No answer.

"FRANK!!!"

Now you see him, now you don't.

CASE CLOSED.

MAYBE IT'S BEST if we talk to Orlando Bones alone right now. "I know you're busy," I say to Nadira, "but we'll try to find you later."

"Good luck," she says sincerely. Then she checks her watch again. "Perhaps it's for the best—I can talk to my intern before meeting Zip!" Then she quickly gathers her items into a satchel and dashes out of the tent.

"Alone at last," Orlando Bones says as he gestures for us to take a seat in the spare folding chairs.

We all sit down, and Frank immediately starts wiggling his tooth.

"Seems like you didn't want Nadira around," I say.

Orlando laughs a little too loudly. He adjusts his fedora. "About that . . . I don't know who I can trust. Maybe Nadira is trustworthy, but maybe not, and I just don't want to roll the dice on it. You see, I'm afraid that someone is going to steal the treasure in the catacombs before we get there."

"Why are you so sure someone's going to steal it?" Eliza asks. "When no one knows what it is?"

Orlando's eyes dart toward the front of the tent, and he drops his voice. "But we *do* think we know what it is. And if other valuable artifacts have gone missing, then it's a certainty that the biggest prize in human history will too. The treasure is in danger—and we must reach it. Before someone else does."

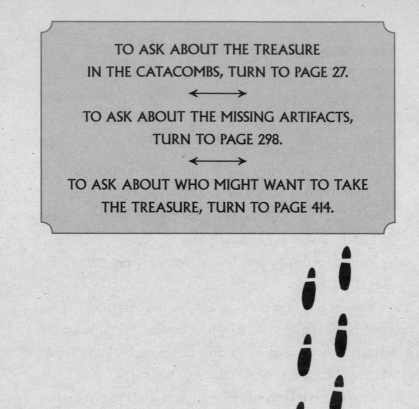

TO ASK ABOUT THE TREASURE
IN THE CATACOMBS, TURN TO PAGE 27.

←→

TO ASK ABOUT THE MISSING ARTIFACTS,
TURN TO PAGE 298.

←→

TO ASK ABOUT WHO MIGHT WANT TO TAKE
THE TREASURE, TURN TO PAGE 414.

I LOOK OVER Eliza's shoulder at the paper she stole from Dr. Amanda Mandible. It's a brochure for something called Harmonia Clay, whatever that is. It has a picture of Amanda on it . . . and another woman I don't recognize. I read the words.

HARMONIA CLAY™
GLOW LIKE A GODDESS

ABOUT HARMONIA CLAY™

Studies have shown that bentonite clay is rich in magnesium, iron, sodium, potassium, and calcium—all healthy nutrients that your skin needs to shine. As you apply bentonite clay to your face, toxins beneath the skin rise to the surface and are extracted upon removal of the mask. With our soothing facial treatments, you can be your most radiant self, even from the comfort of your own home.

Our six all-natural, hydrating flavors:
Honey, to cleanse pores and rejuvenate
Charcoal, to absorb oil and exfoliate
Milk, to stimulate cell growth and moisturize
Aloe vera, to activate your skin and refresh
Avocado, to slow signs of aging and nourish
Green tea, to reduce puffiness and heal

I look up. "So . . . Dr. Mandible is starting a skincare company with her wife? And they're calling it Harmonia Clay?"

"Don't forget the T-M!" Frank says.

Eliza nods. "Harmonia Clay—"

"T-M!" Frank shouts.

"—*clearly* has some link to the Necklace of Harmonia."

"And," I add, "it explains why we saw her in the tunnels yesterday. She was testing the soil or clay or whatever, and collecting it."

"I wonder if the clay in this area of Greece is exceptional, or whether the special properties come from being near the Necklace of Harmonia."

I think for a second. "That would give her a motive to steal the necklace, for sure. But what about the other artifacts? Why would she need those?"

Eliza thinks for a moment. Then she says, "It takes

a lot of money to start a company. She could sell the artifacts for millions, then use that as seed money to pay for Harmonia Clay's production and marketing costs."

"I don't want her to be guilty." Frank pouts. "She gave me lollipops."

"We should confront her with this brochure," Eliza says. "She won't be able to fake-smile her way through our interrogation then."

"Do you think . . ." I trail off. Eliza looks at me with a furrowed forehead. I take a deep breath and continue. "But what about my hunch about Nadira Nadeem? Because what we saw on her computer yesterday was pretty incriminating."

Eliza looks a little disappointed and defiant. "How about this—whoever we see first, we talk to?"

And she storms out of Dr. Mandible's tent. I sigh in frustration and hurry after her.

The sun is blazing. I can't believe it's been a full twenty-four hours since I last saw Mom. I don't know how I can even keep investigating while she's missing, except I know that the closer I get to the culprit, the closer I get to Mom. With each passing hour, I feel more and more certain that they're linked.

Eliza has stopped behind a tent, watching Professor Phineas Alistair Worthington and Smarty Marty having some sort of heated conversation that grows louder with every sentence.

"*I* have a doctorate!" the professor says.

"Perhaps they shouldn't have let you graduate!"

"How *dare* you—"

"Are you going to tell me about Harmonia's death or not?" Smarty snaps.

Professor Worthington jeers at her. "If you really could do my job better than I could, then I suspect you'd already know about Harmonia's fate. It seems you're not as good a researcher as you say you are!"

Smarty stomps away in a huff. Professor Worthington takes off his glasses and pinches the bridge of his nose.

"Well, a deal's a deal," Eliza says, shrugging at me. "He *is* the first person we've seen." And then she rushes out to question him without even asking me about it! What gives?

"That was an impassioned argument," Eliza says to the professor.

He jumps and holds his hand over his heart. "You gave me a fright! But I'm pleased to see you again. How are your young and moldable minds?"

"Your mind is moldy, not mine!" Frank says.

"Do you fight with Smarty often?" Eliza asks.

He frowns. "I didn't get a PhD in classical studies

to be undermined by a twenty-two-year-old almost-valedictorian with a bachelor's degree," he says snootily. "She is insufferable, and I once attended a dinner party with a dozen moral relativists."

"Oh, yeah, sure, I can see how that would be insufferable," I bluff.

"She even thinks she can do *your* job better than you. She wanted directions to the ruins of the fire."

My heart skips a beat. "She did? When?"

"Yesterday morning. Just shortly after your mother asked for them."

Eliza and I exchange a dark look.

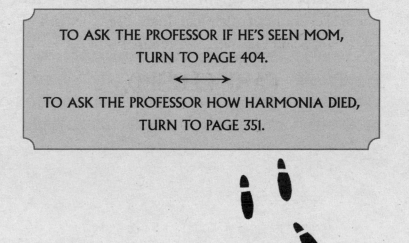

TO ASK THE PROFESSOR IF HE'S SEEN MOM,
TURN TO PAGE 404.

←——————→

TO ASK THE PROFESSOR HOW HARMONIA DIED,
TURN TO PAGE 351.

WE HAVE TO throw sand at the snakes! It's the only thing I can think of to stop them from approaching.

I grab a fistful of sand and lob it. Eliza does too. Frank just mopes on the sand mound.

I pitch more and more sand at the serpents. They hiss angrily, but nothing happens. They don't stop approaching.

"I don't understand! Why didn't it work? They don't even have eyelids!"

Eliza groans. "Oh no! I just remembered—snakes have a membrane over their eyes to protect their corneas from irritants."

The serpents coil up my legs. Maybe I could fight one snake, but I can't fight hundreds. I see the flash of white fangs, and I know . . . we're hisssssstory.

CASE CLOSED.

I KNOW WE didn't get to talk to Nadira Nadeem earlier, when we dismissed her from our initial conversation with Orlando Bones. But she's so nice. Now I'm wondering if she has ideas about where the real artifacts could be.

"So . . . if you're not selling artifacts from the dig, then do you have any idea where the real artifacts might be?"

She purses her glossed lips. "If I knew that, then we wouldn't have had to hire you."

"So you don't have any suspicions?" Eliza asks.

"I'd assume, at this point, you probably have more leads and more suspicions than I do."

I think she's probably right about that. Even Nadira isn't cleared from my suspect list yet. At least not until we further understand what the items are that she's making bank on . . . and why exactly she's selling them.

> TO ASK NADIRA WHY SHE'S SELLING THE ITEMS,
> TURN TO PAGE 127.

"WE SHOULD CHECK out Nadira Nadeem's workspace," I say. "After all, Orlando Bones didn't trust her enough to include her in our intro chat. Maybe we can figure out why he's suspicious of her."

Her desk is organized, maybe even more so than Eliza's desk at school, which is saying something. Frank sits down at Nadira's swivel chair and shakes her mouse to wake up her computer. Locked, unfortunately. I open her desk drawer. Inside, there are all sorts of color-coded calendars and schedules.

Eliza picks ups a calendar and flips through it.

"What are you doing?"

"Finding out when she'll be back—seems like we have thirty minutes until her meeting with Professor Worthington is over. And I'm also, even more importantly, seeing if maybe she wrote down a password for her computer."

"Um, don't you think someone this organized has a clean uncluttered brain that can remember all her passwords?"

Eliza shakes her head. "Actually, I think exactly the opposite. We know Nadira is smart—she speaks more than one language. And we know she's detail oriented. Someone that methodical would know that it's unsafe to have the same password for all your devices. Therefore, she probably has too many passwords to remember." She continues flipping through the calendar. Eventually, she hums.

"What did you find?"

"Was it a lollipop?" Frank asks.

I roll my eyes. "Give it a rest with the lollipops, Frank."

"Pshhh. You're a lolli*poop*."

"If you two are finished," Eliza says. "It seems like Nadira has a few different passwords written down."

"Great!" I say. "Let's try them all."

"We probably shouldn't. Sometimes electronic devices are programmed to lock you out if you guess the wrong password too many times. We need to figure out which of these seven passwords is the right one."

"How do we do that?"

"Take a look at this," Eliza says, excitedly showing me the page in Nadira's calendar. I'm glad to see her enthusiasm for puzzles is back . . . but maybe it's because *she* found this one.

DAILY PASSWORD:
Four days before the day after the day before yesterday

Sunday	Monday	Tuesday	Wednesday	Thursday	Friday	Saturday
126	142	178	236	259	284	321

"So her code changes each day?" I say.

"What's today?" Frank asks.

"Thursday."

THE SOLUTION TO THE PUZZLE
WILL LEAD YOU TO YOUR NEXT PAGE.

←——→

TO ASK ELIZA FOR A HINT, TURN TO PAGE 48.

WE NEED TO steer Bones to the excavation pit! I flank his left side, and Eliza and Frank follow me. With our bodies between him and the parking lot, Bones starts veering to the right, weaving between columns and people. And there are *so many people*. I don't think a single archaeologist is in the pit during lunch hour.

"Out of my way!" he growls as he turns back to look at us. He keeps glancing over his shoulder.

I can use this!

"Mr. Bones," I shout, "you should look at the necklace!"

"Huh?"

"Trust us."

He continues to run, gazing between the bag and us—not looking where he's going. Not paying attention to the hole up ahead.

"Look out!" one of the archaeologists calls.

"Why? *Aaaaaaaugh!*" Orlando Bones yowls as he falls into the pit.

"Quick! Grab the ladder!" Eliza shouts.

We yank the ladder up and pull it out of the pit before Bones even gets to his feet.

"LET ME OUT OF HERE!" he bellows, trying to claw up the sides of the pit. But it's useless.

Then, suddenly, he seems to remember the catacombs, and he makes a mad dash for the entranceway.

371

Which makes no sense to me because there's only one entrance, which is also the exit. Maybe he wants to hide down there, but if he stays there too long, well . . . I guess the catacombs will live up to their name.

We run around the perimeter. Bones is halfway across the covered pit. I wait until he's just a few feet away from the archway before calling out, "Aren't you going to look at our necklace?"

"*My* necklace," he growls.

"Actually, it's MY necklace!" Frank says proudly.

"What?" Bones kneels in the dirt, zips open my bag, and reaches in. "No. *No.* This can't be! Impossible!" He pulls out the necklace. During the chase, the clay crumbled into several parts and some of the jewels popped off.

"Rest in pieces," Frank says dramatically.

Eliza puts a hand on her brother's shoulder. "The forgery had a good life. You did well, Frankie."

"I think you mean I did *good.*"

"I most certainly did not!" she says.

Bones looks up at us, red-faced and livid. "You—this is all your fault! *Why* couldn't you just go into the catacombs? Why couldn't you do the one thing I hired you to do?"

"You hired us to find missing artifacts," Eliza says.

"No, I hired you to go into the catacombs! I went as

far as I could, alone, by myself. But there's a spot at the end, only big enough for a child. And I thought, *what* child could I get to go in there? Who would be up for the danger? Who would hand deliver the Necklace of Harmonia to me?"

"So you hired us?"

"I came across an article about a case you solved back in the States—with a missing actress. And the more I researched you, the more I thought, They'd be perfect. My next move was to steal some artifacts so I could justify hiring you. Then I bought your tickets out here."

"But we weren't as easily manipulated as you thought we'd be," Eliza says.

"You kept messing up my plans," he says, shaking with anger. "All three of you. When you arrived, I would have wagered anything that it'd be easy to get you to take the bait. All I had to do was pique your curiosity with the catacombs and the treasure, and I'd be headed for a payday. But *nooooo*, you had to invite Nadira into our first conversation, and she would not let me talk about the tunnels! Then, when you still had no interest in exploring them, I kidnapped your mom, thinking that *of course* you would retrieve her. Am I really to believe you didn't go searching for your own mother?"

"We didn't believe for one second that she was in the

catacombs," I say. "Where is she?"

Bones hesitates for a moment. He knows this is his last bargaining chip. "Get me out of here, and I'll pony up the info."

It's tempting. *Really* tempting. But . . .

"No," I say. "We found the artifacts without your help. We can find her too."

"You kids are relentless," Bones says, slumping to the ground. He puts his cheek on the dirt and begins to moan. And finally the rest of the task force catches up.

"Now, now, Mr. Bones," Nadira Nadeem says. "It doesn't do to carry on like this."

He wails in response.

"We've called the police, sir," Smarty says. "They're on their way. Now that a position is opening on the special task force, do you think you could write a letter of recommendation for me? For your job?"

Bones groans.

At last I hear sirens in the distance, and that is when Orlando Bones finally accepts that there's no way out of this. "Okay, kids," he says. "Your mom is on my boat, docked in the Gulf of Corinth. You beat me. You win. And winner takes all."

Two hours later, we're sitting at the dig.

Smarty took us to retrieve Mom, which would have

374

been a nicer gesture if she didn't spend the whole ride bragging to us about how *she* could have found the artifacts in half the time, if only she had been given our resources.

I had expected to find Mom weak or in trouble, but she was as lively as ever. She had chewed through her duct tape binding and had unlocked the door of the cabin, even while still tied to a chair. If she had a few more hours, I'm pretty confident she would have busted herself out of there.

She is, after all, a Serrano. Resourcefulness is in our blood.

When we got back to the dig, we each gave statements to the officers there. And since we are minors, Mom sat in on each one. Eventually she pieced the story together from hearing three accounts.

And now we're sitting on the edge of the pit, drinking coffee (Mom) and eating cookies (the rest of us), while Mom confirms that we *truly* did not go into the tunnels after she left.

"But really?" Mom says.

"Yes, really!"

"And you didn't even peek in there?"

"Nope," I say.

"I just can't believe it. I can't believe you actually *listened* to me when I said something was too dangerous!

I've never been more proud!"

"Of course we listen to you!"

"You did excellent work," Mom says. "You three should be so happy with yourselves right now."

I bite into another cookie, but it doesn't make me feel any less glum. "Mom, how can I feel happy right now? If the person who hires us is the culprit, I assume that means we don't get paid."

"What about the necklace?" Frank says. "We can be paid in treasure!"

Eliza shakes her head. "They can't give us the necklace. We're the only ones who can fit in the tunnels once we get farther into the catacombs, apparently."

"So let's do it! Now! Hurry up! Faster!" Frank folds his arms. "Why are you all still sitting there?"

"Because," I say, "we did the job we were hired to do. We uncovered an artifact thief. We returned the artifacts. Nadira was right—the catacombs were never relevant to our job."

"But *treasure*," Frank insists.

"That is a mystery that the catacombs are going to keep."

"I think that's very wise of you, mijo," Mom says, hugging me close. She ruffles my hair. "Just look at you three—growing up right before my very eyes. So very responsible!"

376

"Am not, am not, *am not*!" Frank insists, and to prove it, he slips down the ladder into the excavation pit and starts running toward the doorway to the catacombs.

"FRANK, NO!" Mom hollers, climbing into the hole after him.

Eliza chuckles. And a rush of warmth floods me. I couldn't have done any of this without Eliza—I never would have come up with this brilliant forgery plan. I would have had us roaming aimlessly in those dangerous and deadly catacombs.

I feel like I'm finally seeing her, not just for her brain but for *everything* she brings to the table. For her logic and calm. For her cunning plans. For the way she makes decisions driven by facts and evidence. Going forward, this is how we have to be. Perfect equals compromising, communicating, and working in tandem.

"You can't get me! Neener neener!" Frank shrieks as he runs in circles around the perimeter. Poor Mom is very winded.

"Some things never change," Eliza says.

I grin. "And some things do."

CASE CLOSED.

"SLOW DOWN, MOM! If you get next to them, we can see who it is."

Mom gently puts her foot on the brakes. We coast slowly as the other car speeds up. We're neck and neck—I look to the left, and . . .

Nothing.

The windows on the sides are tinted too. We have no idea who's following us.

"We can't see in!" Eliza says, disappointed.

It *has* to be somebody from the dig, right? Nadira, Bones, Smarty, Professor Worthington—all of them knew we had found something. Or knew, at least, that we were leaving the dig.

The silver car speeds up. They drive away, leaving us in the dust. I relax against the car seat and breathe a sigh of relief. Maybe it was all in my head. . . .

I don't remember falling asleep, but Mom is shaking me awake. "Get up, Carlos. We're here."

I open my eyes. A ridiculously tall mountain is looming above me. I can't even see the top. The peak is hidden in the clouds.

I gulp. "We're really going to climb that thing?"

"We're going to have to," Eliza says solemnly.

I grab the Necklace of Harmonia from up front. Now that I have the chance to look at it up close, I can see it's exactly how Professor Worthington described it: two snakes wrapped around each other with their mouths making a clasp and lots of glittering jewels. I slip it into my backpack for safekeeping.

We start up the path, our backpacks stuffed with the water bottles and granola bars Mom bought and the emergency first-aid kit from the car. There are a few serious hikers who pass us. No one could mistake us for serious hikers. But we have a quest. We have to keep going.

Rock after rock after rock. I start to remember why I'm not really an outdoors person. This is tedious, I'm tired, and we're not even halfway up.

"I bet I can beat you to the top!" Frank says.

"I bet you can too," I say.

We walk, we climb, we groan, we sweat. Finally I feel like we're making some progress. Still not even close to the top, but we're up pretty high now. The view is incredible—the valley stretches on for ages.

I turn back to the mountain. We've reached a pass where the climb is literally a rocky stairway to the sky. The stones are uneven. I really, really hope we don't fall. We just have to be slow and careful.

I put my hand on a rock, to climb up. But I see something that stops me dead in my tracks. On the rock I'm touching, someone has etched a drawing into the stone:

two snakes intertwined. In *exactly* the same shape as the snakes entwined on the Necklace of Harmonia. I step closer to the snakes. It's subtle, but instead of forking, their tongues make the shape of an arrow.

To the left, there's a very narrow cliff ledge. I'm certain—more certain than anything in my life—that we have to take it.

"This way!" I say, edging off the path. The ledge is frightening. There's no railing, and one wrong step off the shelf could send us plummeting down. We shuffle sideways. Very slowly. And just when I start to wonder if I made a bad call, I see another snake. It's pointing around the bend.

"Just a little farther," I say encouragingly.

"Carlos, I hate you right now," Eliza whimpers.

"MOM?" I call. She is far behind us. A snail could go faster on this ledge.

"I'm okay!" she yells. "Keep going! I'll catch up!"

Okay. We keep going until the ledge becomes a wider platform that leads to a cave. But for the cave, we need our flashlights. We dig them out of Eliza's backpack and click them on.

The cave is shallow. There's a whole bunch of tiles of different shapes on the back wall, and underneath, a stockpile of items: a seashell, a hammer, metal lightning bolt, a golden wheat stalk, a trident, a lyre, a sword, a

380

tiara, a staff, a bow and arrow, and a helmet.

But what catches my eye is a rock in the center of the cave. It has a circle on it, surrounded by a triangle. At each point of the triangle is a carving of a different animal: a vulture, a donkey, and a dove.

I pull the Necklace of Harmonia out of my bag and rest on the circle. The pendant fits perfectly, like it was made to sit there. But . . . nothing happens.

"Is something supposed to happen?" I ask Eliza.

"I don't think we're done yet," she says. "We did the circle part—putting the necklace in its proper place—but I feel like we're missing the triangle part."

"So we have to find a vulture, a donkey, and a dove?"

Eliza reaches into her backpack and pulls out a book. She thumbs through the pages until she gets to a spread about the Greek gods. She shows me the page. "Look! A vulture is the symbol of the god Ares—Harmonia's real father. A donkey is the symbol of Hephaestus—spurned lover and maker of the cursed necklace. And a dove symbolizes Aphrodite—Harmonia's mother, Ares's lover, and Hephaestus's wife."

"This is their love triangle."

I think for a moment, then I shine my flashlight on the wall, where Frank is drawing weird S symbols with a piece of chalk he found. "I didn't do it!" he says guiltily.

But actually . . . I think Frank's on to something. There's something about these triangle wall tiles . . . some sort of message they're trying to tell me. I grab the chalk from him and start shading only the triangles.

COUNT THE TRIANGLES.
THE NUMBER OF TRIANGLES IS YOUR NEXT PAGE.

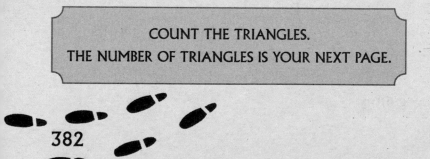

WE NEED TO get the maps from Zip. And if Zip isn't going to share the maps, then we're just going to have to steal them.

We sneak into the work tent. Zip is at the computer, with the light of it glowing on their face. We have to be sneaky . . . we have to be fast.

I tiptoe behind Zip's chair. The real maps have to be around here somewhere—but I don't know which ones they are, so I grab them all.

"Hey!" Zip says, turning around.

I race out of the tent with all the maps in hand. I did it—mission successful!

But when we get down to the catacombs, I realize I still don't know which map is the right one. And without Zip, I'm never going to know. And now that I stole from them, they're never going to help us!

This plan was half-baked and hasty. I clearly didn't map this out well enough.

CASE CLOSED.

I WANT TO hear what Nadira has to say. "Ms. Nadeem, why don't you stay," I say politely, ignoring the pout that appears on Bones's face.

"Yes, of course—I would love to." Nadira pulls up a chair and sits with Bones on the other side of his desk. But while Bones kicks back in his chair, Nadira sits rigid. She smooths out her clothes, and when she's done with that, she starts picking at her nails. She looks tense. . . .

"Why are you so anxious?" Eliza asks, and I know she's wondering the same thing I am: whether Nadira has something to hide.

Nadira smiles. "I'm very nervous about the thefts. Too much has gone missing from our storage shelves, and I've noticed that some members of the team have been acting rather suspiciously. Don't you think, Mr. Bones?"

"What? Oh, yeah," he says glumly. His tone almost makes me feel bad about inviting her to stay. *Almost.*

"At first, I wasn't sure that hiring a detective was necessary, but now I'm glad Mr. Bones insisted." Nadira leans forward and says, "So what do you want to know? I am an open book."

And that's when I feel confident about my decision.

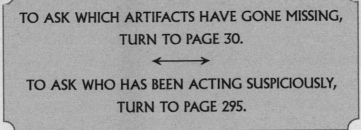

TO ASK WHICH ARTIFACTS HAVE GONE MISSING,
TURN TO PAGE 30.
←——→
TO ASK WHO HAS BEEN ACTING SUSPICIOUSLY,
TURN TO PAGE 295.

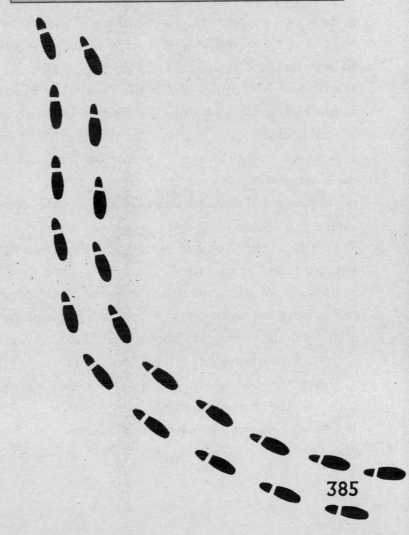

385

WE HAVE TO talk to Professor Phineas Alistair Worthington. It seems clear that he has so much more information than Orlando Bones on the necklace, the history, and the tunnels. He might even have the answers to questions we don't know how to ask.

We finally find the professor eating lunch. He doesn't seem to be very popular—he's all alone, a whole table to himself. Or maybe he wanted to be alone. He seems to be buried in research. He's highlighting passages in a thick book and writing notes in the margins, and next to me, Eliza gasps loudly. She doesn't even like writing in workbooks.

"Are you looking for me?" the professor says, adjusting his glasses.

"Do you mind if we ask you a few questions?" Mom says.

"We have nine hundred ninety-nine thousand billion questions," Frank says.

Professor Worthington looks surprised. "That's not a real number," he says snobbishly, "but by all means." He gestures to the empty table around him. We sit down.

"What are you reading?" Eliza asks.

"Just reviewing the story of Harmonia, daughter of gods—and her cursed necklace."

Cursed necklace? I knew it was valuable . . . but *cursed*?

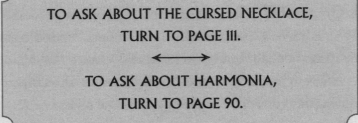
TO ASK ABOUT THE CURSED NECKLACE,
TURN TO PAGE 111.

TO ASK ABOUT HARMONIA,
TURN TO PAGE 90.

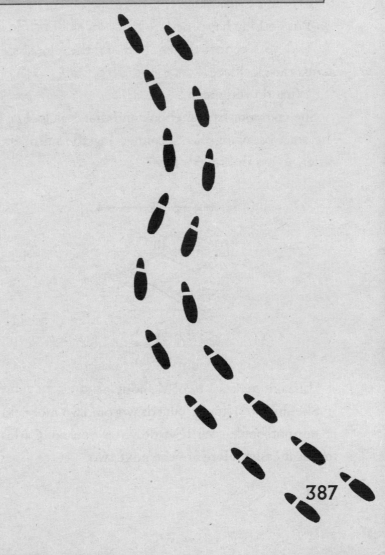

387

UGH. I NEED Eliza's help. "What does this all mean? Why is there a line through the numbers? I tried connecting them all, but it didn't work."

She circles back to me, since Frank is shimmying down the column. "I think your idea of connecting them is an *excellent* idea."

"But nothing happened. . . ."

"Did you connect them *around* the clockface or *across* the clockface?"

"What do you mean?"

She takes out her notebook and draws a clock. Then she starts drawing on it, connecting the numbers, in order, across the clock's face.

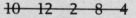

"Eliza, it makes a two!" I shout.

She smiles. "I know." She draws out two more clocks in her notebook. "Write it down as you go, Carlos. It makes it easier. Here are the next two."

388

8 6 4 10 12 2 8

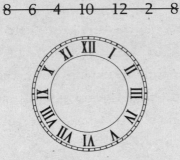

1 11 9 3 5 8

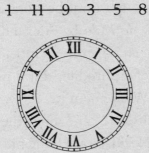

THE SOLUTION TO THE PUZZLE
WILL LEAD YOU TO YOUR NEXT PAGE.

"MR. BONES, I don't understand," I say. "You seem very focused on the treasure in the catacombs . . . but when we talked to Nadira yesterday, she didn't think it was worth our time to explore down there. I thought you hired us to find the missing artifacts. We can't change focus now! Not when we're getting closer to our thief."

Orlando Bones gets up. He walks to a bookshelf behind him and pulls out a giant dictionary-sized thing. Then he flips through until he stops at a picture of a sculpture: *Venus de Milo* by Alexandros of Antioch. I'm certain I've seen a picture of it before.

"A depiction of Aphrodite," Eliza says. "The Greek goddess of love. What about it?"

"It's not that I don't care about the other artifacts. It's just that the Necklace of Harmonia versus the other artifacts . . . is like the Venus de Milo versus a Play-Doh project."

"I love Play-Doh!" Frank says. "It's fun to eat."

"You're not supposed to eat that," Eliza scolds.

"It's colorful for my tummy!"

I shake my head and stand up, so that Mr. Bones knows I'm serious. "We are detectives, not treasure hunters, not bodyguards. I understand that the necklace is your focus, but ours is finding the missing artifacts and the thief."

Mom beams at me proudly.

390

Bones scoffs. "You're stacking the deck against me." Then he looks down at the work on his desk and starts scribbling on papers. So we leave.

Outside, the treasure-hunting team is also gathering. All our suspects are huddled near the medical tent: Nadira, Leech, Smarty Marty, Zip, and Professor Worthington. Even Dr. Mandible—who we haven't even talked to yet, except very briefly yesterday—has a medical kit and is prepping to go down into the tunnels. Everyone is going, it seems, except Orlando Bones, who hasn't emerged from his tent.

As they head out, I realize now is the *perfect* opportunity to go through their stuff. And if I had to pick somewhere to start . . .

Our top two suspects: Nadira Nadeem and Richard Leech.

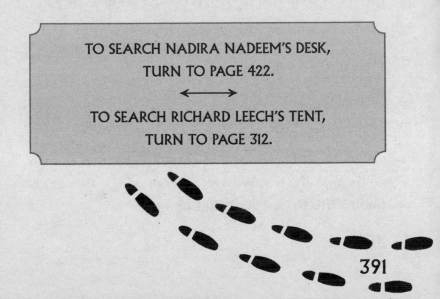

TO SEARCH NADIRA NADEEM'S DESK,
TURN TO PAGE 422.

←——→

TO SEARCH RICHARD LEECH'S TENT,
TURN TO PAGE 312.

I DON'T KNOW how to explain it, but instinct is calling me deeper into the catacombs. I'm like a fish on a line.

And I can just hear Eliza's voice in my head reminding me that fish on a line end up dead. I quiet that thought.

"Just a little bit farther," I say. "Then we'll turn back around, I swear."

These catacombs are unnaturally cold and surprisingly empty. When Orlando Bones said that the necklace was housed down here, I thought it would be . . . fancier? More elaborate. Instead it's just stones and cobwebs. And so far I've seen no booby traps.

"Um, Carlos?" Mom says. I turn around and notice that she is stooped over. The ceiling has gotten so low that she can barely stand. "I don't know how much farther I can go in this tunnel. It doesn't seem to be adult sized."

"For some reason it's getting smaller and smaller," Eliza says from up ahead.

"So . . . is this a dead end?" I say.

"No," Eliza says, hunching. "I think there's something up ahead! Come look!"

I stoop as I walk, and so does Frank, even though he technically doesn't have to. Poor Mom, though, is finding this to be a very tight squeeze.

Up ahead is a wall with some weird symbols. Lots of triangles and circles—it looks like witchcraft.

"Alchemy," Eliza says. "Just like the archway out—"

Thump.

It's unmistakable—the sound of a footstep behind us.

Eliza and I go rigid. Mom whips around with the flashlight. No one's there.

"Let's go," Mom says sharply.

We rush back to the exit. The person is in front of us—I can see a shadow!

THUNK. ZZZZZZT.

A fence drops in front of us, and it's coursing with electricity. We've fallen right into a booby trap! But why is there electricity in this catacomb? There's *no way* they had electricity in ancient Greece.

"We have to turn the electricity off!" Mom says.

"Here!" Eliza cries, pointing to a small box at the bottom of the fence. "Resetting the circuit breaker will stop the electricity! Just follow the words *circuit breaker* through the box—and don't get electrocuted!" Eliza says, as Frank (of course) puts a finger out to poke the fence.

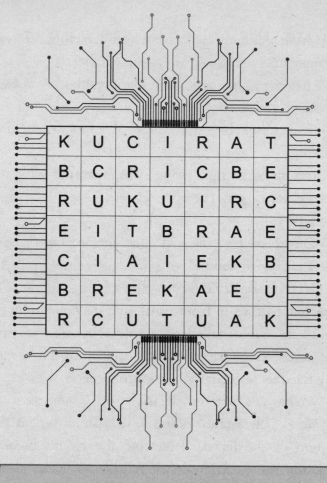

K	U	C	I	R	A	T
B	C	R	I	C	B	E
R	U	K	U	I	R	C
E	I	T	B	R	A	E
C	I	A	I	E	K	B
B	R	E	K	A	E	U
R	C	U	T	U	A	K

THE PATHWAY FORMS A NUMBER.
ADD ONE HUNDRED TO THE NUMBER AND
TURN TO THAT PAGE.

←——→

TO ASK ELIZA FOR A HINT, TURN TO PAGE 318.

I HAVE A hammer, right? I have to swing it toward Bones. Maybe that will keep him back!

I heave the hammer over my shoulder—it is *super* heavy. Then I swing it around like a baseball bat. Only—it lodges into the wall.

Rumble . . . crack!

Rocks start falling. Bones runs out of the cave, but Eliza, Frank, and I are too deep inside. "Everybody duck!" I yell.

"Duck? Where?" Frank says. "Quack quack!"

The cave collapses, and when the rumbling finally stops, I look up. There's a wall of rocks blocking our way out. We're trapped! Eliza claws and claws, but the rocks are too big to move. We're stuck until Mom or someone else finds us.

I tried to be bolder . . . but I ended up boulder.

CASE CLOSED.

"**WHAT EVIDENCE DO** you have that someone's been in the tunnels?" I ask.

Orlando Bones finally comes alive. There's a twinkle in his eye, and he readjusts his fedora. It's like he's been waiting all day for someone to ask him this question. "First off, we haven't been able to go very far into the tunnels. We are still waiting on Zip for maps of the catacombs. Because Keira Skelberry got so seriously injured from a booby trap, I've instructed everyone that we must only go inside as a team. But . . . there have been a few times we've gone in and found a set of muddy footprints."

Mom looks up from her notebook. "Mud? Where did the mud come from? The dirt here is dry."

"No idea. Clearly someone has gotten deeper into the catacombs, without the rest of us. We also found an abandoned lantern. Still warm to the touch."

Nadira taps her foot impatiently, like this is all a waste of her time. It's obvious that she's not interested in talking about the catacombs.

Eliza clears her throat, and Orlando looks at her. "Is it possible," she says, "to put a camera angling at the mouth of the catacombs? That way, you can catch the intruder on tape."

"You must think I'm an easy mark. Tried that already, and the footage shows nothing!"

"Why do you think someone wants to get into the catacombs alone, without the rest of the team?" I ask.

"So they can steal what lies deep within—the greatest prize in the world."

TO ASK ABOUT THE GREATEST PRIZE
IN THE WORLD, TURN TO PAGE 172.

I DECIDE TO go with Eliza's idea—hide from Mr. Bones.

Eliza and I crouch behind Nadira Nadeem's desk, and Frank dives under Orlando Bones's desk.

"MR. BONES!" Smarty calls repeatedly until he comes in.

I can tell he's already annoyed. He crosses the room, and I hold my breath.

"You called for me?" Bones marches across the tent and sits down at his desk. He puts his feet out . . . right on Frank. "What the—what are you doing here?"

"*That's* what I called to tell you!" Smarty says. "Someone's in *trouble*!"

"What are you kids doing in here?" Bones says. "And why aren't you investigating where I asked you to investigate?"

"Cause!" Frank says.

"Cause why?"

"BEcause!"

Bones growls in frustration. "Where are the other two?"

Smarty points in our direction.

"I thought I told you where the next theft is going to happen—in the catacombs. I thought I told you that the Necklace of Harmonia was more important than all the other artifacts combined."

"You—"

"I blame myself," Bones interrupts loudly. "I bet on the wrong horse. Clearly detective work isn't your forte."

It sounds like we're getting fired. But we *can't* get fired. "Please, Mr. Bones, don't fire us!"

"Fire you?" He laughs. "I paid for your time. So I'm reassigning you. From now on, you'll be on artifact cleaning duty. Wear gloves and goggles. Smarty here will set you up with tiny brushes. I think you'll find that this is a much better line of work for you."

One tiny mistake, and we've been brushed aside.

CASE CLOSED.

UGH. FIGURING OUT Dr. Mandible's password feels like filling out a worksheet for science class. I need help.

I look over at Eliza, who is buried deep in a book.

"I did my part already," she says, without even looking up. "Ask someone else."

Someone else? There's only Frank, who is right now digging deep into the lollipop jar.

"I know my ZYXWVUTs," he says, reciting the alphabet backward. That's right—he's just starting to read. But what help could he really give me on a puzzle that requires so much reading?

I don't understand. Eliza loves puzzles. She *always* gives me help. Maybe if I ask really nicely and flatter her a bit . . .

Or maybe I should just give in to the idea of Frank.

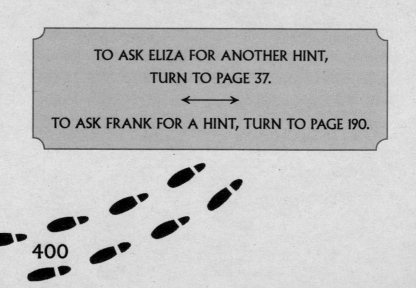

TO ASK ELIZA FOR ANOTHER HINT,
TURN TO PAGE 37.

←——→

TO ASK FRANK FOR A HINT, TURN TO PAGE 190.

I'LL TOSS A trowel across the parking lot. Since it's made of steel, it's sure to make a noise when it hits the concrete. Smarty will investigate, and that's when we'll climb into her trunk.

I pitch the trowel across the parking lot. Perfect practice for Little League. Only—throwing a trowel is *nothing* like throwing a baseball. And it's not going nearly as far as I intended. In fact, it's headed right for—

CRASH.

The trowel hits Smarty's front windshield, and the glass spiderwebs into a thousand pieces.

Smarty shrieks—first in surprise, then in anger.

"Quick!" I say, pulling Eliza and Frank toward Smarty's car. Maybe we can still hide in her trunk. But she's circling her car like a shark around its prey. "YOU!" she says, lunging toward us. She grabs my backpack, pulls the zipper open, and sees nineteen trowels inside. "You'll pay for this!"

Unfortunately, the evidence against us was overwhelming. And the car repairs were more than we could afford.

Las Pistas Detective Agency was forced to throw in the trowel.

CASE CLOSED.

"CAN WE LOOK at the disk, Mr. Bones?"

He nods and slides it across his desk. "Be very careful."

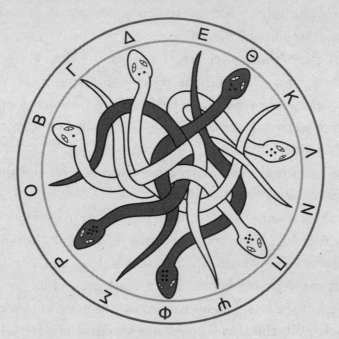

Eliza and I move closer. The snakes crisscross the face, like they're tangled in a giant knot. All around the snakes, in a border around the top of the disk, are Greek letters . . . but different from the letters that are on the side.

"What does the message say on the top?" I ask.

"You'll have to ask Nadira . . . or Professor Worthington. I don't know Greek at all. I don't even know classical studies that well. I'm definitely the brawn, and not the brains, of this operation."

It seems weird that he would be leading this expedition if he doesn't know anything about Greece or classical studies, and I can tell Eliza feels the same from the way she purses her lips.

"How did you get this job again, Mr. Bones?" Eliza asks.

"The lead archaeologist, Keira Skelberry, and I are old pals—we've worked a few digs together. Played some bang-up games of poker after hours. She phoned me, and I'm here because the timing worked out."

"She called you from the hospital?" I ask.

He shakes his head. "No, she fell into one of those ancient booby traps after the task force arrived on the scene. One day after we arrived."

I look at Mom, whose face is stony.

"Here," he says cheerfully, gesturing to the disk. "Check this out! It's like the royal flush of artifacts!"

Delicately, I pick it up. It's surprisingly heavy.

"We haven't been able to do anything with it," Orlando says after I put it down again.

"Because it's a puzzle," Eliza says.

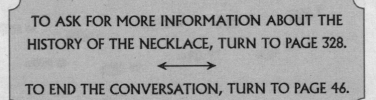

TO ASK FOR MORE INFORMATION ABOUT THE HISTORY OF THE NECKLACE, TURN TO PAGE 328.

TO END THE CONVERSATION, TURN TO PAGE 46.

"DO YOU KNOW where my mom is?" I ask Professor Phineas Alistair Worthington.

"I gave her directions to the last known location of the Necklace of Harmonia yesterday. That is all I know."

I squint at him. Is it possible that he could have followed Mom? Intercepted her? Kidnapped her?

"You told Smarty where to find the ruins?" Eliza asks.

"Indeed."

So now Professor Worthington and Smarty have jumped to the top of my suspect list. "What else did you tell Smarty?"

"I gave her some information about Harmonia—she was *very* curious about that. Of course, the moment she insulted me, I abruptly concluded our mini lesson and refused to share any more of my knowledge. Hence the quarrel you've just witnessed."

"What *did* you talk to her about?" I ask.

"The necklace and these catacombs. I stopped short of telling her how Harmonia died."

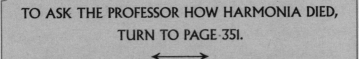

TO ASK THE PROFESSOR HOW HARMONIA DIED,
TURN TO PAGE 351.

←——→

TO ASK WHY EVERYONE KEEPS CALLING THE
TUNNELS THE "CATACOMBS," TURN TO PAGE 290.

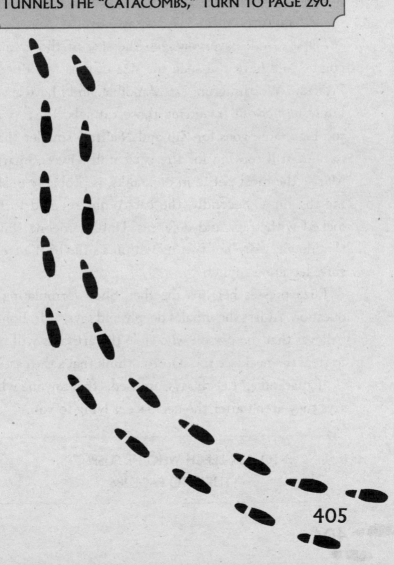

"WHAT ABOUT THE necklace?" I ask Leech.

"What about it?"

"Are you planning on taking that?"

"Couldn't, even if I tried."

Eliza and I look at each other, confused.

"What do you mean?" Eliza says.

"First of all, have you seen the size of those catacombs, and have you seen the size of me? Mr. Bones, Professor Worthington, Dr. Mandible, and I have absolutely *no hope* of traversing those tunnels. We're way too big. Same goes for Zip and Nadira—smaller than us, but still too big for the catacombs. Even Smarty Marty, the most petite in our ranks, is probably pushing the limit. Secondly, the catacombs seemed to be locked with traps and defenses. Until someone shuts that down, we're not getting within a mile of the treasure, let alone an inch."

Eliza presses her lips together. She's formulating a question. At last she inhales deeply and says, "Mr. Bones believes that the person who stole the artifacts will try to steal the necklace too. Do you think that's the case?"

"I guarantee," Leech says, amused, "that anyone who says they aren't after the necklace is lying to you."

TO ASK LEECH WHO HE SUSPECTS,
TURN TO PAGE 186.

"YOU SAW THE disk that Mr. Bones has?" I ask.

"Ah, yes," Professor Worthington says, leaning over the book in front of him. He purses his lips in distaste. "The disk Mr. Bones couldn't comprehend, no matter how hard he tugged and twisted." His tone seems to suggest that he doesn't think very highly of Orlando's methods. "I told him that something like this requires your *mind*, not your muscle."

"You think it's a puzzle?" Eliza says excitedly.

"But of course!"

"Do you have a copy of what the translation said— around the side of the disk?"

"I thought Nadira already did a translation . . . ancient and powerful necklace, blah blah blah, lying dormant in a catacomb, blah blah blah, brave adventurers welcome to test your mettle."

"What's Greek for blah blah blah?" Frank says, suddenly interested.

I ignore Frank. "Do you have an exact translation?"

"I could, if I saw the disk again. Mr. Bones hasn't let it go since we found it."

"Well, with all the artifacts going missing around here, can you blame him?" Eliza says.

Professor Worthington simply peers at us over his glasses.

"Have you seen anything suspicious?" I ask. "Or any-*one* suspicious?"

407

"I'm afraid I can't help you there. I mostly keep my nose buried in a book. My focus is solely on finding the Necklace of Harmonia. I have no interest in your job."

I think part of our job is to find the necklace too. But I don't tell Professor Worthington that. The last thing I need is for him to follow us into the catacombs. And speaking of that . . . I think it's time we go check them out.

"What do you think—" Eliza says, but I interrupt her.

"Thank you so much for your time," I say, standing up. Mom seems surprised, but she follows my lead. Eliza rises too, looking mildly irritated. Frank doesn't get the picture until I waggle a candy bar. He almost always follows the chocolate.

"What was that about?" Eliza asks when we're out of earshot. "I had more questions to ask Professor Worthington!"

"No need!" I say. "We have everything we need."

"You have everything you need," Eliza says. "I still wanted more."

"Sorry," I say. "I just thought . . . usually when one of us gets excited about a lead . . ."

She crosses her arms. "What lead?"

"The catacombs! I think we should go check them out. It's where Bones thinks the necklace is—and where he encouraged us to go. I think we need to see them for ourselves. Maybe we can find something the grown-ups missed."

"Well, I think we should go to where the house burned down with the necklace in it," Eliza says. "If we go to the last known location of the necklace, we might be able to figure out what happened. We don't *know* that the necklace is in the catacombs, but we do know—for sure—that it was at that house."

"You think we'll find something thousands of years later?" I say skeptically. "Eliza, crime scenes don't last that long. It's not like they put caution tape on the ruins for all of history. I'm sure anything that we could have found there is long gone by now. I'm certain the catacombs are the key to this mystery—we have to go there."

"Well, whatever you want," she says coolly. She's shutting down.

I look at Mom for advice, and she raises an eyebrow at me. I'm not sure if that's the expression for "Follow your gut, Carlos!" or "Trust your friend, Carlos!" and I wish I could read my mom's face better.

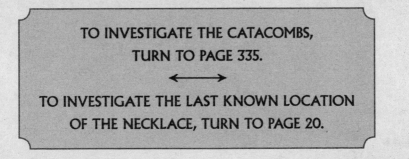

TO INVESTIGATE THE CATACOMBS,
TURN TO PAGE 335.

←——→

TO INVESTIGATE THE LAST KNOWN LOCATION
OF THE NECKLACE, TURN TO PAGE 20.

"WHAT WERE YOU doing in the tunnels?"

"I wasn't in the tunnels."

Eliza and I look at each other.

"Yes, you were!"

"No, I was not."

I frown. "I know what this is. It's called gaslighting."

"I like to light up with gas too!" Frank says.

"Please don't," I beg of him. I turn back to Dr. Mandible. "You're trying to make us doubt ourselves by pretending something we know to be true isn't true. But it *is* true." My head is spinning.

"Does it have something to do with what's in your drawer?" Eliza asks.

Dr. Amanda Mandible holds her fake smile so perfectly. It doesn't falter for an instant.

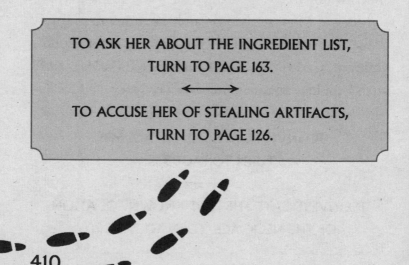

TO ASK HER ABOUT THE INGREDIENT LIST,
TURN TO PAGE 163.

←——→

TO ACCUSE HER OF STEALING ARTIFACTS,
TURN TO PAGE 126.

I CLICK ON the voicemail. There's one missed call and one voicemail waiting for him from a number he didn't save in his phone.

I play the message on speaker.

"Hi, Richie Rich, my man! This is Chad DuPont. Just wanted to let you know we're all set for the opening of your private collection. Your artifacts are looking great. I told you—it's nice to *own* them, not borrow, yeah? When you return, let's hope you bring a few more trophies with you. Especially that necklace, man. That legendary—" He curses *very* emphatically, and Frank gasps. "—necklace! That would be such a draw. If you manage to nick that, you can double—no, *triple*—the cost of admission. But if it's too high-profile to keep, you can sell it. I know some other collectors who would bid a pretty penny for that necklace. Either way, you're going to make *bank*. Keep me posted on your new gets. See you stateside!"

The voicemail ends.

We look at each other, stunned. My hands are trembling, and I grip the phone tighter. I can't believe we just cracked this case! "This is proof," I say, breathless.

"Maybe," Eliza says, unconvinced.

"What do you mean, *maybe*?"

"I'm just wary. Until we find the artifacts, this case isn't over."

411

"So let's go confront Leech!"

She looks at me like she doesn't think it's a good idea. But I'm tired of her disagreeing with me all the time. I walk out of the tent, and I just have to hope she follows.

Outside, the dig is quiet. I guess everyone is in the pit, and it's too early for lunch. Being by ourselves, with just the towering columns and the scattered ruins, is creepy. I miss the flurry of activity and noise.

We wander over to the excavation pit. I'm thinking we're going to have to call into the catacombs for Leech, but as we look down, we see the special task force climbing up the ladder.

"Stupid map," Smarty Marty grumbles as she reaches the top. "Absolute incompetence."

"What's wrong?" Eliza asks her.

"Nothing! Just Zip messing up the map for the *fifth* time."

"Messing up how?" I ask.

"We ran right into a wall. Literally. I wish Mr. Bones would let me take over for Zip!" Then she storms off.

The mood of the team is down, except for—curiously enough—Zip. They don't seem as depressed or embarrassed as I would be if I had just made the same mistake five times in a row. They look very even-keeled. And is it just my imagination, or is there the smallest upturn at the corners of their mouth?

Zip disappears, following Smarty into their work tent. Professor Worthington, Dr. Mandible, and Nadira Nadeem come up the ladder next. And Leech is last.

"Excuse me, Mr. Leech, but we need to talk to—"

"No," he says, stomping past us. He practically runs to his tent to avoid talking to us. But when he gets inside, I hear a furious scream.

Uh-oh.

Richard Leech comes storming out of the tent. "Somebody's been through my *stuff*!" he bellows. "Someone's gonna pay for this!"

He pulls out his phone. Is he calling the police?

Suddenly my pocket starts ringing at full volume. Richard Leech is using his first phone to call his second phone! I try to silence it, but it's too late—

Leech swivels in our direction. He glares at me. He is *seething*.

TO RUN FROM LEECH, TURN TO PAGE 225.

←——→

TO FACE LEECH HEAD-ON, TURN TO PAGE 71.

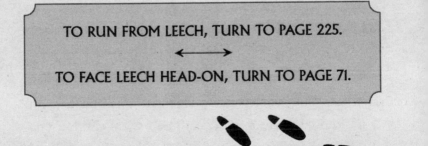

413

IF THERE'S ONE thing I know about mysteries, it's this: *always* start with the suspects. Motive, means, opportunity. Figuring this out will give us the key to who might be behind the thefts.

"You seem to think someone is going to steal the treasure," I say. "Who might want to?"

"ME!" Frank says.

"Oh, I don't know," Orlando says, throwing his hands up in the air. "I'm not sure who I suspect."

"You don't have *any* suspicions at all?" Eliza says.

He rubs the stubble on his chin. "No."

Eliza sighs, frustrated. I'm beginning to think she wishes we'd kept Nadira Nadeem in the room for this conversation, since Nadira had many suspects in mind. Eliza looks at me with an annoyed expression, but she can't be mad at *me* for that, can she? I made a call, just like I always do when we're on a case.

I don't really have time to worry about it. It's in the past. Now all we can do is focus on Orlando Bones.

"Look, the stakes are high," Bones says. "We can sit here all day and talk about the members of the special task force, but that's not the important thing."

Eliza shakes her head, incredulous. "How can you say that? The whole reason we're here is because you don't know which of your teammates you can trust!"

"The whole reason you're here," he says excitedly, "is

to help me keep the treasure at the end of the tunnel safe. It's more valuable than all the missing artifacts combined."

"But if we know who took the artifacts," Eliza argues, "then we'll know who's going to take the treasure, right? Which leads us back to *this* conversation—talking about the suspects!"

I know Eliza's super logical and methodical, but I don't know why she's being so combative. It's like she's trying so hard to take the lead that she's forgetting not to annoy the client. I stare pointedly at her, hoping she understands my glance, but she opens her mouth to argue again.

Time to jump in quick with a new topic of conversation!

TO ASK ABOUT THE MISSING ARTIFACTS, TURN TO PAGE 298.

←——→

TO ASK WHAT'S AT THE END OF THE TUNNEL, TURN TO PAGE 27.

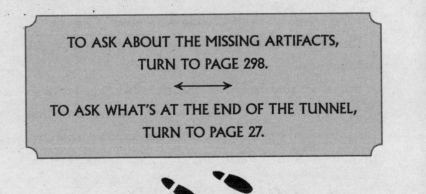

WE HAVE TO grab the necklace. It's sitting on the podium . . . *right there.* I throw my flashlight at Bones. He ducks. I lunge forward and grab the necklace.

"GOT IT!" I cry.

The room starts hissing. Fire is rising between the columns, one flame at a time, going around in a circle. We have to get out of here before we're surrounded!

"Let's go!" I cry, running for a gap where the fire hasn't yet appeared.

"Oh no you don't!" Bones shouts, grabbing me by the ankle. "Give me my necklace!"

Woosh! Woosh! Woosh! The flames go up in every archway, trapping us in the room. With Orlando Bones.

"Well," he says. "Good thing I have a deck of cards with me. We can pass the time and play for the necklace."

"You want us . . . to gamble with you?" Eliza says.

I snort. "No dice!"

"Yeah! Go fish!" Frank shouts.

But after five hours of the fires blazing, he deals us in for rummy. We agree . . . reluctantly. But since this fire doesn't seem to be stopping anytime soon, we might as well turn a crummy time into a rummy time.

CASE CLOSED.

"WHAT ARE YOU doing down here?"

"Isn't it lovely in these catacombs?" Bones says, as if he's talking about the weather in September and not some creepy, cold cave. "I hope you've come to enjoy it. And if you haven't, you will have at least a few days to learn to love it before you dehydrate. Oh, or is the river freshwater? Then you'll have a few weeks before you starve."

"What are you talking about?" Eliza says, her voice shaking.

"From the tremor in your voice, I would bet that you already know what I'm talking about. I'd put good money on it. Now. Hand over the necklace, young man."

Frank backs up a step.

"You," I say. "You're the artifact thief."

"Bingo again!" he says.

"But you hired us!"

"I did."

My head is spinning. "So you stole the artifacts, then hired us to find the artifacts you stole? But why would you want us to investigate a crime *you* were committing?"

But Eliza gets there a second before me. She gasps. "The path up ahead is really tiny. You needed us—or people our size—to get to the necklace. There was no artifact thief. You made it up so you would have an excuse to hire us."

"And all this talk about the necklace being in danger?"

Bones smiles. "I was the danger. Keira Skelberry falling into an ancient trap gave me the idea to set up modern ones to ensure that I was the only one with true access to the catacombs."

"But *why?*" I ask. "Why go through all the trouble of stealing the necklace when it was literally your job to retrieve it?"

"This is the most priceless artifact in the world, and . . ." He hesitates for a moment. "Now that I have no need for you anymore, I suppose I'll show you my hand. Not that it's any of your business, but I . . . I have a gambling problem. I have debts and debt collectors— the shady kind."

"That's who you were on the phone with!" I realize.

Bones nods. "I lied, and you didn't call my bluff. I'm in more trouble than you could possibly imagine. I need more money than I will ever have. If not, I will surely not survive."

"So to be clear," Eliza says coldly, "you're totally okay being responsible for the death of the three of us and Carlos's mom, so long as you get out of *your* problems unscathed?"

"Speaking of my mom, where is she?"

Bones chuckles. "Not in the tunnels. I wrote that letter from 'a friend' to get you to come down here. That was my ace in the hole."

He takes a menacing step forward, and I step back. My sneaker dips into the water, which is shockingly cold. We can't let him have this necklace. But we also don't want to get hurt protecting it either.

TO THROW THE NECKLACE INTO THE WATER,
TURN TO PAGE 78.

←——→

TO RUN BETWEEN HIS LEGS,
TURN TO PAGE 320.

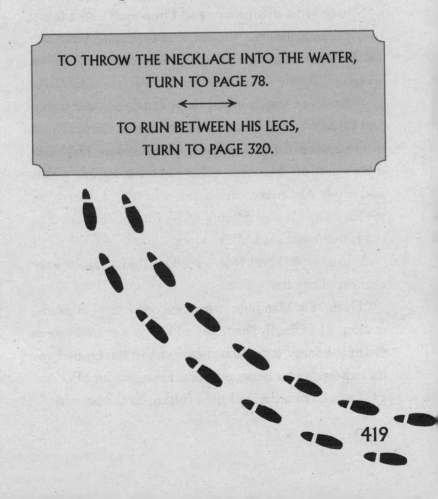

IF I PRETEND to faint, I won't have to answer Mr. Bones's question. I start swaying like I'm woozy. Then I crumple to the floor, my cheek on the dirt.

"Carlos!" Mom yells. "Carlos!"

"He died," Frank says.

"He's not dead!" Eliza says, putting her fingers on my wrist to feel my pulse. "He's just fainted."

"Someone help him!" Nadira says.

Strong arms lift me up, and I'm tossed like a towel over Orlando Bones's shoulder. It isn't until we reach Dr. Amanda Mandible's medical tent that I pretend to wake up.

"Thank you, Mr. Bones. I think a little rest and water, and I'll feel better. You should go back to Nadira."

He ignores me and gingerly places me on Dr. Mandible's patient chair. She takes my temperature, pokes and prods me, makes me drink a bottle of water, has me lie down. It's all getting to be too much. I need to ditch them and get back to work.

"Thank you. I feel fine—really. I'll just take it easy the rest of the day."

"Hush," Dr. Mandible snaps. She continues her examination. Then finally she takes off her gloves and looks at Orlando Bones. "It could be heat exhaustion. Or perhaps it's indicative of a larger ailment. He needs an MRI and a CT scan. I'm ordering him a full medical diagnostic."

420

"So . . . can I go?"

She shakes her head no. "I wouldn't feel comfortable, ethically, as a medical professional, letting you continue on." She turns to Bones. "If he gets injured or sick on the dig, then you could be liable financially. You need to send him home immediately."

Nooooooo! I guess my feint was too convincing.

CASE CLOSED.

WE HAVE TO search through Nadira Nadeem's desk.

"Let's go investigate Nadira," I say.

We turn around and march back into the bosses' tent. Only . . . Orlando Bones is sitting right there. Ooops. I forgot.

"What are you doing here?" he says.

"Um . . . we forgot something," I say, trying really hard to come up with an excuse for why we'd walk into a tent we just left. Is there a question I can ask Bones? Something to cover my tracks?

"What'd you forget?"

Frank puts his hands on his hips. "We forgot to snoop through Nadira's desk!"

Frank! What did you do?

Bones looks surprised for a second. And then mad. "And you were going to do that with me here?"

"We forgot," I say.

"You forgot—even though you spoke to me mere moments ago?" He stands up. "This displays a serious lack of judgment!"

"Sorry, we'll just go now," I say.

"You know what? Perhaps that is best. I'm cashing in my chips. Pack your bags—I'm sending you all the way home."

CASE CLOSED.

"YOU AND ZIP work in this tent together, right?"

"Yes," she says.

"And . . . do you find them suspicious?"

"Not suspicious," Smarty Marty says. *"Incompetent.* I have no idea how they got this job in the first place."

I'm not sure what to say. After all, Smarty questioned our competence as detectives the very moment she met us. I'm starting to wonder if Smarty Marty just thinks she's better than everyone else. Maybe in her eyes, everyone is incompetent . . . except her.

"What do you mean, incompetent?" I ask.

"Zip has *one job*, and they can't even do it properly. On the first day, Mr. Bones asked them to make a map. With the laser scan and computer imaging, no problem, right? Well, Zip took forever and a day to do it. Then when we took the map into the tunnels, it was all wrong! It said there was a path where there was a wall, and the dimensions were off—it was just a complete mess. So Zip had to start over from scratch."

"Everyone's allowed one mess-up."

"It's happened *three times* already. They're on the fourth iteration of the map. I know nothing about computers, but give me an hour, and I'll learn everything I need to know about them, and then *I'll* do a better job!"

That seems to be Smarty Marty's refrain: she thinks she's smarter—and could do a better job—than everyone else.

"So what excuse did Zip have for the map being messed up?" I ask.

"Did a dog eat their homework?" Frank says. "A dog always eats my homework!"

"Frank, you don't have a dog."

Smarty Marty ignores us. "Zip said something about the laser being misaligned and the equipment not working correctly. But way to blame the *machine* for your mistake. It's so irresponsible."

"Because the responsible thing is to own up to your mistakes?"

"No," Smarty Marty says haughtily. "The responsible thing is to not make mistakes in the first place."

"Well sometimes people can't help that, right? Everyone makes mistakes."

"I don't."

"Me neither!" Frank shouts.

Smarty sighs deeply. "Look," she says. "I really have to get back to work. But . . . I have a juicy secret about Richard Leech. If you want it, it's yours."

TO HEAR SMARTY MARTY'S INFORMATION, TURN TO PAGE 239.

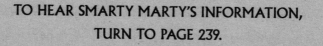

AS MUCH AS I hate to admit it, I think Eliza's right: a drop of blood on the stone makes the most sense.

I step forward. "Do you have anything sharp on you? I can prick my finger, and we can clean it up with antibiotic cream—"

"No need!" Frank says, standing up and grinning. "Just call me Mr. Blood Bank!" And he starts wiggling his loose tooth aggressively.

Eliza cries out. "Frank, you don't have to—"

"OH YES I DO. The tooth fairy is bringing me fifty dollars tonight!"

I shake my head. "You should know, Frank . . . the tooth fairy doesn't dispense fifties."

But he does not listen to me. He wiggles and tugs and pulls and twists. At last, when his baby tooth is on the last string, he yanks it out, and the blood comes rushing. He spits his blood on the stone and holds his baby tooth up to the luminescent cavern ceiling.

"HOORAY!" he cries. "ONE DOWN, SIXTY TO GO!"

"Frank, you're not a shark. You don't have sixty teeth in your—"

The ground begins to rumble. The stone that has Frank's blood on it sinks deeper into the floor. And up rises a marble dais.

And on that dais is a necklace. It's gold, with two

snakes intertwining. Their mouths form the clasp, and their tails curve around a very shiny pearlescent gemstone. Its shimmer looks like a rainbow.

"This is it," Eliza whispers. "We found the Necklace of Harmonia!"

"Pretty!" Frank says. "And even more important, I HAVE A TOOTH!"

"I don't know if that's *more* important," I mutter, and Frank glares at me.

We walk around the pedestal, observing the necklace from all angles. Even if I didn't know how valuable it was . . . I would know just by looking at it.

"Should we take it?" Eliza suggests.

I gulp. "Do we think this is a scenario where if we lift the treasure off the stand, it'll trigger a booby trap?"

"Only one way to find out!" Frank says, and he grabs the necklace from its plinth.

Nothing happens.

I sigh in relief.

But then—

Woosh! Woosh! Woosh! I don't know what chemical reaction happened when we pulled the necklace off, but fire is being activated in the room, and it travels up each of the columns. The room is ablaze.

"RUN!" I scream, and we dash to the very small tunnel. We're shuffling as fast as we can, but it's hard to go sideways. The fire starts to heat up the stones we're stuck between, and everything is suddenly very hot.

At least Frank is up ahead, lightning fast. "You still have the necklace, Frank?"

He doesn't answer.

"FRANK?"

Eliza moves faster, and so do I. The fire is right on our heels—

And then, the door! The one that leads out through the three-headed dog. We open the heavy door and shut it again on the fire. Then we pant on the banks of the inky-black River Styx.

"The necklace?" I pant.

Frank is wearing it.

"Get that thing off—it's cursed!" I yell.

"Cursed, schmursed," Frank says.

"Mom wasn't there," I say. "That was a dead end. You were right all along."

Eliza squeezes my hand. "We'll search until we find her. We're the best detectives I know. But first . . . we have to get out of here."

We turn our attention to the boat. It's a chore, but we know what we have to do: first, Eliza and Frank cross. Then Frank rows the boat back to me. Me to Eliza. Eliza to Frank. Both of them back again.

When it's all over, I never want to see this boat or this river again.

We walk to the tiny crawl door—the one that will take us to the wall of alchemy symbols. Through it, we'll exit the catacombs and go find Mom.

We open the crawl door.

There are legs in front of us, blocking our way. Tall legs in khaki pants. The person kicks, and Frank goes tumbling backward.

"FRANK!" Eliza yells, rushing toward him.

Frank seems more confused than hurt. "What was that?"

"See? *Cursed!*"

Frank sticks his tongue out at me.

I shine my flashlight on the little door. Whoever kicked Frank is coming in now. They crouch down and wriggle through. And as this mystery person gets to their feet, they adjust the fedora on their head—and at once, I realize who it is.

I nearly drop my flashlight.

"Orlando Bones," I say.

He looks at me. Bones usually wears an excitable grin on his scruffy, sweaty face, but he's not smiling now. He's more serious than ever.

"Mr. Bones, did you come here to find us? Because we were about to find . . ."

428

I trail off. From his hardened expression and the way he's obstructing the door, something tells me this isn't a regular check-in. Alarm bells are blaring in my head. This is off.

I try to ease the tension with a chuckle. "Mr. Bones, we can't get out if you don't move."

"Bingo."

TO ASK HIM WHY HE'S IN THE TUNNELS,
TURN TO PAGE 417.

←——→

TO DEMAND THAT HE MOVE, TURN TO PAGE 342.

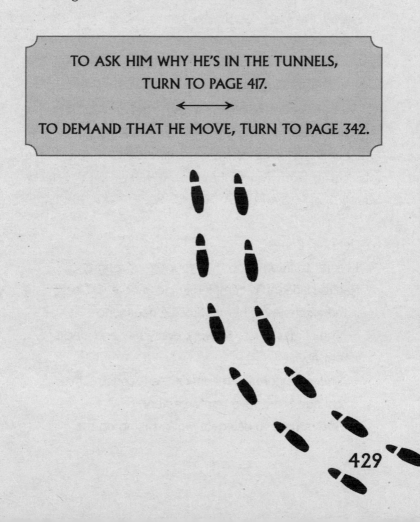

I CLICK ON Orlando Bones's email. A lot of boring stuff. Bills and email names I don't recognize—one user in particular seems to email him a *lot*. I click on one of those emails.

> OB—
> I came to your house to collect what you owe.
> Seems like you're gone. Did you run away? You
> can't run away from your debt.

The email is unsigned.

"So here's confirmation," I say, "that he's in debt."

"And owes someone money," Eliza says.

I keep scrolling through his email. Then I see something from Marta Higgins. "Hey—that's Smarty Marty!"

> Dear Mr. Bones,
> I regret to inform you that your direct report,
> Nadira Nadeem, is completely incompetent. I have
> listed examples of her workplace negligence:
> - She comes in late to work every day and clocks
>   out at five.
> - She does not give feedback, be it constructive
>   critique or positive reinforcement.
> - She refuses to delegate work, taking on the

bulk of the responsibility herself until she is overwhelmed with tasks.

- She is unable to be found most times of the day.
- She does not communicate.
- She has been spotted crying in the corners of dig sites.

I look up. The list goes on for a while. A long, long while. Typical Smarty. She even overachieves at list making.

"Look at the last bullet point!" Eliza says.

- She seems to be acting rather suspiciously. I have noticed that she does not seem very interested in recovering artifacts, or even work in general.

What I am suggesting here is a resolute redistribution of assignments. I am more than capable and ready to stand at the helm and lead this team to the Necklace of Harmonia. Let me prove myself— and my worth—to you. I will find the necklace for you no matter what.

Sincerely,
Marta Higgins

"Well, that was unpleasant," I say. "Clearly, Smarty is eager to prove herself. Maybe too eager. Would she go into the tunnels alone, trying to find the necklace, just to prove her worth?"

"Or . . . more than that," Eliza says. "Would she steal artifacts, just so she could look good and promotable when she 'finds' them?"

Typical Eliza. I have a good thought, and she has a better one. I sigh. "See? I told you we might find good stuff on Bones's computer. I'm a good investigator too, Eliza."

"I never said you weren't!"

Mom whistles very loudly from outside the tent.

"DANGER! DANGER!" Frank chirps.

"Yeah, we got the message!" I say as we close out of the computer.

In walks Professor Phineas Alistair Worthington, exhilarated, nearly bouncing with energy. Mom and Frank come in behind him.

"Well?" the professor says. "Do tell! Did you find anything of note at the fiery ruins?"

Eliza and I accidentally look at each other, and the professor claps. "Oho! That means you *did* find something! Tell me!"

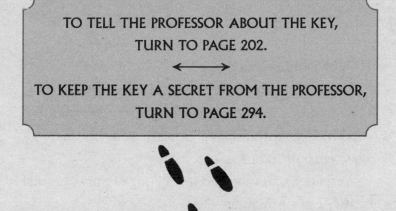

TO TELL THE PROFESSOR ABOUT THE KEY,
TURN TO PAGE 202.

←→

TO KEEP THE KEY A SECRET FROM THE PROFESSOR,
TURN TO PAGE 294.

433

ELIZA'S RIGHT—THE FINGERPRINT idea is better. And I'm not so stubborn that I can't see that.

I nod, and she stands up.

"We will reveal the location of the necklace," she says, "once everyone gives us a fingerprint sample."

"Why is that necessary?" Smarty says, and there's a collective murmur of assent.

"Yes, I don't feel comfortable giving out my personal identifying information—"

"This doesn't feel proper," Orlando Bones says, stepping forward.

"You have nothing to worry about if you have nothing to hide. If you don't give us your fingerprint, we'll assume you're guilty."

Everyone nods. One by one, we collect their fingerprints.

Then we take the print off a shard of a vase. All we need is a match!

1. Richard Leech.
2. Nadira Nadeem.
3. Smarty Marty.
4. Orlando Bones.
5. Zip.
6. Amanda Mandible.
7. Phineas Alistair Worthington.

TAKE THE NUMBER OF YOUR SUSPECT
AND ADD THREE HUNDRED.
THEN TURN TO THAT PAGE.

←→

TO ASK ELIZA FOR A HINT,
TURN TO PAGE 60.

WE HAVE TO talk to Nadira Nadeem about Smarty's letter. And we find her in her natural state—running from one side of the dig to the other with a clipboard.

"Can we talk to you for a second?" I ask her.

"If you can keep up!"

We have to run to keep pace with her. That's how fast she's walking.

"We found a complaint email from Smarty Marty to Orlando Bones," I say.

"Oh? What's the complaint about?"

"Er . . . you, actually," I say, feeling awkward.

I expect Nadira to stop walking, but she walks even faster. We're near the edge of the pit.

"She said you come late and leave early, that you refuse to share work with your teammates, and that you're always overwhelmed."

"Not true!"

"And," Eliza adds, "she said you've been crying at the corner of the dig—is that true?"

"What? Why would I be crying?" Nadira says quickly.

"We were hoping you could tell us that," Eliza replies.

"Show-and-tell time!" Frank says.

Nadira increases her speed. Why do I get the sense that she is trying to run away? "Are you stressed out?"

436

I ask her. "I know you have a lot on your plate. Do you get any time for yourself? How's your personal life?"

"My personal life? Why are you . . ." She turns her head to look at me. Her eyes are wide with panic as she continues to power walk. "Who said anything about tha—AHHHHHHHH!" It's like I'm watching it in slow motion. Nadira trips and falls—right over the edge of the pit.

I can't help but feel responsible because of our reckless questioning—especially knowing that Nadira is often multitasking and distracted. With four different fractures, Nadira Nadeem retires from archaeology, her career in ruins.

CASE CLOSED.